July 2015

1 1 AUG 2015

CHURCH END
LIBRARY
020 8359 3800

1 8 NOV 2015

− 8 FEB 2016

317121

D0810028

ease return/renew this item by the
ast date shown to avoid a charge.
oks may also be renewed by phone
d Internet. May not be renewed if
required by another reader.

www.libraries.barnet.gov.uk

BARNET
LONDON BOROUGH

30131 05358851 0

LONDON BOROUGH OF BARNET

THE *Best*
{BRITISH}
Short Stories
2015

NICHOLAS ROYLE IS the author of more than 100 short stories, two novellas and seven novels, most recently *First Novel* (Vintage). His short story collection, *Mortality* (Serpent's Tail), was shortlisted for the inaugural Edge Hill Prize. He has edited seventeen anthologies of short stories, including *The Time Out Book of New York Short Stories* (Penguin), *'68: New Stories by Children of the Revolution* (Salt) and *Murmurations: An Anthology of Uncanny Stories About Birds* (Two Ravens Press). A senior lecturer in creative writing at the Manchester Writing School at MMU and head judge of the Manchester Fiction Prize, he also runs Nightjar Press, publishing original short stories as signed, limited-edition chapbooks.

Also by Nicholas Royle:

NOVELS
Counterparts
Saxophone Dreams
The Matter of the Heart
The Director's Cut
Antwerp
Regicide
First Novel

NOVELLAS
The Appetite
The Enigma of Departure

SHORT STORIES
Mortality

ANTHOLOGIES (as editor)
Darklands
Darklands 2
A Book of Two Halves
The Tiger Garden: A Book of Writers' Dreams
The Time Out Book of New York Short Stories
The Ex Files: New Stories About Old Flames
The Agony & the Ecstasy: New Writing for the World Cup
Neonlit: Time Out Book of New Writing
The Time Out Book of Paris Short Stories
Neonlit: Time Out Book of New Writing Volume 2
The Time Out Book of London Short Stories Volume 2
Dreams Never End
'68: New Stories From Children of the Revolution
The Best British Short Stories 2011
Murmurations: An Anthology of Uncanny Stories About Birds
The Best British Short Stories 2012
The Best British Short Stories 2013
The Best British Short Stories 2014

THE *Best*
{ BRITISH }
Short Stories
2015

SERIES EDITOR **NICHOLAS ROYLE**

SALT

CROMER

PUBLISHED BY SALT PUBLISHING
12 Norwich Road, Cromer, Norfolk NR27 0AX

All rights reserved

Selection and introduction © Nicholas Royle, 2015
Individual contributions © the contributors, 2015

The right of Nicholas Royle to be identified as the editor of this work has
been asserted by him in accordance with Section 77 of the Copyright,
Designs and Patents Act 1988.

This book is in copyright. Subject to statutory exception and to provisions
of relevant collective licensing agreements, no reproduction of any part may
take place without the written permission of Salt Publishing.

First published by Salt Publishing, 2015

Printed in Great Britain by Clays Ltd, St Ives plc

Typeset in Paperback 9/12

*This book is sold subject to the conditions that it shall not, by way of trade
or otherwise, be lent, re-sold, hired out, or otherwise circulated without the
publisher's prior consent in any form of binding or cover other than that in which
it is published and without a similar condition including this condition being
imposed on the subsequent purchaser.*

ISBN 978 1 78463 027 0 paperback

1 3 5 7 9 8 6 4 2

In memory of Graham Joyce (1954–2014)

CONTENTS

Introduction   ix

HILARY MANTEL
The Assassination of Margaret Thatcher   1
August 6th 1983

JULIANNE PACHICO
Lucky   22

BEE LEWIS
The Iron Men   38

JONATHAN GIBBS
Festschrift   45

JENN ASHWORTH
Five Thousand Lads a Year   63

NEIL CAMPBELL
LS Lowry/Man Lying on a Wall   69

EMMA CLEARY
Lightbox   73

JIM HINKS
Green Boots' Cave   79

USCHI GATWARD
The Clinic   84

TRACEY S ROSENBERG
May the Bell Be Rung For Harriet   95

HELEN SIMPSON
Strong Man   102

MATTHEW SPERLING
Voice Over   113

K J ORR
The Lake Shore Limited   128

TAMAR HODES
The First Day   145

ALAN McCORMICK
Go Wild in the Country   149

HELEN MARSHALL
Secondhand Magic   159

CHARLES WILKINSON
Fresh Water   183

REBECCA SWIRSKY
The Common People   198

ALISON MOORE
Eastmouth   205

JULIANNE PACHICO
The Tourists   214

JOANNA WALSH
Worlds From the Word's End   229

Contributors' Biographies   239
Acknowledgements   244

INTRODUCTION

I HAVE A shelf at home – I won't tell you what I call it – where I keep particular books, or books by particular authors, more to the point. There might be a novel there by an author who once declined to write a short story for an anthology I was editing on the grounds that he didn't 'get out of bed for less than a grand'. You might find a short story collection featuring an introduction by its author in which he quotes at length from his own fan mail. (Publishers, please stop encouraging pathological narcissists.) There could be books by people who have repeatedly given me – or writers I admire, or in fact anyone at all – unreasonably bad reviews, who clearly take an unsettling degree of pleasure in wielding the axe. Bad reviews are easier to write than good ones, and some writers and critics – as bloodthirsty as they are lazy – specialise in them. There might well also be a collection by a writer previously featured in this series who made a fuss about the fee offered for the use of her story – each writer is offered the same fee and anyone requesting a higher fee, for whatever reason, is given one more chance to accept the original fee before being advised, politely, of the offer's withdrawal.

In my head, at least, I have started a new shelf, for *publishers* who refuse permission to allow a story to be reprinted on the grounds that the fee offered is too low. This situation has the potential to arise where an author publishes a short story collection, with a major publisher, and control of the rights rests with the publisher rather than the author. Some publishers understand what we are trying to do here; there's no point in publishing a series called *The Best British Short Stories* if we don't include what are, in the editor's opinion, the best British short stories. Among the stories first published in 2014 by British writers was one by a Booker Prize-winning novelist and short story writer – it was the title story from his latest collection – and it was, again in my opinion, one of the best of the year, but his publisher was not prepared to allow the story to be reprinted for the fee on offer. It's hard to see the sense in this, since publication in this series does not preclude publication elsewhere. Who knows if the author was even given the choice?

Fortunately, HarperCollins allowed the reprint of Hilary Mantel's 'The Assassination of Margaret Thatcher 6th August 1983' (just as Mantel and her agent had been happy to allow the reprint of other stories earlier in this series); the story caused a furore when it was published, ahead of the collection of which it would be the title story, in the *Guardian*. Offended politicians and ex-politicians on the right lined up to denounce Mantel, unaware, perhaps, of the story's place in a tradition of similar works by JG Ballard, Christopher Burns, Frederick Forsyth and others.

Another highly acclaimed short story writer, Helen Simpson, is represented in this volume, and in the series for the first time, with 'Strong Man', a story first published in the *New Statesman*, which, it is pleasing to note, continues to commission one or two original short stories a year. The BBC is one of the UK's staunchest supporters of the short story, broadcasting dozens of stories on Radio 4 and Radio 4 Extra and continuing to back the BBC National Short Story Award; Radio 3's *The Verb* should not be missed either. Jenn Ashworth's story, 'Five Thousand Lads a Year', was broadcast on Radio 4.

Perhaps one of the most encouraging developments in

short story publishing in recent years, the rise of the single short story publication – in the form of a chapbook or pamphlet – has been partly driven by Daunt Books, who have been putting out beautifully designed small-format perfect-bound booklets for a couple of years now. 'The Tourists' by Julianne Pachico was irresistible; the same author popped up in the now essential *Lighthouse* journal with 'Lucky'. The same issue of *Lighthouse* yielded 'Lightbox' by Emma Cleary. Knives Forks and Spoons Press of Newton-le-Willows produce poetry pamphlets and last year they published Neil Campbell's short but perfectly formed short story collection *Ekphrasis*, from which 'LS Lowry/Man Lying on a Wall' is taken.

There's an international flavour to this year's volume, and not only because of the presence of two or three authors enjoying dual nationality. 'Secondhand Magic', by Helen Marshall, who was born and raised in Canada, is taken from her second collection, *Gifts For the One Who Comes After* (ChiZine Publications), while Tamar Hodes, born in Israel, published 'The First Day' in *Wiltshire View*. Irish journals *Gorse* and *Dublin Review* were where Jonathan Gibbs's 'Festschrift' and K J Orr's 'The Lake Shore Limited', respectively, appeared for the first time. Bee Lewis's 'The Iron Men' was published by a Danish magazine for English teachers, *Anglo Files*.

Short stories can turn up in academic journals. 'May the Bell Be Rung For Harriet', by Tracey S Rosenberg, was published on the Brontë Society website and reprinted in *Brontë Studies* after it won the society's short story competition judged by Margaret Drabble. 'Green Boots' Cave', by Jim Hinks, well known to readers and writers as an editor at Comma Press, was published in *Short Fiction in Theory and Practice*.

Short story anthologies are still being published, but by smaller publishers, so they might need more seeking out. Alison Moore's 'Eastmouth' was one of the highlights of superior horror volume *The Spectral Book of Horror Stories* (Spectral Press), which editor Mark Morris hopes will be the first in a series inspired by countless Pan and Fontana anthologies of the 1960s and 1970s. Unthank Books continue to publish some very good work in their *Unthology* series edited by Ashley Stokes and Robin Jones, including 'Fresh Water' by Charles Wilkinson. 'Worlds from the Word's End' by Joanna Walsh was first published in *Best European Fiction 2015* (Dalkey Archive Press) edited by West Camel.

Magazines – whether online or print, or both – probably remain the first place to go to find new short stories. Matthew Sperling's 'Voice Over' and Alan McCormick's 'Go Wild in the Country' were both published online in *The Literateur* and *3:AM Magazine* respectively. Former fiction editor of *3:AM* Susan Tomaselli edits twice-yearly journal *Gorse*, mentioned above, one of the most exciting recent arrivals on the scene.

Making an increasingly important contribution to the world of the short story is the Word Factory, run by poet and founder of the *Sunday Times* EFG Short Story Award Cathy Galvin and her team, with its packed programme of readings and masterclasses, short story club and mentorship schemes. Rebecca Swirsky and Uschi Gatward are both former Word Factory mentees; their stories, 'The Common People' and 'The Clinic', appeared online in *Litro* and in print in *Structo* respectively.

There was, last year, good work published in *Ambit*, *Black Static* and *Confingo*, a new magazine from Manchester edited by Tim Shearer and featuring stories by John Saul, Adrian Slatcher and Vanessa Gebbie. In the pages of horror magazine *Black Static*, Stephen Hargadon loomed into view on two occasions, exploring the boozers, tower blocks and transport routes of Manchester as well as recording its voices; he has a good eye and a good ear. *Ambit* is transitioning after the retirement in 2013 of long-serving founder-editor Martin Bax. The new team, headed by Briony Bax with Kate Pemberton as fiction editor assisted by Gary Budden and Mike Smith, is finding some gems among a huge number of submissions, which are invited to coincide with twice yearly openings of their new 'portal'. *The Mechanics' Institute Review* continues to showcase interesting work by Birkbeck creative writing students alongside contributions last year from Hari Kunzru, Alex Preston and Julia Bell. Also worthy of note was *Everything is Spherical: An Anthology of Dyslexic Writers* (Rebelling Against Spelling Press) edited by Naomi Folb and Sarah Fearn.

Going by feedback, short story writers themselves number not insignificantly among the readership of this series. It's unlikely that any individual writing short stories in Britain today hasn't heard of the Arvon Foundation, as anyone who has been there, whether as punter or tutor or guest reader, tends to proselytise on its behalf, and I am no exception, so, just in case there is a soul reading this who writes and wants to write better, and doesn't know about Arvon, check them out. They have three centres – Lumb Bank (West Yorkshire), the Hurst (Shropshire) and Totleigh Barton (Devon) – where week-long themed residential courses are taught by practising writers. There is nothing quite like the atmosphere that develops during an Arvon week, or indeed a week at Moniack Mhor, which was Arvon's centre in Scotland, until, in a canny reflection of the zeitgeist, they recently became independent.

NICHOLAS ROYLE
Moniack Mhor
Inverness-shire
April 2015

THE *Best* {BRITISH} *Short Stories* 2015

HILARY MANTEL

THE ASSASSINATION OF MARGARET THATCHER AUGUST 6TH 1983

APRIL 25TH 1982, DOWNING STREET: Announcement of the recapture of South Georgia, in the Falkland Islands.

Mrs Thatcher: Ladies and gentlemen, the Secretary of State for Defence has just come over to give me some very good news . . .

Secretary of State: The message we have got is that British troops landed on South Georgia this afternoon, shortly after 4pm London time . . . The commander of the operation has sent the following message: 'Be pleased to inform Her Majesty that the White Ensign flies alongside the Union Jack in South Georgia. God save the Queen.'

Mrs Thatcher: Just rejoice at that news and congratulate our forces and the marines. Goodnight, gentlemen.

Mrs Thatcher turns towards the door of No.10 Downing Street.

Reporter: Are we going to declare war on Argentina, Mrs Thatcher?

Mrs Thatcher (pausing on her doorstep): Rejoice.

Picture first the street where she breathed her last. It is a quiet street, sedate, shaded by old trees: a street of tall houses, their facades smooth as white icing, their brickwork the colour of honey. Some are Georgian, flat-fronted. Others are Victorian, with gleaming bays. They are too big for modern households, and most of them have been cut up into flats. But this does not destroy their elegance of proportion, nor detract from the deep lustre of panelled front doors, brass-furnished and painted in navy or forest green. It is the neighbourhood's only drawback, that there are more cars than spaces to put them. The residents park nose-to-tail, flaunting their permits. Those who have driveways are often blocked into them. But they are patient householders, proud of their handsome street and willing to suffer to live there. Glancing up, you notice a fragile Georgian fanlight, or a warm scoop of terracotta tiling, or a glint of coloured glass. In spring, cherry trees toss extravagant flounces of blossom. When the wind strips the petals, they flurry in pink drifts and carpet the pavements, as if giants have held a wedding in the street. In summer, music floats from open windows: Vivaldi, Mozart, Bach.

The street itself describes a gentle curve, joining the main road as it flows out of town. The Holy Trinity church, islanded, is hung with garrison flags. Looking from a high window over the town (as I did that day of the killing) you feel the close presence of fortress and castle. Glance to your left, and the Round Tower looms into view, pressing itself against the panes. But on days of drizzle and drifting cloud the keep diminishes, like an amateur drawing half-erased. Its lines soften, its edges fade; it shrinks into the raw cold from the river, more like a shrouded mountain than a castle built for kings.

The houses on the right-hand side of Trinity Place – I mean, on the right-hand side as you face out of town – have large gardens, each now shared between three or four tenants. In the early 1980s, England had not succumbed to the smell of burning. The carbonised reek of the weekend barbecue was

2

unknown, except in the riverside gin palaces of Maidenhead and Bray. Our gardens, though immaculately kept, saw little footfall; there were no children in the street, just young couples who had yet to breed and older couples who might, at most, open a door to let an evening party spill out on to a terrace. Through warm afternoons the lawns baked unattended, and cats curled snoozing in the crumbling topsoil of stone urns. In autumn, leaf-heaps composted themselves on sunken patios, and were shovelled up by irritated owners of basement flats. The winter rains soaked the shrubberies, with no one there to see.

But in the summer of 1983 this genteel corner, bypassed by shoppers and tourists, found itself a focus of national interest. Behind the gardens of No.20 and No.21 stood the grounds of a private hospital, a graceful pale building occupying a corner site. Three days before her assassination, the prime minister entered this hospital for minor eye surgery. Since then, the area had been dislocated. Strangers jostled residents. Newspapermen and TV crews blocked the street and parked without permission in driveways. You would see them trundle up and down Spinner's Walk trailing wires and lights, their gaze rolling towards the hospital gates on Clarence Road, their necks noosed by camera straps. Every few minutes they would coagulate in a mass of heaving combat jackets, as if to reassure each other that nothing was happening: but that it would happen, by and by. They waited, and while they waited they slurped orange juice from cartons and lager from cans; they ate, crumbs spilling down their fronts, soiled paper bags chucked into flowerbeds. The baker at the top of St Leonard's Road ran out of cheese rolls by 10am and everything else by noon. Windsorians clustered on Trinity Place, shopping bags wedged on to low walls. We speculated on why we had this honour, and when she might go away.

Windsor's not what you think. It has an intelligentsia.

Once you wind down from the castle to the bottom of Peascod Street, they are not all royalist lickspittles; and as you cross over the junction to St Leonard's Road, you might sniff out closet republicans. Still, it was cold comfort at the polls for the local socialists, and people murmured that it was a vote wasted; they had to show the strength of their feelings by tactical voting, and their spirit by attending outré events at the arts centre. Recently remodelled from the fire station, it was a place where self-published poets found a platform, and sour white wine was dispensed from boxes; on Saturday mornings there were classes in self-assertion, yoga and picture framing.

But when Mrs Thatcher came to visit, the dissidents took to the streets. They gathered in knots, inspecting the press corps and turning their shoulders to the hospital gates, where a row of precious parking bays were marked out and designated DOCTORS ONLY.

A woman said, 'I have a PhD, and I'm often tempted to park there.' It was early, and her loaf was still warm from the baker; she snuggled it against her, like a pet. She said, 'There are some strong opinions flying about.'

'Mine is a dagger,' I said, 'and it's flying straight to her heart.'

'Your sentiment,' she said admiringly, 'is the strongest I've heard.'

'Well, I have to go in,' I said. 'I'm expecting Mr Duggan to mend my boiler.'

'On a Saturday? Duggan? You're highly honoured. Better scoot. If you miss him he'll charge you. He's a shark, that man. But what can you do?' She fished for a pen in the bottom of her bag. 'I'll give you my number.' She wrote it on my bare arm, as neither of us had paper. 'Give me a ring. Do you ever go to the arts centre? We can get together over a glass of wine.'

I was putting my Perrier water in the fridge when the doorbell rang. I'd been thinking, we don't know it now, but we'll look back with fondness on the time Mrs Thatcher was here: new friendships formed in the street, chit-chat about plumbers whom we hold in common. On the entryphone there was the usual crackle, as if someone had set fire to the line. 'Come up, Mr Duggan,' I said. It was as well to be respectful to him.

I lived on the third floor, the stairs were steep and Duggan was ponderous. So I was surprised at how soon I heard the tap at the door. 'Hello,' I said. 'Did you manage to park your van?'

On the landing – or rather on the top step, as I was alone up there – stood a man in a cheap quilted jacket. My innocent thought was, here is Duggan's son. 'Boiler?' I said.

'Right,' he said.

He heaved himself in, with his boiler man's bag. We were nose to nose in the box-sized hall. His jacket, more than adequate to the English summer, took up the space between us. I edged backwards. 'What's up with it?' he said.

'It groans and bangs. I know it's August, but —'

'No, you're right, you're right, you can never trust the weather. Rads hot?'

'In patches.'

'Air in your system,' he said. 'While I'm waiting I'll bleed it. Might as well. If you've got a key.'

It was then that a suspicion struck me. Waiting, he said. Waiting for what? 'Are you a photographer?'

He didn't answer. He was patting himself down, searching his pockets, frowning.

'I was expecting a plumber. You shouldn't just walk in.'

'You opened the door.'

'Not to you. Anyway, I don't know why you bothered. You can't see the front gates from this side. You need to go out of here,' I said pointedly, 'and turn left.'

'They say she's coming out the back way. It's a great place to get a shot.'

My bedroom had a perfect view of the hospital garden; anyone, by walking around the side of the house, could guess this.

'Who do you work for?' I said.

'You don't need to know.'

'Perhaps not, but it would be polite to tell me.' As I backed into the kitchen, he followed. The room was full of sunlight, and now I saw him clearly: a stocky man, thirties, unkempt, with a round friendly face and unruly hair. He dumped his bag on the table, and pulled off his jacket. His size diminished by half. 'Let's say I'm freelance.'

'Even so,' I said, 'I should get a fee for the use of my premises. It's only fair.'

'You couldn't put a price on this,' he said.

By his accent, he was from Liverpool. Far from Duggan, or Duggan's son. But then he hadn't spoken till he was in at the front door, so how could I have known? He could have been a plumber, I said to myself. I hadn't been a total fool; for the moment, self-respect was all that concerned me. Ask for identification, people advise, before letting a stranger in. But imagine the ruckus that Duggan would have caused, if you'd held his boy up on the stairs, impeding him from getting to the next boiler on his list, and shortening his plunder opportunities.

The kitchen window looked down over Trinity Place, now seething with people. If I craned my neck I could see a new police presence to my left, trotting up from the private gardens of Clarence Crescent. 'Have one of these?' The visitor had found his cigarettes.

'No. And I'd rather you didn't.'

'Fair enough.' He crushed the pack into his pocket, and pulled out a balled-up handkerchief. He stood back from the tall window, mopping his face; face and handkerchief were both crumpled and grey. Clearly it wasn't something he was used to, tricking himself into private houses. I was more annoyed with myself than with him. He had a living to make, and perhaps you couldn't blame him for pushing in, when some fool of a woman held the door open. I said, 'How long do you propose to stay?'

'She's expected in an hour.'

'Right.' That accounted for it, the increased hum and buzz from the street. 'How do you know?'

'We've a girl on the inside. A nurse.'

I handed him two sheets of kitchen roll. 'Ta.' He blotted his forehead. 'She's going to come out and the doctors and nurses are lining up, so she can appreciate them. She's going to walk along the line with her thank-you and bye-bye, then toddle round the side, duck into a limo and she's away. Well, that's the idea. I don't have an exact time. So I thought if I was here early I could set up, have a look at the angles.'

'How much will you get for a good shot?'

'Life without parole,' he said.

I laughed. 'It's not a crime.'

'That's my feeling.'

'It's a fair distance,' I said. 'I mean, I know you have special lenses, and you're the only one up here, but don't you want a close-up?'

'Nah,' he said. 'As long as I get a clear view, the distance is a doddle.'

He crumpled up the kitchen roll and looked around for the bin. I took the paper from him, he grunted, then applied himself to unstrapping his bag, a canvas holdall that I supposed would be as suitable for a photographer as for any tradesman. But one by one he took out metal parts, which, even in my ignorance, I knew were not part of a photographer's kit. He began to assemble them; his fingertips were delicate. As he worked he sang, almost under his breath, a little song from the football terraces:

~

'You are a scouser, a dirty scouser,
You're only happy on giro day.
Your dad's out stealing, your mam's drug-dealing,
Please don't take our hub-caps away.'

'Three million unemployed,' he said. 'Most of them live round our way. It wouldn't be a problem here, would it?'

'Oh no. Plenty of gift shops to employ everybody. Have you been up to the High Street?'

I thought of the tourist scrums pushing each other off the pavements, jostling for souvenir humbugs and wind-up Beef-eaters. It could have been another country. No voices carried from the street below. Our man was humming, absorbed. I wondered if his song had a second verse. As he lifted each component from his bag he wiped it with a cloth that was cleaner than his handkerchief, handling it with gentle reverence, like an altar boy polishing the vessels for mass.

When the mechanism was assembled he held it out for my inspection. 'Folding stock,' he said. 'That's the beauty of her. Fits in a cornflakes packet. They call her the widowmaker. Though not in this case. Poor bloody Denis, eh? He'll have to boil his own eggs from now on.'

It feels, in retrospect, as if hours stretched ahead, as we sat in the bedroom together, he on a folding chair near the sash window, his mug of tea cradled in his hands, the widow-maker at his feet; myself on the edge of the bed, over which I had hastily dragged the duvet to tidy it. He had brought his jacket from the kitchen; perhaps the pockets were crammed with assassin's requisites. When he flung it on the bed, it slid straight off again. I tried to grab it and my palm slid across the nylon; like a reptile, it seemed to have its own life. I flumped

8

it on the bed beside me and took a grip on it by the collar. He looked on with mild approval.

He kept glancing at his watch, though he said he had no certain time. Once he rubbed its face with his palm, as if it might be fogged and concealing a different time underneath. He would check, from the corner of his eye, that I was still where I should be, my hands in view: as, he explained, he preferred them to be. Then he would fix his gaze on the lawns, the back fences. As if to be closer to his target, he rocked his chair forwards on its front legs.

I said, 'It's the fake femininity I can't stand, and the counterfeit voice. The way she boasts about her dad the grocer and what he taught her, but you know she would change it all if she could, and be born to rich people. It's the way she loves the rich, the way she worships them. It's her philistinism, her ignorance, and the way she revels in her ignorance. It's her lack of pity. Why does she need an eye operation? Is it because she can't cry?'

When the telephone rang, it made us both jump. I broke off what I was saying. 'Answer that,' he said. 'It will be for me.'

It was hard for me to imagine the busy network of activity that lay behind the day's plans. 'Wait,' I'd said to him, as I asked him, 'Tea or coffee?' as I switched the kettle on. 'You know I was expecting the boiler man? I'm sure he'll be here soon.'

'Duggan?' he said. 'Nah.'

'You know Duggan?'

'I know he won't be here.'

'What have you done to him?'

'Oh, for God's sake.' He snorted. 'Why would we do anything? No need. He got the nod. We have pals all over the place.'

Pals. A pleasing word. Almost archaic. Dear God, I thought, Duggan an IRA man. Not that my visitor had named his affiliation, but I had spoken it loudly in my mind. The word, the initials, didn't cause me the shock or upset it would cause, perhaps, to you. I told him this, as I reached in the fridge for milk and waited for the kettle to boil: saying, I would deter you if I could, but it would only be out of fear for myself and what's going to happen to me after you've done it: which by the way is what? I am no friend of this woman, though I don't (I felt compelled to add) believe violence solves anything. But I would not betray you, because . . .

'Yeah,' he said. 'Everybody's got an Irish granny. It's no guarantee of anything at all. I'm here for your sightlines. I don't care about your affinities. Keep away from the front window and don't touch the phone, or I'll knock you dead. I don't care about the songs your bloody great-uncles used to sing on a Saturday night.'

I nodded. It was only what I'd thought myself. It was senti-ment and no substance.

'The minstrel boy to the war is gone,
In the ranks of death you'll find him.
His father's sword he has girded on,
And his wild harp slung behind him.'

My great-uncles (and he was right about them) wouldn't have known a wild harp if it had sprung up and bitten their bottoms. Patriotism was only an excuse to get what they called pie-eyed, while their wives had tea and gingernuts then recited the rosary in the back kitchen. The whole thing was an excuse: why we are oppressed. Why we are sat here being oppressed, while people from other tribes are hauling themselves up by their own ungodly efforts and buying three-piece suites. While we are rooted here going la-la-la auld Ireland (because at this distance in time the words escape us) our neighbours are patching their quarrels, losing their origins and moving on, to modern, non-sectarian forms of stigma, expressed in modern songs: you are a scouser, a dirty scouser. I'm not, personally. But the north is all the same to southerners. And in Berkshire and the Home Counties, all causes are the same, all ideas for which a person might care to die: they are nuisances, a breach of the peace, and likely to hold up the traffic or delay the trains.

'You seem to know about me,' I said. I sounded resentful.

'As much as anybody would need to know. That's to say, not that you're anything special. You can be a help if you want, and if you don't want, we can do accordingly.'

He spoke as if he had companions. He was only one man. But a bulky one, even without the jacket. Suppose I had been a true-blue Tory, or one of those devout souls who won't so much as crush an insect: I still wouldn't have tried anything tricky. As it was, he counted on me to be docile, or perhaps, despite his sneering, he trusted me to some small extent. Anyway, he let me follow him into the bedroom with my mug of tea. He carried his own tea in his left hand and his gun in his right. He left the roll of sticky tape and the handcuffs on the kitchen table, where he'd put them when they came out of his bag.

And now he let me pick up the phone extension from the bedside table, and hand it to him. I heard a woman's voice, young, timid and far away. You would not have thought she was in the hospital round the corner. 'Brendan?' she said. I did not imagine that was his real name.

He put down the receiver so hard it clattered. 'There's some friggin' hold-up. It'll be twenty minutes, she reckons. Or thirty, it could even be thirty.' He let his breath out, as if he'd been holding it since he stomped upstairs. 'Bugger this. Where's the lav?'

You can surprise a person with *affinity*, I thought, and then say, 'Where's the lav?' Not a Windsor expression. It wasn't really a question, either. The flat was so small that its layout was obvious. He took his weapon with him. I listened to him urinate. Run a tap. I heard splashing. I heard him come out, zipping his trousers. His face was red where he'd been towelling it. He sat down hard on the folding chair. There was a bleat from the fragile canework. He said, 'You've got a number written on your arm.'

'Yes.'

'What's it a number of?'

'A woman.' I dabbed my forefinger with my tongue and slicked it across the ink.

'You won't get it off that way. You need to get some soap and give it a good scrub.'

'How kind of you to take an interest.'

'Have you wrote it down? Her number?'

'No.'

'Don't you want it?'

Only if I have a future, I thought. I wondered when it would be appropriate to ask.

'Make us another brew. And put sugar in it this time.'

'Oh,' I said. I was flustered by a failing in hospitality. 'I didn't know you took sugar. I might not have white.'

'The bourgeoisie, eh?'

I was angry. 'You're not too proud to shoot out of my bourgeois sash window, are you?'

He lurched forward, hand groping for the gun. It wasn't to shoot me, though my heart leapt. He glared down into the gardens, tensing as if he were going to butt his head through the glass. He made a small, dissatisfied grunt, and sat down again. 'A bloody cat on the fence.'

'I have demerara,' I said. 'I expect it tastes the same, when it's stirred in.'

'You wouldn't think of shouting out of the kitchen window, would you?' he said. 'Or trying to bolt down the stairs?'

'What, after all I've said?'

'You think you're on my side?' He was sweating again. 'You don't know my side. Believe me, you have no idea.'

It crossed my mind then he might not be a Provisional, but from one of the mad splinter groups you heard of. I was hardly in a position to quibble; the end result would be the same. But I said, 'Bourgeoisie, what sort of polytechnic expression is that?'

I was insulting him, and I meant to. For those of tender years, I should explain that polytechnics were institutes of higher education, for the young who missed university entrance: for those who were bright enough to say *affinity*, but still wore cheap nylon coats.

He frowned. 'Brew the tea.'

'I don't think you should sneer at my great-uncles for being cod-Irish, if you talk in slogans you found in skips.'

'It was a sort of a joke,' he said.

'Oh. Well. Was it?' I was taken aback. 'It looks as if I've no more sense of humour than she has.'

I indicated, with my head, the lawns outside the window, where the prime minister was shortly to die.

'I don't fault her for not laughing,' he said. 'I won't fault her for that.'

'You should. It's why she can't see how ridiculous she is.'

'I wouldn't call her ridiculous,' he said, mulish. 'Cruel, wicked, but not ridiculous. What's there to laugh at?'

'All things human laugh,' I said.

After some thought, he replied, 'Jesus wept.'

He smirked. I saw he had relaxed, knowing that because of the friggin' delay he wouldn't have to murder yet. 'Mind you,' I said, 'she'd probably laugh if she were here. She'd laugh because she despises us. Look at your anorak. She despises your anorak. Look at my hair. She despises my hair.'

He glanced up. He'd not looked at me before, not to see

me; I was just the tea-maker. 'The way it just hangs there,' I explained. 'Instead of being in corrugations. I ought to have it washed and set. It ought to go in graduated rollers, she knows where she is with that sort of hair. And I don't like the way she walks. "Toddles", you said. "She'll toddle round." You had it right, there.'

'What do you think this is about?' he said.

'Ireland.'

He nodded. 'And I want you to understand that. I'm not shooting her because she doesn't like the opera. Or because you don't care for – what in sod's name do you call it? – her accessories. It's not about her handbag. It's not about her hairdo. It's about Ireland. Only Ireland, right?'

'Oh, I don't know,' I said. 'You're a bit of a fake yourself, I think. You're no nearer the old country than I am. Your great-uncles didn't know the words either. So you might want supporting reasons. Adjuncts.'

'I was brought up in a tradition,' he said. 'And look, it brings us here.' He looked around, as if he didn't believe it: the crucial act of a dedicated life, ten minutes from now, with your back to a chipboard wardrobe glossed with white veneer; a pleated paper blind, an unmade bed, a strange woman, and your last tea with no sugar in it. 'I think of those boys on hunger strike,' he said, 'the first of them dead almost two years to the day that she was first elected: did you know that? It took sixty-six days for Bobby to die. And nine other boys not far behind him. After you've starved yourself for about forty-five days they say it gets better. You stop dry-heaving and you can take water again. But that's your last chance, because after fifty days you can hardly see or hear. Your body digests itself. It eats itself in despair. You wonder she can't laugh? I see nothing to laugh at.'

'What can I say?' I asked him. 'I agree with everything you've said. You go and make the tea and I'll sit here and mind the gun.'

For a moment, he seemed to consider it. 'You'd miss. You're not trained at all.'

'How are you trained?'

'Targets.'

'It's not like a live person. You might shoot the nurses. The doctors.'

'I might, at that.'

I heard his long, smoker's cough. 'Oh, right, the tea,' I said. 'But you know another thing? They may have been blind at the end, but their eyes were open when they went into it. You can't force pity from a government like hers. Why would she negotiate? Why would you expect it? What's a dozen Irishmen to them? What's a hundred? All those people, they're capital punishers. They pretend to be modern, but leave them to themselves and they'd gouge eyes out in the public squares.'

'It might not be a bad thing,' he said. 'Hanging. In some circumstances.'

I stared at him. 'For an Irish martyr? Okay. Quicker than starving yourself.'

'It is that. I can't fault you there.'

'You know what men say, in the pub? They say, name an Irish martyr. They say, go on, go on, you can't, can you?'

'I could give you a string of names,' he said. 'They were in the paper. Two years, is that too long to remember?'

'No. But keep up, will you? The people who say this, they're Englishmen.'

'You're right. They're Englishmen,' he said sadly. 'They can't remember bugger-all.'

Ten minutes, I thought. Ten minutes give or take. In defiance of him, I sidled up to the kitchen window. The street had fallen into its weekend torpor; the crowds were around the corner. They must be expecting her soon. There was a telephone on the kitchen worktop, right by my hand, but if I picked it up he would hear the bedroom extension give its little yip, and he would come out and kill me, not with a bullet but in some less obtrusive way that would not alert the neighbours and spoil his day.

I stood by the kettle while it boiled. I wondered: has the eye surgery been a success? When she comes out, will she be able to see as normal? Will they have to lead her? Will her eyes be bandaged?

I did not like the picture in my mind. I called out to him, to know the answer. No, he shouted back, the old eyes will be sharp as a tack.

I thought, there's not a tear in her. Not for the mother in the rain at the bus stop, or the sailor burning in the sea. She sleeps four hours a night. She lives on the fumes of whisky and the iron in the blood of her prey.

When I took back the second mug of tea, with the demerara stirred in, he had taken off his baggy sweater, which was unravelling at the cuffs; he dresses for the tomb, I thought, layer on layer but it won't keep out the cold. Under the wool he wore a faded flannel shirt. Its twisted collar curled up; I thought, he looks like a man who does his own laundry. 'Hostages to fortune?' I said.

'No,' he said, 'I don't get very far with the lasses.' He passed a hand over his hair to flatten it, as if the adjustment might change his fortunes. 'No kids, well, none I know of.'

I gave him his tea. He took a gulp and winced. 'After . . .' he said.

'Yes?'

'Right after, they'll know where the shot's come from, it won't take any time for them to work that out. Once I get down the stairs and out the front door, they'll have me right there in the street. I'm going to take the gun, so as soon as they sight me they'll shoot me dead.' He paused and then said, as if I had demurred, 'It's the best way.'

'Ah,' I said. 'I thought you had a plan. I mean, other than getting killed.'

'What better plan could I have?' There was only a touch of sarcasm. 'It's a godsend, this. The hospital. Your attic. Your window. You. It's cheap. It's clean. It gets the job done, and it costs one man.'

I had said to him earlier, violence solves nothing. But it was only a piety, like a grace before meat. I wasn't attending to its meaning as I said it, and if I thought about it, I felt a hypocrite. It's only what the strong preach to the weak: you never hear it the other way round; the strong don't lay down their arms. 'What if I could buy you a moment?' I said. 'If you were to wear your jacket to the killing, and be ready to go: to leave the widowmaker here, and pick up your empty bag, and walk out like a boiler man, the way you came in?'

'As soon as I walk out of this house I'm done.'

'But if you were to walk out of the house next door?'

'And how would that be managed?' he said.

I said, 'Come with me.'

He was nervous to leave it, his sentry post, but on this promise he must. We still have five minutes, I said, and you know it, so come, leave your gun tidily under your chair. He crowded up behind me in the hall, and I had to tell him to step back so I could open the door. 'Put it on the latch,' he advised. 'It would be a farce if we were shut out on the stairs.'

The staircases of these houses have no daylight. You can push a time-switch on the wall and flood the landings with a yellow glare. After the allotted two minutes you will be back in the dark. But the darkness is not so deep as you first think.

You stand, breathing gently, evenly, eyes adapting. Feet noiseless on the thick carpets, descend just one half-flight. Listen: the house is silent. The tenants who share this staircase are gone all day. Closed doors annul and muffle the world outside, the cackle of news bulletins from radios, the buzz of the trippers from the top of the town, even the apocalyptic roar of the aeroplanes as they dip towards Heathrow. The air, uncirculated, has a camphor smell, as if the people who first lived here were creaking open wardrobes, lifting out their mourning clothes. Neither in nor out of the house, visible but not seen, you could lurk here for an hour undisturbed, you could loiter for a day. You could sleep here; you could dream. Neither innocent nor guilty, you could skulk here for decades, while the alderman's daughter grows old: between step and step, grow old yourself, slip the noose of your name. One day Trinity Place will fall down, in a puff of plaster and powdered bone. Time will draw to a zero point, a dot: angels will pick through the ruins, kicking up the petals from the gutters, arms wrapped in tattered flags.

On the stairs, a whispered word: 'And will you kill me?' It is a question you can only ask in the dark.

'I'll leave you gagged and taped,' he says. 'In the kitchen. You can tell them I did it the minute I burst in.'

'But when will you really do it?' Voice a murmur.

'Just before. No time after.'

'You will not. I want to see. I'm not missing this.'

'Then I'll tie you up in the bedroom, okay? I'll tie you up with a view.'

'You could let me slip downstairs just before. I'll take a shopping bag. If nobody sees me go, I'll say I was out the whole time. But make sure to force my door, won't you? Like a break-in?'

'I see you know my job.'

'I'm learning.'

'I thought you wanted to see it happen.'

'I'd be able to hear it. It'll be like the roar from the Roman circus.'

'No. We'll not do that.' A touch: hand brushing arm. 'Show me this thing. Whatever it is I'm here for, wasting time.'

On the half-landing there is a door. It looks like the door to a broom cupboard. But it is heavy. Heavy to pull, hand slipping on the brass knob.

'Fire door.'

He leans past and yanks it open.

Behind it, two inches away, another door.

'Push.'

He pushes. Slow glide, dark into matching dark.

The same faint, trapped, accumulating scent, the scent of the margin where the private and public worlds meet: raindrops on contract carpet, wet umbrella, damp shoe-leather, metal tang of keys, the salt of metal in palm. But this is the house next door. Look down into the dim well. It is the same, but not. You can step out of that frame and into this. A killer, you enter No.21. A plumber, you exit No.20. Beyond the fire door there are other households with other lives. Different histories lie close; they are curled like winter animals, breathing shallow, pulse undetected.

What we need, it is clear, is to buy time. A few moments' grace to deliver us from a situation that seems unnegotiable. There is a quirk in the building's structure. It is a slender chance but the only one. From the house next door he will emerge a few yards nearer the end of the street: nearer the right end, away from town and castle, away from the crime. We must assume that despite his bravado he does not intend to die if he can help it: that somewhere in the surrounding streets, illegally parked in a resident's bay or blocking a resident's drive, there is a vehicle waiting for him, to convey him beyond reach, and dissolve him as if he had never been.

He hesitates, looking into the dark.

'Try it. Do not put on the light. Do not speak. Step through.'

~

Who has not seen the door in the wall? It is the invalid child's consolation, the prisoner's last hope. It is the easy exit for the dying man, who perishes not in the death-grip of a rattling gasp, but passes on a sigh, like a falling feather. It is a special door and obeys no laws that govern wood or iron. No locksmith can defeat it, no bailiff kick it in; patrolling policemen pass it, because it is visible only to the eye of faith. Once through it, you return as angles and air, as sparks and flame. That the assassin was a flicker in its frame, you know. Beyond the fire door he melts, and this is how you've never seen him on the news. This is how you don't know his name, his face. This is how, to your certain knowledge, Mrs Thatcher went on living till she died. But note the door: note the wall: note the power of the door in the wall that you never saw was there. And note the cold wind that blows through it, when you open it a crack. History could always have been otherwise. For there is the time, the place, the black opportunity: the day, the hour, the slant of the light, the ice-cream van chiming from a distant road near the bypass.

And stepping back, into No.21, the assassin grunts with laughter.

'Shh!' I say.

'Is that your great suggestion? They shoot me a bit further along the street? Okay, we'll give it a go. Exit along another line. A little surprise.'

Time is short now. We return to the bedroom. He has not said if I shall live or should make other plans. He motions me to the window. 'Open it now. Then get back.'

He is afraid of a sudden noise that might startle someone below. But though the window is heavy, and sometimes shudders in its frame, the sash slides smoothly upwards. He need not fret. The gardens are empty. But over in the hospital, beyond the fences and shrubs, there is movement. They are beginning to come out: not the official party, but a gaggle of nurses in their aprons and caps.

He takes up the widowmaker, lays her tenderly across his knees. He tips his chair forward, and because I see his hands are once more slippery with sweat I bring him a towel and he takes it without speaking, and wipes his palms. Once more I am reminded of something priestly: a sacrifice. A wasp dawdles over the sill. The scent of the gardens is watery, green. The tepid sunshine wobbles in, polishes his shabby brogues, moves shyly across the surface of the dressing table. I want to ask: when what is to happen, happens, will it be noisy? From where I sit? If I sit? Or stand? Stand where? At his shoulder? Perhaps I should kneel and pray.

And now we are seconds from the target. The terrace, the lawns, are twittering with hospital personnel. A receiving line has formed. Doctors, nurses, clerks. The chef joins it, in his whites and a toque. It is a kind of hat I have only seen in children's picture books. Despite myself, I giggle. I am conscious of every rise and fall of the assassin's breath. A hush falls: on the gardens, and on us.

High heels on the mossy path. Tippy-tap. Toddle on. She's making efforts, but getting nowhere very fast. The bag on the arm, slung like a shield. The tailored suit just as I have foreseen, the pussy-cat bow, a long loop of pearls, and – a new touch – big goggle glasses. Shading her, no doubt, from the trials of the afternoon. Hand extended, she is moving along the line. Now that we are here at last, there is all the time in the world. The gunman kneels, easing into position. He sees what I see, the glittering helmet of hair. He sees it shine like a gold coin in a gutter, he sees it big as the full moon. On the sill the wasp hovers, suspends itself in still air. One easy wink of the world's blind eye: 'Rejoice,' he says. 'Fucking rejoice.'

LUCKY

HER PARENTS AND brother are going to spend the holiday weekend up in the mountains at the neighbour's country house. When asked she says no, she's not up to it – the long drive on those endlessly winding roads always makes her car-sick – and she shakes her head, sticks out her tongue and makes a face like she can already feel the nausea. She's been up there several times anyway, knows what it's like: she's seen the automatic shampoo dispensers in the bathroom that fill her hands with grapefruit-scented foam, the shiny mountain bikes that have never been ridden propped up on the porch, the indoor fish pond and the seashell-patterned ashtrays. She always gets so bored, sitting in a white plastic chair and batting away flies while the adults drink beer out of green glass bottles and talk, talk, talk for hours about things she either doesn't care about or doesn't understand. When she hears the word *guerrilla* she'll picture a group of men dressed up in gorilla suits, roaming through the jungle while carrying rifles, wearing black rubber boots with yellow bottoms, and she'll have to choke back laughter to prevent Coca-Cola from snorting out of her nose. The sinewy meat and burnt black corn from the grill always get stuck in her teeth and hang down from her upper molars like vines for Tarzan, and she'll inevitably end up prodding them with her tongue for the rest of the weekend.

So no, she tells her mother again, but thank you, and she brushes strands of blonde hair away from her eyes, smiling sweetly.

'Well fine then,' her mother says, a little sharply. 'That means I'm going to have to tell Angelina that she can't have the holiday weekend off like she planned and that she has to spend it here with you. Was that church thing of hers this weekend or next?' She says this last part to her husband, who shrugs without looking up, still fiddling with the car radio knobs. One of the announcers is saying in a highly amused voice, *Communist rebels? Those words don't even mean anything any more. You might as well call them cheese sandwich rebels.* Her brother makes a face at her through the car window and she makes a face right back.

'Just do me a favour then, sweetie,' her mother says. 'As long as you're going to be here all weekend.' She glances across the street at the neighbour's house, the grey automatic gates barred shut, shards of glass glistening on top of the stone walls. 'If the phone rings,' she says, 'or the doorbell sounds, let Angelina deal with it. And do make sure she tells any men who ask that we're not in the country any more. Could you do that for me?'

'What kind of men?' she asks.

Her mother tucks a strand of hair behind her ears, blond like hers except for the grey at the roots. 'You know what kind I mean,' she says in her soft accent.

So they want their revolution? the radio asks. *Listen, I'll tell you what I'd do to them!* Her mother's head flicks sharply towards her husband, and he quickly switches it off.

After they drive away she finds her mother's cigarettes almost immediately, hidden at the bottom of one of the woven baskets Angelina brings back from her village marketplace.

She smokes one under the trees by the pool, taking quick little puffs, watching carefully for Angelina at the window. What she didn't tell her mother is that she has plans to meet up with her friends at the mall on Monday. Katrina's chauffeur will take them there, dropping them off at the entrance, where they'll hover just long enough to make sure he's gone. Then they'll cross the highway together, ducking fast across the busy intersection, laughing and running past the wooden sticks of chicken sweating on grills and giant metal barrels of spinning brown peanuts, the clown-faced garbage cans and men in zebra costumes directing traffic. The plan is to head to the other mall across the street, the one with the upper floors still closed off with yellow electrical tape from when the last bomb went off. On the first floor is the food court that serves Cuban sandwiches and beer in lava lamp containers. That's where the members of the football team will be, older boys with their hair slicked back and glistening. She and her friends are going to sit at the wooden picnic tables and yank their jeans down as far as they can go, tug their tank top straps aside to reveal the smallest hints of bra straps, peach and pink and black. She has this way of crossing her legs at the ankles, tilting her head to the side and smiling as though whatever is being said is the most interesting thing in the world and there's nowhere else she'd rather be. She'll accept their smiles, their eyes scanning her up and down, their low murmurs of approval, even the high-pitched whistles of *Blondie*, with the same icy sense of destiny that she accepts everything else in her life.

Later that night she's sitting on the couch reading one of her Arthurian fantasy novels, another one filled with knights kneeling before queens and saying things like My lady, perchance you have misunderstood me. She never needs to raise her eyes to know where Angelina is or what she's doing – the sound of her black plastic sandals slapping against the floor tiles is like a noise made by the house itself. Without looking she knows when Angelina's opening the silverware drawer, lighting the candles to chase away flies, setting the last of the dishes on the table. The radio in the kitchen crackles loudly with static, drowning out the newscasters' gruff voices.

She's almost at the end of the chapter when she feels a stubby finger gently tracing her scalp. 'We really need to fix your hair, *mija*,' Angelina says, in that same shrill, high-pitched voice she's been listening to her whole life. 'It's bad to have it in your eyes all the time like that.'

'That won't be necessary,' she says, not looking up from the page.

When Angelina's hands linger close to her face, she uses the book to push them away, ducking irritably from their overwhelming smell of onions and stale, powdered milk. She turns a page as the sandals slap slowly back to the kitchen.

During dinner she drips a giant spoonful of curry sauce onto her plate and swirls around the lettuce leaves and onion slices to make it look like she's eaten something. When she pushes the chair back from the table Angelina is already there, reaching for her plate with one hand and squeezing the flesh on her lower arm with the other. 'My God, but you're skinny!' Angelina says, the same high-pitched shrill. 'Eat more! How are you going to fight off men?'

'Could you please not touch me?' she says, jerking her arm away, but the tiny nugget of pleasure that's formed inside her just from hearing the word *skinny* is already giving off warmth.

Angelina says something else, speaking in a low voice this time, but her words are muffled beneath the trumpets of the national anthem, blasting from the kitchen radio, in its usual slot just before the news.

'What?' she says, but Angelina's already abruptly turned away, her white apron swirling through the air like a cape.

'Don't worry about it, *mija*,' Angelina says, not looking back. 'It's nothing.'

She doesn't wake up till mid-morning. Because Katrina and the others won't be coming by until Monday, she doesn't shave her legs and wears a baggy pair of yellow basketball shorts instead of jeans. The day is already uncomfortably hot. She heads outside to the pool and smokes a cigarette under the grapefruit tree, careful to stand in the shade to protect her skin. It never feels like a holiday weekend to her until she's smoked, until she gets that jumpy feeling in her stomach that makes her want to stand very still. In the distance she hears the low rumble of the neighbour's automatic gates opening, the crunching of car wheels on the gravel road, and she takes another long, slow drag.

Back in the kitchen, she opens the refrigerator and drinks directly from the pitcher of lemonade, ice cubes clanging against the glass. As she puts the pitcher on the counter there's a loud blast of the doorbell. It echoes through the house, followed by six blunt buzzes, as though it's a signal she should recognise.

'Angelina!' she calls out. She waits but there's no sound of sandals slapping against the floor tiles, heading to the front door.

The buzzing is long and sustained this time. 'Christ,' she says. 'Angelina!' When she was very young she would just stand in the middle of a room and scream Angelina's name over and over again, not stopping until she came running, apron flying out behind her, but that's not the kind of silly immature thing she would do now.

She takes another long swig of lemonade to hide her cigarette breath, just in case it's one of her mother's friends. It would be just like her to send someone to check up. As she walks down the hallway it's hard to decide what feels worse,

26

the damp cloth of the T-shirt sticking to her armpits or the sweaty bare skin of her collarbones. At the front door she runs her fingers through her hair, tucking strands carefully behind her ears.

The first door is made of heavy brown wood, covered in stickers Angelina gave her years ago, with a yellow bolt that slides easily open. The second door is made of white criss-crossing bars, forming diamond-shaped gaps that reveal the front yard and crackly bushes, the dried-out banana trees and dry brown hedge surrounding the property. Behind the hedge is the neighbour's automatic gate, the gravel road leading to the main highway, and beyond that are the fields of sugar cane and palm trees, the eucalyptus forests and the mountains.

Standing a few steps away is a man. He's grinning in a way that makes him look slightly embarrassed, rocking on his heels, arms crossed behind his back.

'Well, here I am,' he says. 'Let's go.'

He's wearing a shapeless brown robe, hanging off him as if empty, the creases flat. His feet are bare and caked in red clay, legs thin and hairless.

'Sorry I'm late,' he says. He brings an arm forward, a dirty plastic bag hanging from his wrist. 'It took me a lot longer to get here than I thought. I came as fast as I could.'

The plastic bag sways back and forth, hitting the front of his thigh. 'Lord, am I thirsty. Does that ever happen to you, when you have to walk a long way?' He licks his lips with a dark purple tongue. 'Never mind, don't worry about answering now. We'll have lots of time to talk.'

'Can I help you?' she says, taking a step back.

The man's face suddenly becomes a mass of deeply ingrained lines. He isn't old or wrinkled but his face is still cracked with deep splits, as if only just recently patched together. 'You mean she didn't tell you I was coming?' His voice comes out high-pitched and sad in a way that sounds deeply familiar to her, like something she's been listening to her whole life, though she cannot say why or how.

'Daddy!' she calls out over her shoulder, her voice echoing down the hallway. 'There's somebody here to see you!'

'Princess,' he says, the lines in his face growing even deeper. 'Come on. Don't do that. You know that I know they're not here.'

She stares at the lines. Some are thin like strands of hair, others deep like someone gouged the skin out with a scalpel. She takes another step back, tucking her body behind the brown door so that only her head is poking out. He kneels and starts ripping grass out of the ground, letting it fall in a tiny pile.

'I just don't understand why she didn't tell you,' he says. 'I spoke with her about it the other day and she said it would be fine. It doesn't make any sense.' His voice gets more high-pitched and shrill the longer he talks.

'Look, I don't even know you,' she says. It creates a sudden fluttering in her chest to use a loud voice like that, to be rude without caring, like the time she saw her father slap the hands of the street children reaching for her ice cream on the park picnic table.

'Don't know me?' His mouth turns downwards. 'Don't know me from Adam, huh? Have you heard that expression?' He rubs a hole into the ground, sticks his index finger in it and wiggles it around before covering it up again.

'At least it's a beautiful day,' he says, 'for us to run.' Just like that his head snaps up and he looks directly at her, narrowing his eyes in a way that makes her stomach leap and hit the back of her throat.

'Are you ready,' he says, 'to run?'

'Sorry,' she says. 'I'm sorry I can't help you.' She's closed the door to the point that she's looking at him through the thinnest crack possible, torso leaning forward in an L-shape.

'Hey,' he says, rising quickly to his feet, blades of grass drift-ing down from his robe. *'Mija.* Seriously. How lost are you? I'm here to help *you* —'

'I'm sorry,' she says again, right before closing the door completely, not finishing her sentence: *I don't have the key.* She's staring at the Bert & Ernie sticker now, plastered there by Angelina years ago, their smiles bright and beaming as they drive their firetruck down the street. The jumpy feeling in her stomach is still there.

Angelina's room is at the back of the house, next to the washing machine and the stacks of cardboard boxes filled with champagne. She forces herself to walk there as calmly and slowly as possible, the doorbell blasting and buzzing. The pale green door is covered with a giant Baby Jesus sticker, dimpled elbows raised smilingly heavenwards. On the floor lined neatly against the wall is a pair of black plastic sandals. She places her hand on the center of Baby Jesus' face, but doesn't push down. 'Angelina?' she says, softly at first, then louder. 'Are you there?'

She checks the rest of the rooms in the house, just to be sure. She checks her parents' bedroom, her brother's, her own (also with a Baby Jesus sticker on the door). She makes sure the back doors are locked and tugs experimentally at the bars over the windows.

With Angelina gone, she has no choice but to prepare lunch herself. She props the fridge door open with her torso, scoop-ing the rice and lentils out of the Tupperware containers with her hands curved like claws. The doorbell is still going, one long sustained note. By now the annoyance is bubbling inside her like the sudsy bubbles fizzling at the top of a shaken Coca-Cola bottle. She's already rehearsing the words in her head, picturing herself standing furiously in front of Angelina, arms akimbo, head tilted just like her mother's that time she addressed the electricity repairman, the one she suspected of stealing from them. *How could you do that*, she'll say. *Unacceptable. You know that I've never been left home alone before – completely un-fucking-acceptable. Good luck finding another job; I hope your bags are packed and ready. Are they ready?*

It's only that evening – when Angelina still isn't back, when she cannot get through to her parents, when their cellphones ring and ring – that she starts to get the feeling that something is happening.

The first thing she does is phone Katrina. She'll know what to do – she'll send her chauffeur along with the bodyguard; they'll come and take her away. But the telephone is silent when she presses it against her ears, the plastic heavy in her hands. She flicks the lightswitch back and forth a dozen times, pushes her thumb down on the TV power button as hard as possible, but the screen stays black and silent. She turns on Angelina's radio, the ridged wheel imprinting her fingertip as she rapidly surfs through the hisses and crackles. She finally finds a programme that seems to consist (as far as she can understand) of a fuzzy voice ranting endlessly about the need to drive out all the rebels, smoke them out of the mountains, exterminate them all, punctuated by short blasts of the national anthem. It creates a tight feeling in her chest. She switches the radio off, pries out the tiny yellow batteries with a kitchen knife and puts them away in the drawer with the silver bell Angelina used to ring to announce dinner. She spends the rest of the day in her bedroom, curtains shut tight, watching Disney movies on her laptop. The battery dies seconds before the Beast's magical transformation into a handsome prince, and after that she just lies there without moving, knees tucked near chin, ears tensed for the sound of car wheels on the road, keys rattling, the doorknob turning.

The next day is Monday, the holiday – Katrina's chauffeur never arrives. By mid-afternoon she heads outside to check the generator, more in hope than expectation. It's located in the back yard by the garage, bars across the door to prevent stray dogs and street people from sneaking in and sleeping. She stands there rubbing her arms, studying the thick braids of red and green wires, the forest of rust-encrusted switches. The gardener was the only person who knew how it worked, back when the power would go out due to bomb attacks in the city centre. He'd head to the back of the house, wiping his hands off on his denim shorts and two minutes later, as if by magic, the lights would fly back on. Her brother would whoop, bolting to the computer room, her parents smiling in forehead-crinkling relief as the soothing tones of BBC broadcasters returned, and she would blow out the candles and pick the wax off her algebra homework with her nails. Now, as she stands there by herself, she takes a last long, slow look at the impenetrable cluster of wires and switches, before trudging slowly back to the house.

The computers in the office seem like medieval relics. The screens stare at her, blank and impassive as grey-faced children asking for coins at traffic lights. In the end, she closes the door and bolts it. It's not like there's anything else in the room that's useful anyway: her parents' skis from Yale, faded blue and pink tapestries covered in dead moth wings, the wooden toucans and leopards she played with as a child, their eyes coloured in with washable markers, Christmas presents from Angelina that she opened politely before stuffing them away, brightly patterned shirts and alpaca shawls she'd never dream of wearing, not even alone in her bedroom.

If necessary they'll come for her. She's certain of it. Some kind of international peacekeeping army. Professional rescuers, speaking Norwegian, blue berets. Pale faces pressing smilingly against the white bars of the door, extending their arms as she runs to the kitchen to get the keys out of the blue wicker basket on top of the fridge. Their uniforms will smell like dairy, and they'll take her away in a shiny black car with squeaky plastic seats. Embassy members, the international community.

She won't just be left here. She won't be forgotten.

Mostly she wanders through the house, drifting from one room to another. The days blend lifelessly together, thick grey fuzz growing over each one like the dust accumulating on the unspun fan blades. She spends hours reading her fantasy novels, lying stomach-down on the bed. She reads childhood favourites, like a novelisation of *Star Wars: A New Hope* with half the pages missing, ending shortly after the scene where Luke bursts into Leia's cell: *My name is Luke Skywalker, and I'm here to rescue you.* She stares at the page for hours, the words blurring until they could be saying *cheese sandwich, cheese sandwich* over and over again.

She never puts anything away. She starts eating the canned food her parents reserved for parties, strange things like silvery fish floating in red sauce and olives in slimy black liquid, and leaves jars of sticky jam and cans of condensed milk licked clean and shiny on the kitchen counters. She rummages through school papers, re-reads syllabuses from long-ago classes (eighth-grade English with Mr Rover, World History with Mrs Márquez). She finds ancient notes Angelina wrote to excuse her from PE swimming class, every letter in each misspelled word painfully scrawled out in shaky capital letters. She opens her mother's make-up drawer, spills peach-coloured powder all over the sink, smears herself with eye shadow, ignores Angelina's high-pitched cries in her head: *Mija, what a mess! What do you think you're doing?* She pulls dusty boxes out of the closet and plays never-ending games of Monopoly, moving the tiny silver pieces around the board in infinite rotations: the dog, the thimble, the shiny boot last of all.

One night she feels both brave and desperate enough to

stand outside by the pool and hug the grapefruit tree. It's so quiet she can hear the water move, gently lapping against the concrete walls. She strains her eyes as she looks towards the mountains, almost convincing herself that she can see the fires, as small as the orange dots burning at the end of her cigarettes. She wills herself to smell smoke and gunpowder, hear the explosions and gunshots of incoming American forces, foreign backup support. Scrunching her eyes and pressing her face against the scratchy tree trunk, she can almost hear the helicopters, the clang of the metal doors as they slide open, the thud of the knotted rope ladder as it hits the ground by her feet. But when she opens her eyes there's only ever the scratchy grey fungus draped over the tree like a fisherman's net.

Back in her bedroom, she presses her face against the window, standing on her tiptoes, attempting to see over the stone walls into the neighbour's yard. But all she sees is the sunlight, glistening off the shards of glass, and the motionless metal face of the automatic gate, still silently shut.

Later, she stands outside of Angelina's room, hand resting on Baby Jesus' face. Looks down at the sandals, waits for the picture to form itself in her mind. Angelina, dressed in her white apron (what else could she be wearing?), carefully unlocking the front door, heading outside. Dawn is breaking, the earliest morning birds are singing. Or maybe it's still dark, the sky speckled with stars. Angelina's humming, hands in her pockets; Angelina's frowning, face scrunched up in her classic sour scowl. No matter what she imagines, the picture always abruptly ends the moment Angelina rounds the hedge corner, apron swirling through the air. Walking busily, purposefully, on her way to – what? Towards who?

Sometimes, she thinks she hears the slapping sound of black plastic sandals hitting floor tiles echoing through the house, and turns her head sharply. But there's never anything there.

One morning she awakes abruptly to the sound of someone banging on the door, the same insistent sound ringing out again and again. It takes her a second to realise that she's horizontal instead of vertical, fantasy book resting heavily on her chest. She struggles out of bed, dragging the bedsheets on the floor, dressed in her mother's fancy silk nightgown and saggy pink underpants (she ran out of clean pairs of her own long ago). Yellow dust motes float through the air, following her down the hallway as she stumbles forward, still dazedly clutching the book to her torso like a shield.

Once again she just barely opens the door, so that only her face can be seen. He's holding a walking stick, beating the bars like a monk ringing church bells in one of her Arthurian novels.

'Oh,' he says, his face framed in the diamond-shaped gap, 'you came!' His eyes widen in what is unmistakably delight. The whites of his eyeballs are lined with yellow and red; the cracks in his face look deeper and darker than ever. There's a low-pitched rumbling in the distance she hasn't noticed until now, the sound of a low-flying plane or helicopter. He's dressed in the same robe, but the plastic bag is gone, his feet no longer bare; instead he's now wearing a pair of shiny black rubber boots with yellow bottoms. For some reason the sight of those boots make her feel the most frightened she's ever been in her life; goosebumps break out on her neck and sour liquid leaks from her tonsils.

'Be a good girl,' he says. 'Open the door.'

'It's locked,' she says. She's turning away when he presses his face against the bars and reaches out, fingers fluttering urgently towards her.

'*Mija*,' he says. 'Time to go.'

'Could you please not touch me?' She uses the book to roughly push his hands away. The buzzing of the helicopter or plane returns for a bit, circles overhead, is replaced by a single engine. He says something else, speaking in a low voice, but his words are muffled beneath the sound of shots rattling out. She flinches.

'Don't worry about it, *mija*,' he says. 'It's nothing.'

This time, she looks directly at him. But he's already abruptly turned away, the hem of his robe swirling through the air like a cape.

The tiles feel cool and steady under her feet as she backs away. The book clatters loudly against the floor as it falls. She watches herself, dragging the bed sheets along the floor, heading towards the back of the house, to the washing machine and boxes of champagne. She's standing in front of the Baby Jesus sticker, spreading her fingers on his face, pushing down hard. The door opens easily. It only takes a few seconds to take everything in: the bed with thin yellow sheets, the window with scratchy brown curtains, everywhere the strong smell of soap. She opens the closet but there are only rows of white dresses hanging headless and limbless from hangers, aprons limp, no shoes to be seen. There are thick gobs of candle wax on the windowsill by the altar. On the floor by the bed, propped up by the wall, is a framed photograph of the three of them: she, her brother and Angelina. Hair hanging in her eyes, smiling sweetly.

She crawls into the bed, dragging the sheets with her, the sharp smell of mothballs itching her sinuses.

She thinks, *I have got to figure this out.*

She thinks, *If only I had more time.*

She doesn't know it yet but there's something waiting for her. It could be a future or it could be something else. It could be the plastic accelerator of a car pressing stickily against her leg, the man's wet fingers on her legs trembling as he helps her pull her saggy underpants back up from her ankles, mumbling over and over again *I'm sorry, I'm so sorry, I didn't mean to hurt you, mean to hurt you*. Or maybe she's in an enormous orange tent next to the raging, overflowing river on the border, one orange tent among many, where she wakes up at the same time every morning to stare at the silhouette of a lizard crawling across the fabric, and think about how she needs to head to the Red Cross tent to get into the line early. Or maybe she's running through a field, grass stinging against her legs and an aluminum taste in her mouth, the thudding footsteps and clink of machetes against belt buckles behind her getting louder and louder.

Or maybe it'll be something else. It could still happen. She could be lucky. She could be sitting in the giant concrete shell of a classroom in Europe or Australia, her pen moving slowly across a notebook, her eyes never leaving the professor as he speaks at the opposite end of the table.

It's still possible. But for now all she has is the round ball of the keychain in her hand, the rattling metal, and as she watches the keys dangle from her fingers, she thinks about how there's not a single key among the many that she recognises, not a single one she can pick out and say with confidence, this key opens that door, opens this one. None of it belongs to her and none of it ever has, in the same way that nothing in the house was ever hers and the tightly clenched muscle squeezing out blood in her chest has never really been hers either. For now there's only the cool metal in her hand that rattles loudly as she lifts her hands towards the dirty silver lock.

'Oh!' he says. The door makes a loud scraping sound against the ground as it swings open. 'You clever girl.' He lets out a deep sigh that could also be a groan of pain. Behind him the hedge rustles and she turns her head sharply. It could be the flash of a white apron or the metallic shine of a machete. It feels like noticing the shadow of her own half-closed eyelid, something that had always been there and should have been seen at least a thousand times before.

BEE LEWIS

THE IRON MEN

THE OTHERS THINK sunset is the best time, but I prefer sunrise. There is something comforting about seeing my shadow stretching out in front of me, a visual marker of the hours and days to come. I could be a sundial. The beach is quieter in the morning and each new day brings with it a promise that bends the horizon. The joggers stick to the promenade, their pounding heels driving the world forward. In the evenings, they run along the shoreline, blotting my view. I don't jog. I stand and absorb the air, my pores soaking up the sodium chloride and the ozone, which in fact isn't ozone, it's dimethyl sulphide.

Sometimes, there are horses and riders. They gallop past, sending clods of sand flying and leaving crescent moons in their wake. The horses are fleeting but I can feel them long before they come into view. Their hooves beat a tribal rhythm, replacing the thrum of my heart. I feel them at first in my feet, then my knees, then my pelvis, until finally they splinter up through my chest and out of my skull. Just as quickly, they are gone.

A bit further down the beach from me, Paddy contemplates the world around him by paddling in the spume. He started coming here before I did, after his wife had an affair.

He doesn't talk about it, but he wears the pain on his face like
decay. He smiles across at me and I can tell he is happiest in
that exact moment, with infinitesimal photons beaming down
on him and the foamy sea tickling his ankles. Man and nature.

A little girl in a red coat squeals and runs along the sand.
Here, in north-west England, the sand is mainly silicon
dioxide, better known as quartz, but in the Caribbean, say,
it would be calcium carbonate, created by millions of years
of shellfish habitation. The girl's flowery Wellingtons splash
through the rivulets of water, coursing down from the dunes to
the sea. She is carrying a sun-bleached stick that is almost as
tall as her and, up ahead, a Jack Russell is barking encouragement. Two adults come into view. They must be her parents.
They walk slowly, deliberately, hands in animated conversation. The woman has long hair that snakes in front of her face
in the breeze as she listens to her companion. He calls to the
girl and she stops, before turning towards him, knees bent as
though ready to sink into the sand. The adults catch up with
the girl and, taking her hands in theirs, swing her between
them. The dog yaps and circles them, wanting to join in.

I used to be afraid of dogs. I have been ever since I was a little
boy and our neighbour's dog barked all through the night.
The sound invaded my dreams, giving me night terrors, where
wolves chased me through the rain-glistening streets. Years
later, my morning walk to work would take me past a small
scrub of green, where the dog walkers congregated. It was a
daily test of my mettle. I challenged myself to go by without
giving off the scent of fear. Now I think of it, it's possible I
was more afraid of their owners. One morning, a quiet lady
in a blue, quilted jacket, stopped me. Her black Labrador sat,
patiently waiting.

'You don't like dogs, do you?'

I looked at her closely, unnerved by the intervention, not

sure how to respond. Would she think me a coward? And would I mind if she did?

'No, not really. I can't read them, you see. I can't tell what they are thinking.'

She looked at me, her eyes level, steady, and said, 'It's simple really. They want love and security, a place to sleep and food to eat. They are not so different from you and me.'

Her words stayed with me, coating my heart. I started looking out for her, Julia, and Jet, the Labrador. They'd walk part of the way to work with me. It took me a while to find the courage to ask her out, but I needn't have worried, we fitted together like hydrogen and oxygen. The result was something bigger than just us on our own. I asked her to be my wife and we lived together, not far from here. When our daughter, Sally, was born, we moved to a larger house further up the coast, but still close enough to the school I taught at.

I miss teaching the wonders of chemistry and physics to shiny-faced students, innocent with untapped potential. I try not to think of it too often. Not on days like this, when the haematite sea meets the mercury horizon.

My arms ache to hold my daughter. I look out, across the Irish Sea, and imagine her running along the shoreline, like the little girl with the stick and the Jack Russell. She'd be nearly twenty now.

There is another man standing close by. He, too, stares out to sea and breathes in deeply. I wonder if he can he smell the chemicals from the oil refinery at Stanlow. He sees me looking and half salutes; brothers in arms. He takes his clothes off and folds them in a neat pile next to where he is standing. Then he resumes staring, scanning the horizon for something he has lost.

Loss. It hits me in the guts again, and each time the blow hurts just as much as the first time. Sometimes, I see my pupils, heads bent in concentration, or chewing the ends of their pens, daydreaming. Without warning, I remember Sharon's face staring up at me as I stand at the front of the class, chalking the chemical formulas onto the board. She wore her red hair tied back in a single ponytail, a frown of concentration pleating her features. She was always an easy student to teach because she tried hard. Not especially clever, but able to apply herself well and her natural curiosity blossomed with the extra tuition I gave her.

My home life was more than I ever expected to have. Julia filled the house with love, while filling the cupboards with cakes and treats for Sally and me. We spent our weekends walking across these dunes, or further up the coast at the nature reserve, feeding the red squirrels. Our happiness came from simple things. All we needed was a car, a picnic rug and a Thermos flask. When it changed, no-one seemed to care what my opinion was.

I spend my time here reciting poetry. Not for me, the words of Larkin, Yeats or Heaney. I recite the Periodic Table, running my tongue over the elements, trying them on for size. My favourites are the noble gases: helium, neon, argon, krypton, xenon and radon. They sound to me like a potent task force of mythological super heroes. I marvel at the elegance and simplicity of the building blocks of the universe. We are made of stars. When the sun dies, and this world ends, the elements in the Periodic Table will remain and combine to form something new. Life is a series of chain reactions.

Sometimes, I can go many days without thinking of Sally or Julia or Sharon. But then something will remind me. It always does. I hate the rain the most, because the rain reminds me. I picture Sharon again, standing in the rain at the bus stop, shoulders sloping with hopelessness.

'Hop in, I'll give you a lift. You'll be soaked.'

Sharon got into the car, silent and grateful. Giving her a lift home seemed like the right thing to do – it wasn't out of my way. It became a regular thing. We mostly talked about school and her homework or her guinea pigs, but one day she was monosyllabic on the journey home and when we pulled up outside her house, there were tears in her eyes.

Sharon sat still, the effort to speak taking all her concentration.

'Dad's gone and Mum won't stop crying.'

Fat, salty tears spilled down her cheeks and misery seeped out of every pore. I put my arm around her shoulder and pulled her close to me, like I would when Sally fell and scraped her knee, or when she'd fallen out with her best friend. I'd learned how from watching Julia.

'It will be okay, sweetheart. It will be okay.' I stroked her hair and no-one was more surprised than me, when Sharon reached up to kiss me. I pulled away, brushed it aside; thought it best to ignore it. Then I stammered something I don't remember and said goodbye. Sharon looked sad, then angry and stormed up the short path to her front door. I drove away from her house, to a chorus line of twitching curtains.

By the time I got to school the following day, it was clear that I wouldn't be able to ignore the problem. I was called to the Headmaster's office. His round, porcine eyes bored into me and his throat-clearing underlined his disquiet.

'I . . . ehm . . . think it best if . . . ehm . . . suspended . . . need to investigate . . . serious allegations . . . ehm . . . best for you and . . . ehm . . . the child.'

The Headmaster actually meant for the benefit of the school, but was too cowardly to say so. The sound of his embarrassment rings in my ears still.

It didn't seem to matter to anyone that I didn't touch her, that I wouldn't do that. The words were out there, causing their own chain reaction, and people chose to believe what was convenient, over what was the truth. I try to blot out the memory of the gaggle of reporters camped outside the house; Julia's accusing face; my suitcase packed and waiting for me in the hall when I got home. The headlines in the papers were hard to bear. Not just for me, but for my family. I remember seeing Sally for the last time. Her puzzled face, her outstretched arms, her plaintive call for her Daddy. A wave of pain crashes over me.

I was charged, of course, and there was a trial. My defence barrister quickly stripped fact from fiction and the jury understood that it was a schoolgirl crush, not reciprocated in any way by me. After all the months leading up to the trial, the matter was dealt with in just 48 hours. At any other time, the efficiency would have delighted me. I was exonerated. Except it wasn't as easy as that. Mud sticks – I won't go into the physics of it – but it does. By that time, Julia had taken Sally away and it was too late to take back the barbs she'd thrown.

My life changed, decayed, oxidised. The iron in my heart fused with the hydrogen and oxygen that used to be Julia and me. The cascades of tears that I cried bound the new compound and, deep inside, the rust started to eat away at me. Day after day, I stood and stared out, until one day, I was powerless to stop the change. It began in my feet; they became leaden, heavy, as I slowly turned to iron. Now, my body is delaminating. The sea sloughs layers of rust and metal, like skin. The end result will be the same as if I had been buried in the ground. I will break down into my component elements and disperse, returning to the stars. All that remains of the old me is my consciousness – and even that will evaporate in time.

In another life, I would have liked to be a Classics scholar. The geometry and philosophy of the ancient Greeks fires my imagination almost as much as their contribution to the Periodic Table. Another day has passed and Apollo's fiery chariot will soon disappear in the west. We are bathed in the golden glow that Paddy calls 'God-light'. I'm aware of another presence nearby. This time, it's an older man and, as he sheds his clothes to absorb the dying rays of the sun, he nods and mouths over to me, 'Bankruptcy.' He turns away from me to stare out to sea like the rest of us. The iron in the haemoglobin carrying oxygen from his lungs thickens and multiplies, turning him to metal from within. His movements slow as the change takes place and, before sunset, he is one of us.

We number nearly a hundred now. We stretch for miles over the sands, silent, contemplative. We all have our stories. In our quiet, determined way, we look out to the horizon, reflecting on the events that brought us here. Each one of us stands apart from the rest, but we maintain the collective communion of hope. Time passes whilst ferrous oxide ravages our outer shells, returning us to the universe. The view I have changes daily, a moving landscape before me. I don't have to go anywhere to see the world turning. It's all here.

JONATHAN GIBBS

FESTSCHRIFT

CAN THERE BE, can there honestly be a more stirring monument to the depthless mysteries of the male mind than this: that there exists, for each and every one of us, a lifetime tally of sexual accomplishment? A number it is given to few to know precisely, but an empirically valid one nonetheless. It is the figure you look back on, on your deathbed, and, proverbially, would never wish lower than it is. Not, you understand, the number of distinct sexual partners, which is after all a more manageable and quantifiable statistic, but of the individual acts themselves, stacked up in fair years and fallow.

It was my ex-husband who uncovered to me this most secret measure of the world. We were in bed, and he said, in the moment after he rolled himself off me, lying there beset already by gasps of laughter, that he wasn't even sure if that one *would count* (the laughter starting mid-thrust – or, more precisely, at the completion or apex of a thrust, when he'd said, having suddenly ceased all movement, as if struck dumb, or religious, I think I've come.

You *think* . . .

I can't tell. Can you tell?).

What do you mean, *count*? I said.

You know, he said, flopping the back of a hand onto my tummy. If it'll count. In my running total.

That mystical number, he went on, when he saw I'd no idea what he was talking about, that I'll be able to look back on, as I draw my last breath, and only ever wish it had been higher than it was.

I've no idea what you're talking about.

It's what people say, isn't it? No one ever says, when they look back on their life, that they wish they'd had less sex.

Is that what they say, I said.

I don't mean to seem flippant, or maudlin, but this is what I was thinking of, as I lay in my wide and comfy conference bed, in my well-appointed conference hotel, and thought of my friend and mentor Leonard Peters, asleep as he probably was – as I hoped he was: soundly, painlessly – in some other room of this hotel, in this other country of the world, hours away by plane from our native land.

And I conjured my ex-husband, as I sometimes do in times of stress, or insomnia, or self-pity, and I turned on one elbow to face him. What about this, then, I said. What about my feelings for this man, feelings of pity and – yes, perhaps – of regret? This man I respect, immensely, that I have spent most of my professional life actively and instinctively respecting, but who I declined to go to bed with when he asked – or not even asked, really, but merely obliquely indicated his wish to do so. Whom I turned down when he drunkenly – probably – courageously – probably – and regretfully – definitely – propositioned me, that one time. Which he never did again. He was most considerate about it.

And now, looking back, I think – and this is the maudlin bit – what would have been the harm, in the grander scheme of things, if I had said yes? No question but that I've said yes in instances I regretted – and sometimes regret to this day –

far more than I would most likely have had cause to then, and instances too that were no less free of the taint of the workplace. I've failed to say no to worse men, men far inferior to him in character, and for all I know in bed too. And he was harmless, of that I'm sure. A fuck would have been a fuck. He'd divorced not long before, and was of an age of which I understand, now, the strange and desperate disorientation, and I was recently on the scene, and it was Christmas, and I think it just came over him, the animal need to pitch yourself forward, reach after something, steady yourself.

Work is the measure of all things – this is a belief of mine, perhaps even a maxim – and when you have sat across a boardroom table from someone in a departmental meeting for even five minutes there can be, there can surely be no surprises for you when you face them in the bedroom. Leonard was harmless – *is* harmless – and what harm can it have done to have slept with him that once? So that now, when he looks back on his life, he has one less regret. Or two fewer regrets; for, knowing him as I do, the regret that he never got to sleep with little old me would surely have been compounded by the second regret, following quick on its heels, and lasting far longer, that he had asked me at all.

So why ask me, you might say, blinking and widening your eyes in that way you do when I wake you up from wherever it is you sleep, when I think you back into existence.

Or, just as likely, you'd say, When was this? Was this when we were married?

You've turned onto your side, now, too, and so we lie facing each other, a foot of rumpled bed between us. We are mirrored, our heads propped on hands. You say it jokingly, camply, as if what you really want to say is, Was it because of *me* that you turned him down? Out of *fidelity* to our *marriage*? But you don't say any of these things. What you say is, Why are you asking me this now? And I see that you're serious, that you've seen through me, or through yourself, as conjured by me, and so I have to answer you.

This morning, during the coffee break before the second morning session – each coffee break a late Beckett play, one of the ones with diagrams instead of dialogue – I slipped away for a cigarette, as much to get some air on my face as for the thing itself, to rinse out my brain a little with traffic noise.

My smoking spot here, that a member of staff showed me on the first day, is a small courtyard down a dog-leg corridor from the suite of seminar rooms. Courtyard too grand a word. Poured concrete walls on three sides, with thick skeins of cables running along them and then disappearing around the corner, and, if you looked up, a single thin horizontal wire that trailed from it a creeper of some kind. It was only that, the green waterfall of toxic-looking leaves, and the off-set square of blue sky beyond the rising storeys, that told you where you were – or that you were somewhere even at all. At home I'm down to one cigarette a day, and have been since . . . well more or less since the divorce papers came through, thank you very much. I'm only really a smoker at conferences and the like, these days. It's so much more useful a vice now that so few people do it.

This, time, however, I had barely taken that first deep, and deeply freighted, breath, before I heard the door open behind me, and a man came through it. Having, clearly, followed me.

'Hi there,' he said. 'Mind if I join you?'

I had the elbow of my cigarette arm cupped in my other hand, and I waved the tip of the cigarette in as tight an ellipse as I could manage without seeming rude.

'Nice spot,' he said, and tamped a cigarette on his pack, as he looked up and around him. He looked at me to see if I was responding, was perhaps looking up, too, as if I hadn't noticed how nice my spot was until I'd had it pointed out to me. I kept my eyes on him, though, and sucked on my cigarette. He seemed to take this on the chin; he nodded, tucked the pack back into his shirt pocket, and lit up, with a match from a book from the hotel bar. Perhaps he'd been driven to it, too. He had slicked-back unwashed hair with winding streaks of grey in it, the hair thick enough to swallow them whole and spit them out again, further back. Though the voice was American, he looked Greek, or something like it. Handsomeness part-way compressed by the great gentle fist of poor diet and age.

'So you know Leonard how?' he said.

'Manchester,' I said. I waited a moment, then went on. 'Manchester, England? He was my PhD supervisor, and then I got a job there.'

He made a show of looking for my name badge, which I wasn't wearing.

'Eleanor Prose. Like the bad joke.'

'Eleanor *Prose*. *Right*. No, no jokes at all.'

He seemed impressed, and asked about my keynote address – which I will be giving in something under twelve hours, now, as I lie here, facing you, thinking all this through, trying to find a way out through its far end – and I said something in reply about his paper, which he had given that morning and of which I retained more than I pretended to.

He smoked faster than me, and when he came to the end of his cigarette he brushed it down the wall to dislodge the burning tip, which fell, complete, like a scab from healed skin. It landed and lay on the floor like a dead insect, iridescent. He placed his shoe over it.

'If Leonard could see me now. Shit. Makes me fucking hate myself.'

He shook his head, but this time when he looked at me my incomprehension must have shown. He gestured with the butt he still held. 'Leonard,' he said.

'Leonard.'

'You know, Leonard.'

He stopped – stopped speaking, stopped himself in the act of speech – then started again. 'Leonard, you know . . .'

The point at which he realised he was going to have to tell me was also the point at which he no longer had to.

So much that is spoken in life is redundant. Verbal communication as an overlapping and repetitive series of superfluities. White noise, chatter, birdsong. A doily all cutwork and no mat.

Leonard had lung cancer.

Leonard had lung cancer and he was dying of it. Everybody knew it. How could I not know? How did he, how could that *be*? It was far gone, my new Greek-looking friend told me, beyond all beyonds, and everybody knew. The fact that everybody knew was clear from his shock at the fact that I didn't. Everybody there, at the conference, everyone but me. The other speakers, my peers, friends and colleagues that would sit facing me the following afternoon – the coming afternoon, now – in the main lecture theatre, when I spoke to them about Leonard, his career and his work: they all knew. The early career academics from Bangkok and Sao Paolo: they knew. The grad students from the host university, smart and crisp as new-baked macaroons in their conference clothes, that stood aside at the coffee table, at my approach: they knew. That they withdrew and conversed in whispers when I approached was not because of me, my books and ideas and the fact of my presence, here in a hotel in their city, pumping thin black coffee from a vacuum flask along the trestle table from them, but because of me, how I could walk around like this oblivious when Leonard was dying of cancer, dying, as good as dead.

I had been intending, for the second morning session, to sit in on a seminar featuring my old friend and colleague Derek Boener, also once of Manchester, but I didn't. Instead I went to listen to a fringe panel that Leonard was chairing. So like him, to rock up to his celebratory conference, his Festschrift, the pinnacle of his career, a lovingly constructed peak from which he could survey the forest that has sprung up around the globe, all grown from seeds carried on the four winds from his originating tree, and instead of listening to us all sound off grandly about how important it all was, he'd head up a panel of grad students from Bupkiss, Ohio, or Dubrovnik or wherever, who are actually taking his ideas and doing something with them. Not leaving them in any decent state in the process, it has to said, but that's Leonard for you. And grad students. I slunk into the back row, to sit with the other no-goodniks, slid my tablet onto my lap as cover, and watched him. His ease at the table, leaning first to his left then his right, pouring glasses of water for the presenters, one of whom was actually visibly shaking with nerves. Taking off his watch and placing it, in that classic trope of academia, on the table in front of him. A combination of gaucheness and verve that would have been disarming, if I hadn't already been thoroughly, comprehensively disarmed, dismembered, irradiated.

The first presenter, the nervy one, stood up, went to the computer and opened her slideshow. The sheaf of papers in her hands, as she faced us, shivered, a constant, delicate movement. I thought of my father sifting flour in the kitchen. Mid-twenties, smartly turned out, she could have been me, twenty years ago. I'd puked in the loos ten minutes before I gave my first conference paper. That's still the taste of academia, to me, the acid bite of reflux. She wasn't shaking from nerves, the girl, she had a condition, multiple sclerosis or somesuch. I slipped a pill of chewing gum into my mouth, fervently wishing it were cyanide, and rested a hand like a visor over my eyes to watch. She talked, and people listened, sure enough, but the rushing in my ears was easily enough to drown out any words.

Instead, I watched him. What I was looking for, I don't know.

I do know. I was looking for the mark of death. Such a thing must exist. In the realm of the cancerous, at least. My auntie Evelyn died of cancer of the stomach, and you could see it in her from half a mile away. She, too, was prone to vomiting, the confused response of the body to something inside it, that it wanted to get outside, and that it thought it could simply wash out with the rest of the garbage. There was no mark on Leonard, though, that I could disentangle from the general marks of age, which is nothing more than death smudging you with its thumb, smearing your features, letting you know you're not forgotten, you haven't been passed over. Christ, listen to me.

I'm listening.

When the session ended I headed out quickly to the foyer to ambush Derek, positioning myself by some fabric-covered display boards with A4 sheets tacked on them. He was practically the last person out of his room, swept out on a wave of admirers, all flagrantly nodding and smiling and listening and talking as they manoeuvred themselves around him, never quite jostling, never quite flinging him to the floor and ripping the flesh from his skeleton.

I reached in and pulled him out by the sleeve, firing a barely human grin at the nearest hanger-on, and marched him over to the window.

'Did you know?' I said, practically hissing out the question.

Of course he knew.

How was it that I didn't know, was the real question. Had I been under a rock for the last twelve months? The information had been disseminated sensitively, but rationally. Someone must have told me. Probably Leonard did himself. (Could it have ended up in spam?) Or had I simply not processed the information, let it pass undigested through my system?

'Look,' he said. 'We're going for lunch. Come along.' He nodded to where Leonard was coming into the foyer, with his own coterie – did they know? Surely they knew – but then how could they even *talk* to him if they did?

I backed away, giving another smile that this time was surely no more than a flinch, and slipped myself into the general exodus. Flinch. Such a beautiful word.

'You alright?' someone said. It was my American friend, walking at my side.

He took out his packet of cigarettes and nodded towards the door. Then, when I shook my head, asked if I wanted to go and get a bite to eat.

Why does everyone want to go for lunch? What does it signify, lunch? Does it even have a point? Stand facing the wall and eat a sandwich. Eat a burger or a kebab if you must. Eat a cigarette. Lunch is just a question of what you want to end up smelling of afterwards, and as such – yes, I know it's your line – rather like sex.

I went back to my room, where I'm lying now, and lay on my bed and stared at the ceiling. Alone with my thoughts. Those interlopers.

Well, you say, as we stare at each other, here in the dark, with only the small, incidental sounds of a hotel room to accompany us. Little noises, like creatures, like insects that you are quite happy to share the space with. What do you want me to say, you say. That you're a heartless bitch with sociopathic tendencies? All that 'I don't do networking, I don't do chit-chat, life's too short' bollocks: that it's just a cloak for an innate lack of sympathy? Or not a lack, an incapacity. Is that what you want to hear?

It's nothing I wouldn't have heard from you before, I think. In which case – I know, I know – what's the point in conjuring you here in the first place? If I'm just going to put old words in your mouth, what's the point?

Well, that's your call, you say. I mean, if I came out and said:

that's all a lie, it's not you, not really. Would you even believe me? If I said that your manner, that people take as frosty, or disdainful, or even repellent – I'm *exaggerating*, no one's ever told me they think you're repellent, not in so many words – if I said that wasn't who you are; at heart you're a sweetie, and can be discovered as such, and considered as such, so long as no one treats you as such. If I said all that, you wouldn't believe me, would you?

No, I say. No I wouldn't.

I spent the afternoon in one of the few sessions conducted in the native language of our hosts. Which I don't speak. But which is, I had thought, and now had confirmed for me, enchanting to listen to. The delightful play of intonation, rising and falling as if according to some foreign tide, with only the odd imported Anglicism to make one wish oneself entirely deaf.

In the evening there was a formal do, organised and official, and I decided I had to go. It was that or pack my bags, write an email of abject, career-scuttling apology, and leave. It was in a hall over in the old part of the university, cool stone walls and the floor a stunning pattern of tiles, blue, white and yellow, almost sickeningly regular, like fractals.

Catering staff, the click of heels on tiles, drinks on trays, and a small music ensemble tuning up in the corner, bending their heads over their instruments like wise old birds, a quartet made up of various former colleagues of Leonard's. A tribute, a surprise, they would be playing a mixture of folk and classical and whatever the music was they played here, in this country. The kind of thing you can improvise well enough, if you have half an ear, and know the ground rules. Though no doubt at least one of the serving staff would be dying inside with each lumpen stab and phrase. It's funny, this might be the culmination of an academic career, the Festchrift conference, but where it takes place will be quite random, usually taking over an annual conference like a cuckoo's egg in a warbler's nest. A friend of my father's was a cricketer, and I remember being dragged along to his testimonial, a farewell match from his club, with the meagre takings going to him, to help him on the way in his life beyond the crease. But then sportsmen and women's careers end so soon, whereas academics' just go on and on.

But do they? What actual proper work has Leonard done in the last twenty years? What, for that matter, have I done, in the last five? What will I do in the next twenty, until such a time that I stand there, like Leonard, glass in hand, soaking up the general admiration and love, as if that were some kind of consolation for the approach – for the onset – of death?

We speak of admiration, respect, friendship. But if the expression of that admiration takes the form of the sexual, who's to say that's not appropriate? The sexual gift speaks something that just cannot be said by keynote address, nor by sincere words spoken with rented glass of sparkling wine in hand. Think of the sexual gesture in a relationship, in a *marriage* – think of its manifold ends and uses.

Yes.

Think of it.

I'm thinking.

Even a hug can't do it, the social gesture that mimics the sexual act so brazenly, and insidiously. The bliss of contact, the shock of boundaries overstepped; the breadth of physical coverage, as it happens; the brevity of it, when it's over. And I don't mean that in a facetious way, I say.

I know you don't, you say, and I nod and close my eyes.

You were a good listener, after all, I think. I'm not making *that* up.

These, then, were the thoughts that buoyed along in my wake as I entered the room, took a glass from a tray and insinuated myself into the slow social whirlpool of the evening: that all these clever abstractions – these *ideas* – were a poor stand-in for the physical facts in which they originated, and which they seek to disguise, dispel, refute. Words are a poor cloth in which to dress our acts.

The thought, inserted like the tip of an unbent paperclip under the skin of my pride, that I might actually offer myself, now, in a belated show of esteem, or gratitude, or penance.

There's something I want to tell you, I might say, but I can't tell you it here.

Or, I think we have some unfinished business, Leonard.

What nonsense, you say, and of course you're right.

I wouldn't, couldn't, say that, any more than I could clamp my mouth on his, take him by the tie and lead him, strutting like a whore, from the room. These were just goads, small injuries perpetrated upon myself, to bring myself to myself, put myself in my place, distract myself from the fact that in a few hours I would be standing up in front of everyone and addressing Leonard, and not knowing, not knowing in any manner or form, how I was to do it. What modulation of emotion was I supposed to apply to the words I had written for myself to speak; words that were, after all, not just to him and about him, but of him, from him, using him and his ideas, the bulk of his body of work, as if it could be some kind of compliment to dance around the room in someone's clothes, or clothes you had made out of their clothes, and say, Look at me, even as you're pointing at them. The global forest. The critical ecology. Ideas carried on the wind like seeds. What bollocks.

No wonder I've come as far as I have.

I crossed the room, then, ignoring Derek's discreet wave from one group, my American friend's raised glass from another, and walked directly to where Leonard was, cutting across the aesthetic logic of the tiles as surely as if I were chopping the hands from the statues of saints. I felt falling from me as I went, as if they were items of clothing, all the things I thought I might have said, the prepped and primped and manicured lines, such that I felt sure I looked, to the onlookers, whether they were looking or not, not just naked, but obscene. A middle-aged woman, with no clothes! And no idea of the right thing to say!

Leonard saw me come, and moved to welcome me into his group.

I leaned forward – I was in heels; those were my heels clicking – to hold his arm with my free hand, and press my wrinkled lips against his more wrinkled cheek.

'Leonard,' I said, and he said my name back to me.

'You're looking well,' I said, and drained my face of any possible physical indication that I might mean more by the words than simplest social nicety. Or in fact that I might not. I tried in other words to give the impression that we were both safely beyond the point at which such a statement might be in any way ambiguous or uncertain. Communication as blind exchange, a corrupted potlatch in which blankets are piled up on the shore, in a world where nobody needs blankets. Or where blankets offer no warmth, no protection.

Whether anyone else there was persuaded by this, or even cared, I don't know, but in any case Leonard – graciously, or naively, or just plain normally – seemed to take it at face value, and his acceptance seemed to put the others at ease. They smiled, and let me in their conversation, which was about the fly-past of a dozen hot air balloons they had seen in the skies above the city that day. I stood and listened, trying to mentally align myself with whatever angle they had taken vis-à-vis the whole death and cancer thing. Sure, why not, let's talk about hot air balloons, but are we talking literally, metaphorically, obliquely, palliatively, heartlessly? In any case the music recital started quite soon after this.

And in any case I was soon on my third glass of sparkling wine.

You know where this is going.

You shake your head. How can I, you say.

How can you not?

We sat in rowed semi-circles of seats and listened, and it was good to give myself over to the tedium of the music. To know that we all submitted ourselves to it by way of a tribute to Leonard, his miraculous stoicism, his courage physical and intellectual. That he could be alive, and his death stepping ever closer, and yet that he would choose to sit and listen to music, when all it does, all it can do, is give that death a cue, a rhythm, a dance step by which it may approach.

After we had listened for a while there was a break and the music mutated from a formal recital to a sort of disco, if that's the word (and it's not). The players, as I said, were colleagues or ex-colleagues of Leonard. Or friends. Perhaps they were just friends. Perhaps that is what this was all about. Chairs were moved, instruments plugged into amplification. The players started again, standing now, the tempo altered, though not the music that was played, it seemed to me, and people danced. I couldn't have been more surprised.

You danced, of course, you say.

Of course. Why do you say it like that?

Like what? I was only stating the obvious. I've never known you not dance. You're a good dancer.

Well, thank you.

You're welcome.

I danced, yes, and Leonard danced, whom I suppose I must have seen dance before, at some point, in the twenty-five years of our acquaintance. Our friendship. Our acquaintance. He danced in a way that I found intensely moving. He was like a baby elephant, swaying around the dance floor with a complete lack of coordination or, really, self-awareness, or awareness of others. People sort of ignored him, and sort of acknowledged him, giving him space. An old man, or nearly old man, or nearly dead man, aping the moves and affectations of the young, or of what he thought of as the young – even I knew enough to know that no one danced like that any more. Not that any of the real youngsters danced – they were too uncertain about the social-academic etiquette of how to dance in an ancient hall of an ancient university hosting an international conference that was stuffed with your elders and betters. This wasn't like a wedding, where the celebration of the happy couple's hopes for the future was a licence – or an edict, really – to abandon your usual constraints and dance, damn you, no matter how poorly. The only higher agency that applied here was Leonard's impending death, slinking its way around the outer edges of the group, and our knowledge of it – and how, as a post-grad or early career researcher, you were supposed to express yourself with regards to that through the medium, as they say, of dance, would have been beyond me, I'm sure.

A couple of youngsters did dance, I saw, eventually.

I saw, because one of them, perhaps I'd seen her in the audience, or at the coffee station, was dancing with my Greek-looking American friend, whose name you may have noticed I've refrained from using, out of delicacy, or something like it. She was dancing very close to him, and he to her, and I watched them as I danced. My dancing, as you know, alternates between phases of heightened awareness of the other dancers, and phases of a complete lack of the same. He wasn't a bad dancer, he had a very limited repertoire of moves, but was always moving, slightly, ponderously, rather as if wanting to give the impression that at any moment he was about to start *really* dancing. She, on the other hand, *was* a bad dancer, but was making up for this with a familiar repertoire of affectations that somehow took the place of dancing: placing herself provocatively close to him, shaking her hair, throwing back her head to laugh, responding every time he touched her arm.

They were dancing at the edge of the floor, where perhaps they thought they would be less seen. But they had been seen, I could see. I could see, because he kept looking at me, or for me; every time she lowered her head to drink, or turned her head to look at her friends, who were looking on with something like awe, something like nervous ecstasy, he would shoot a glance over at me. The look in his eyes was one I recognised. It was a plea, a defiance, a confusion: the emotion that rises to the surface of the male psyche whenever it is confronted by something it thinks it wants but isn't sure. When it is confronted by the possibility – such a shock to the male mind – that it doesn't want what it wants to want.

I lie in bed and look at you, and wait for you to say something. You lie there, propped on your elbow, looking back at me, and I feel once again the sharp clenching pain of having done the thing that was right, but which left me bereft. Of the two of us, I was the one who left, yet I am left like this. Left, left, left. Felt, felt, felt. You would help me with this, I feel sure, this snare of words caught in my throat, caught in my mind's throat. You'd get down on your knees on the floor next to me and untangle it, like a mess of cables under a desk.

Perhaps if I had gone to bed with Leonard, that time, things wouldn't have happened the same. Things brought to a head sooner would have sorted themselves out more easily.

What happened with the girl and your . . . American friend, you ask.

The young woman – the girl, really, they are girls at that age, what claim can they have to womanhood? – the girl left the room, to go to the toilet, I assume. If she had gone for a cigarette, after all, he would have gone with her. Unless he was scared of losing sight of me. I watched her go, then danced my way across the floor to him. He stood there, wavering slightly, while the music built itself into another meaningless crescendo. He looked forlorn, as if he'd already had sex and this was the comedown. He looked unequal to the gale of possibilities buffeting around him, all whirling to the rhythm of the violin and the guitar and some kind of drum.

'Hello,' he said.

'Who's that then?'

He knew her, I knew. I could tell. She wasn't just some early career researcher from the other side of the world. She was from his department. I took the glass that he was holding for her from his hand, and drank from it.

'That... Ah.' He laughed, and I smiled for him, for his laugh.

I don't know what I was thinking – perhaps you can help me. Perhaps that's why you're here. To tell me what I was trying to do. Tell me, was I trying to save him from doing something he would regret, something that might cause him harm, even though I owed him no duty of care, and her, certainly not?

And her, was I trying to rescue her from something I'd been busy telling myself all along that I now wish I had never avoided, myself? For he, my American friend, would one day be dying of something – this much was certain – and this notch, this drunken conference notch, this notch with a clever blonde girl half his age, was something that would one day be regretted, if it hadn't taken place.

Or was I acting for none of these reasons, but simply following my own impulses, those clichés, whatever they are, if they even exist any more, I don't know.

And the worst of it is, I fear I won't know your answer, now, when I need it most of all – not now, and perhaps not ever – for, just as I was anticipating your next words, or framing them in my mind, your next kind words – and you knew how to be kind, you do know that, don't you? It's just that you didn't know how not to be cruel, too, how not to be *vicious* – just then, as I say, the body in the bed next to me, there where you'd been lying, looking at me across the foot or so of rucked and fucked-in bedclothes, moved, turned and made a sound that seemed to mark an entry into semi-consciousness, and, as if we'd actually been speaking out loud, you and I, for real, and we'd woken him with our hushed words, his two eyes opened, and looked at me, and the mouth smiled, and it wasn't you, for it was *you*.

JENN ASHWORTH

FIVE THOUSAND
LADS A YEAR

I HAD MY own keys but the screw on the landing walked me down to the seg anyway.

'He's in number four,' he said, 'down the end. Ring the bell if he gets lively.'

He left me to it, even though they're supposed to wait outside. Lazy get. As a civilian, certain rules apply. They don't let the nurses or the teachers sit in a prisoner's pad on their own. It's a security issue, yours and theirs. But over the years here I've gained a bit of respect. There's only one writer in residence so I've had to carve out my own way of working. I banged on the door.

'You in there, mate? Not done a Shawshank on us, have you?'

I already knew the lad's name was Lee and he'd been sent to the block after smashing up his pad. That's generally what the lads do when they want a transfer. Under the old governor, they'd only have to do it once and they'd get shipped out. The lads aren't stupid: if they got themselves into debt with drugs or gambling, it would go like clockwork: smash smash, then off to pastures new.

All that ended under the new governor. She had a totally

different attitude. End of her first month, she called a general staff meeting – officers, civilians, the lot of us. They had to put the establishment on lock-down so we could all get there.

'We won't be manipulated,' she said. 'We will not let prisoners play the system. This is how it's going to be: if a man damages prison property he will go to the segregation unit and he will stay there until he is willing to cooperate with us. No transfers. No exceptions.'

Her wish is our command. The screws call her Maggie behind her back and this is the predicament our Lee, too young and too pig-headed to back down, had found himself in. He had been down there on his own three weeks. He'd upped the ante and stopped eating after two. His personal officer was on long-term sick leave and he wouldn't see a nurse. They couldn't make him. That's the thing. They can lock them up, but they can't *make* them do anything.

'Let me go,' I said, once word got back to me about it. 'I talk to five thousand lads a year. I know how to approach them. I've never made a mistake yet.'

He was laid on the bare springs of the bed – the mattress was on the floor, wet and ripped. The way he was curled up, his face nearly touching the wall, his tee-shirt had ridden up at the back and I could see the bones in his back. His pad was a complete state. The girl from the library had obviously been down to him. He'd shredded the books – there were pages everywhere, scattered all over the show.

'Do me a favour, Lee, and turn around so I can see your face.'

He didn't move. What a lot of people working in prisons don't understand is that you can't just talk at them. You've got to engage them. They start, without exception, by thinking there's something airy-fairy about being a writer. That it isn't quite manly. The first thing I need to do is earn their respect.

So I told him I make more cash doing this than I ever did as a lorry driver. I told him about my caravan in Pembrokeshire, my flat in Andalucía.

'Twenty thousand hits a year on my website, and corporate clients including a major football team and a bank I won't name now, but which you will have heard of. I'm probably earning more than your brief is. Fact.'

You've got to approach them on their own terms. Does a hell of a lot more good than some high-heeled psychology trainee going down there with a smile and a clipboard.

'Do you remember being at primary school? You do remember. You do. You remember Miss grabbing her book and saying, "Come on, lads, pack up and come and sit on the carpet. Time for a story." You remember running, don't you? Running towards that carpet. And her turning the book around so everyone could see the pictures. What was it? Goldilocks? Three musketeers, something like that? You were all up on your knees, weren't you? Craning your necks so you could see what comes next.'

He didn't answer; just put his arms round his head. At least he hadn't nodded off. Most of them go nocturnal after a week or so in the block. He was skinny, jail pale, with prison-done tattoos on his arms. M.U.F.C above his elbow. A heart with some blurred initials in it over that.

'That heart for your mum?' I said. 'The one on your arm?'
Nothing.

'Did you ever call your teacher "Mum"? Course you did. And do you know why? It was because you loved her. You loved her. Because she told you stories.' I always end there, with the same question. 'Now, what's your story?'

The one about the primary school teacher always gets them talking. Doesn't matter who. Prisoners, builders, lawyers. It even works with my clients at the bank. I go to their staff conferences. I do them some poems about teamwork and I always finish with 'Soul Alight', which is a great one about finding your own truth, speaking it clearly, and dancing to its beat. I get them up out of their seats. They're that used to a man in a suit with a power-point that when I turn up, with my scarf and my hair, a fish out of water, they really sit up and listen. I make a difference. They always ask me back. That's how I got the flat in Andalucía, actually. We spend a month there every Christmas, without fail. It's good to get away from things for a while. To chill out for a bit and let the dust settle. I made a YouTube video of me doing 'Soul Alight' and it's got nearly a quarter of a million hits.

I asked Lee to tell me about his family. I'd seen his file. Knew he had a little sister, in the care system somewhere. By the time he gets his Cat D, she'll probably be adopted out, but he could have been looking forward to seeing her all the same. I asked him what her name was. Asked him if on the out, he'd had a dog, a ferret, what cars he were into. Anything. He just laid there. I was on the brink of going when he moved so quickly, swinging his legs round and sitting up on the edge of his bed, that he made me jump.

'Easy,' I said, and he smiled. Just a bit, like he didn't have the energy for much more. He had a black eye, going yellow round the edges. Hair cut close enough that I could see a couple of scars on his scalp. They all have them. Pub fights, beer bottles. It's why they keep their hair short: to show them off. I prefer to let mine grow long, myself. It's a sign to others that I don't conform. My wife says it's my mane. She loves it.

'What is it? What do you want to say to me?' I said.

He shrugged. Most of them will meet your eye after a bit, once trust has been built, but he wasn't there yet. I looked at my watch.

I could have gone, I suppose. I'd given it a fair go. But I can be like a terrier when I get an idea in my head. I sat down next to him. The springs creaked a bit but he was so thin I didn't think it would have any trouble holding us both. He shifted up a bit, but didn't object. Elbows on his knees, head in his hands. I listened to him breathing. I could smell him – bad teeth and rollups, too much sugar in his coffee. Another twenty minutes and I could log this as a session of purposeful activity.

'I know what this is about,' I said. 'I know how things work round here. They've told you they won't consider you for your Cat D unless you do the Alcohol Awareness course.'

He shook his head.

'Anger Management?'

He nodded.

'And you want to get on and do it, but they don't offer it here. You want to progress. You want to see that little sister of yours. And this is your way of getting a transfer. It's worked for plenty of others. They've played the system, why can't you? Except we've had a regime change and her upstairs won't have it. So you're stuck. Does that cover it?'

He wiped his eyes the way they all do, with the heels of his hands, angry with himself. I stood up and pretended I was looking out of the slit they had the cheek to call a window, even though there was nothing outside worth looking at.

'Will you come back tomorrow?' he said, after a bit.

Result, I thought.

'Course I will.'

I ended up going every day. Couldn't log it. It wasn't writing work. Wasn't purposeful. Couldn't even charge for it. One of my pamphlets won an award during that time, and I brought a copy of it in for him. I thought he'd be interested, after all the time we'd spent together, but he shoved it down the toilet. Right in front of me. Same with newspapers.

In the end I came empty handed, made us a pair of brews and sat next to him for an hour. I never got another word out of him. He wasn't interested in writing. No poems. No stories. No song lyrics, no life writing. No flash fictions for the anthology I was organising. Not even a letter. But I went anyway.

What was I thinking? God knows. Maybe I was planning to get a piece out of it for the *Writers' Association Journal.* 'Creativity and Silence: Freedom with Words.' They like that sort of thing.

The battle between the governor and this boy she had never met went on for the best part of another month and he got as thin as a rail. It was scary looking at him. The last time I saw him they'd moved him to the infirmary but it made no difference to him. He'd just lie there, same as usual, not talking. I did him a few poems, but he wasn't listening. You can't make a person speak, any more than you can make them eat.

He did get his ship-out in the end though. They had to bluelight him to the hospital in the early hours of the morning. He was fading fast, and needed feeding up. This were a couple of weeks ago now. I've kept my ear to the ground since, but there's been no news yet. There's still an outside chance he'll come good and see his sister again, or at least I like to think there is. Five thousand lads a year is still a decent margin, though, isn't it?

NEIL CAMPBELL

LS LOWRY/
MAN LYING ON A WALL

I WORKED IN the library at the University of Salford. The Clifford Whitworth Library. I never knew Clifford but I would have wished him well. One morning the train was late. So I walked from Oxford Road, Manchester, to Salford instead. It was a nice day. One of those days where you sit in the office and wish you were outside.

When I got to work a little bit late I was told it was the day for Health and Safety training. Now, my old man worked in a warehouse his whole life. All my life I've sat at desks in front of a computer in warm offices surrounded by women. Anyhow I walked into the meeting and there was this little bloke there, probably about fifteen years younger than me. He said, 'You're late,' and I replied, 'I'm early, you're still here.' Now this meant we got off to a bad start. I was only joking at that point. I sat at the table and looked around it and there were about thirty people sitting there in apparent awe of this guy. I'd never seen any of these people before. And this guy at the front, okay, I know it was his job, but I just feel sometimes that people don't have any *perspective*. He delved into his box of tricks and pulled a skeleton out. And I swear to you, this guy, well, he looked like the guy from *The Office*, had the little goatee

beard and everything, and when he dragged out this skeleton
I almost wet myself. He saw me laughing and I saw in his eyes
that he didn't believe what he was doing. I saw the same in the
eyes of the people sitting around the table. So what the hell
were we all doing there? All of us were just forcing ourselves
to believe it because, well, what choice did we have? I could
see some guys there, the porters, and they were just glad of
the chance to sit down for a while. The ones with the glint in
their eyes like Pete. I used to stand out the back of the library
with him and he used to tell me about Sundays. He said he'd
just go and watch his lad playing football for a few hours and
then come back into work. And he always had these terrible
non-PC jokes that I won't tell you about here. It was like a gen-
erational thing. You had to laugh sometimes; it was the way
he told them. But anyway this guy, what he did then was he
unfolded a desk he'd brought with him and he put a stapler
on the table next to it. And then he reached over and picked
up the stapler. Then he asked us, 'How many times in your
working life do you think you would repeat this motion?' And I
said, 'Never, I haven't got a stapler.' It was not a great joke and
I was never a comedian. But I was hoping to get a laugh at that
point. What happened was that I heard this kind of murmur of
disapproval. And I was wondering what was wrong with everybody. Where was their sense of humour? Couldn't they see
what a waste of time this all was? And you know what came
next: the old bend-the-knees-when-lifting-a-box routine. And
beard-face asked for volunteers, and one of the porters went
and did it. Which was fine, that stuff was part of his job. But
not the lad from accounts. Or the women from payroll, or the
people in personnel. Then the bloke showed us a film with a
man sitting at a desk, all hunched over like Marty Feldman in
Young Frankenstein. And then he stopped the film and asked
us to mark each other's posture out of ten. I said I wasn't doing
that.

There was something about being sat at that desk that reminded me of being at school. When all the boring kids just sat there and did what they were told, and all the ones with any life in them were always getting into trouble. And it was the same in this Health and Safety meeting. And this guy (fifteen years younger than me) said that I had come late and had been a negative influence, and that he was going to put this in a report and that I should go back to the office. And when he said that I wondered why I'd even gone to the Health and Safety thing. You see, they put on these courses and they make everyone do it. I sit in front of a computer. Pete the porter lifts boxes. Yes, sometimes my back aches from sitting on my arse all day. As I got up to leave someone I'd never seen before muttered 'Grow up' and I turned and asked who it was. This old bald bloke said, 'Look, we can take this outside if you want.' And I said 'Fine by me.' And this old guy, well, he never moved.

So I started walking home. And it was still sunny. I looked down at the River Irwell as it shone in a crescent below the traffic roaring along the road. There was a heron down there, sat in a tree and looking down at the water. It didn't move at all and I started to think it was plastic. I kept walking down Chapel Street, past the curve of the old trade union building that was in the opening credits for *A Taste of Honey*. Down near Salford Central I went into the Kings Arms and had a pint. And I left there after two pints. Because I'm not a drinker I was already feeling pretty mellow and down near John Dalton Street, where there's that nice bridge that goes over the Irwell, near that pub called the Mark Addy, and not far from the law courts, well I climbed up on that wall and lay down on it. I had the river to my right and the street to my left. Office workers walked past. I could hear ducks below me. I opened my eyes and saw the sunlight on the water and there were some rowers speeding under the bridge. I thought maybe if I just rolled over and fell into the water that could be something. That could mean something. It would seem that something had actually happened. I went the other way.

There was a formal investigation at work. A disciplinary panel was put together and a meeting arranged for a few weeks later. I was given a big folder full of witness statements and I was asked to write down my own version of events. I was told that I could bring in witnesses of my own. So we had this meeting and I told them that I was having problems at home, and I wrote all that down and a few weeks later I got a formal letter in my pigeonhole. I admit I was nervous. And I opened it and, well, I still had a job. In times like this you're lucky to have a job really.

There was this writer, Sherwood Anderson, that I read about. He said that he owned a paint factory and then one day he just walked off down the railway tracks and out of town.

LIGHTBOX

Elsie wears her picnic dress today, a black and white check. She stares at a crossword puzzle and sips her purple smoothie through a plastic straw. She is sitting at a small table in the grocery store cafe, in front of a huge display of pumpkins. I buy my own smoothie and take a seat. She looks up briefly from tapping at her iPhone, then it beeps and buzzes, pulling her attention back.

I tuck my rucksack under the chair and start to eat an organic cream-cheese bagel. Everything in this store is organic. I never shopped here until Elsie. I thought it was for vegan freaks. She is smiling. 'It was another good session today,' she says. 'I really feel much better about everything.' I'm glad. I used to think Elsie could never have a bad day, until that time she broke down crying. I feel pretty guilty about that now. I scratch the hair on my neck. I'm growing a beard and it itches. She likes men with beards. I swear the perfect man for Elsie looks like a cartoon lumberjack.

When we get home, Elsie takes off her coat and draws the bedroom curtains. Everyone here lives in high-rise boxes. I step out onto the balcony with a bottle of beer and lean against the barred metal railing. There is a rusty tin can at my feet filled with cigarette butts. Elsie was growing tomatoes over the summer but she has already cut everything back. Some geraniums still survive and they chatter in a planter like red mouths conspiring over the street. We live on the fifth floor, just above tree level, and now the orange leaves are deserting their branches. The trees obscure the view a little in summer. This is my favourite time of year, just before all the leaves blow away.

I take out my phone and flip through some sites as I swig my beer. Elsie has uploaded a picture of the berry smoothie poised artfully over the crossword puzzle. One of the solutions was her family name: Palmer. It has a lot of likes already, including some guy she works with. I click his profile picture, scroll through the pages I can. He likes nearly everything Elsie posts online. I think it's cute and all but sometimes I think to myself, Elsie, keep something back for just us, you know? I notice the time and realise she's changing for yoga class. I'm not really in the mood to go today. When I go I feel kind of self-conscious, if you want the truth, but I try to stay at the back where no-one's watching. I'm a novice at yoga and sometimes I just give up and lie there in corpse pose with what the instructor calls a 'soft gaze'. Elsie's been going to yoga for years. I prefer running but Elsie likes to run alone.

I go back inside and poke around inside the fridge. There is some leftover Chinese food and I have this for dinner, while Elsie's out. I do some work at my laptop until the light from the screen is the only light coming from inside the room. I wonder where she is and check my phone. It's unlike her not to let me know where she is or where she's going. I lean back in my chair and look out the glass doors over the city. People move about in their boxes of light across the street. A block away, forty storeys of concrete obscure the night sky – the shining Empire Hotel. On summer nights cameras flash as tourists take pictures of downtown. The top floor of the hotel is a revolving restaurant and above that is a giant neon E. The neon vibrates at the bedroom window when I go to sleep. It's never completely dark here because of the sign, the always-lit corridors and stairwells. It makes me wonder what possessed Elsie to buy lace curtains. I sit in this light for a while. It feels somehow subterranean.

When Elsie finally comes home she looks tired. Her skin is flushed and she's already changed out of her yoga gear. She must have showered at the gym. She hasn't eaten, and she starts banging around the kitchenette, switching the radio on. I love watching her cook, the way she loses herself in the task and in the music. I flick through the stations as she dances, until I find something that matches her movements: 'Happy Together' is playing. We both like sixties music. I nod my head along in time. Her legs are bare, lithe; they make pretty shapes as she pads around the kitchen, singing. She eats standing at the counter. I want to tell her about my day, but she clears her plate and disappears into the bathroom. When we go to bed, neon palpitations creep in through the drapes, keeping me awake.

Elsie leaves earlier than usual for work in the morning. She's already gone when I wake up, late. I go online and check her profile to see if that guy has been bothering her. It's not that I don't trust her, but she's naive, she doesn't realise what men really want when they talk to her. I should probably work today but I feel cooped up and Elsie will be out for hours. I shower and throw on some clothes to take a long walk, closing the door with its brass five-oh-one behind me. The autumnal air is bracing, and it feels good to be outside. I haven't been sleeping well lately. I guess I'm worried about Elsie, about us. Maybe I'm imagining it, but it feels harder to get close to her these days.

Back at the apartment, I make myself a sandwich and a pot of coffee. It's a great sandwich – it really is a good grocery store. I'd never even heard of an heirloom tomato before Elsie.

I go online again and Elsie has written a blog post. It's all about an art project she's doing at college. She's really talented. There are pictures of her laughing and covered in paint. In one photograph, she's raising the paint-streaked palm of her hand to the camera, and in the other hand she holds a paintbrush dipped in red. There are playing cards tucked into her blouse, and she's captioned it with a Lewis Carroll quote. I press my hand against the screen briefly, feeling kind of dumb, but she looks so pretty. The pictures aren't from today and I wonder when this was. Maybe I should ask about her project, or leave a comment. I feel nauseated and I lie down on the sofa. I sleep.

When I wake up, Elsie is home. It's twilight and she moves around the apartment in the semi-darkness. She comes toward me up the hall from the bathroom in her underwear. I'm not sure of the exact colour but in the low light it looks silvery against her pale skin. I think it's new, not just the plain cotton underwear she often wears but the kind of underwear you would call lingerie. She grabs her white robe from the back of the bedroom door and slips it over her shoulders. She glances at herself in the full-length mirror, pulls the pins from her hair, then drops into a sitting position onto the bed. She shakes something in her hand. After a moment I realise it's a pot of nail polish, and she starts painting her toes. Is she going somewhere? While she sits still, waiting for her nails to dry, I feel as if I am holding my breath. A brooding sky streaks the window with rain and the neon hotel sign buzzes into life. She gathers herself, shrugs off the robe and moves to the closet.

She bends to turn on the bedside lamp and a glow emanates from that side of the bed. I move closer to the window. She pulls out a little black dress. I watch her struggle with the zip, wishing I could offer to do it for her. She leaves the room for a while. When she comes back, she slips her feet into a pair of high heels, then flicks out the light.

I don't sleep again that night. Instead, I look out the window at the city, at the apartment blocks that stretch between me and the mountains, the floodlights at the top of Grouse Mountain winking like a giant silver oyster. It's not ski season yet but they still light up the snowless slopes. I'd like to be up there in the mountain air with Elsie. Better yet, we could go up to Whistler and hide out in a cabin, in the woods or next to the lake. The digital clock on the nightstand illuminates the minutes to midnight. Across the street, people cast kinetic silhouettes inside their individual lightboxes, like puppets in a tin theatre. People watching TV with the lights out create a flickering blue variegation in the pattern of largely yellow squares. I pull out my phone to look at the bright screen. She's uploaded a picture of herself, and I realise the dress wasn't black but a deep purple: 'Forest green and plum are my faves for fall!' the caption cries idiotically. She smiles in the picture and holds a glass of red wine. Her lips are stained and reveal a crooked tooth.

She's going somewhere twice a week I don't know about. There are no other signs and she follows the schedule pinned to the refrigerator in nearly every way. Yoga three times a week. Grocery shopping every few days after work. Therapy on Tuesday and Thursday. Art class, library, the coffee shop, all the places she's supposed to go. Just two missing windows I can't account for. I know she can't be having more therapy. She's been doing so much better lately, since I stopped those letters.

On Saturday morning I find her at Starbucks. She sits in the window looking out at the street while I buy coffee. We both like to sit and watch the world go by. A guy next to her is talking on a bluetooth headset and a small white dog sits quietly on the floor next to him, round black eyes following the people coming in and out. Outside, a woman selects flowers from a street vendor, picking up baby's breath, then dahlias in the same shade of orange as the falling leaves. A line of red acacias beautify the sidewalk. A man in a flapping overcoat dashes across the road to make the bus. But he isn't running to make the bus, I realise, as Elsie leans forward and taps on the glass. It's that man, that guy she works with, smartly dressed, clean-shaven, like a fucking advert for cologne. Elsie gets up and rushes out with her latte, the small white dog in tow. I look at the headset man in confusion as the barista hands me my coffee. Then I realise the dog was sitting at Elsie's feet, not his at all. I burn my mouth on the coffee as I take a sip and run after her.

I look left and right as I exit the doors, and notice them further up the street. He is holding the dog leash and they are laughing. He stretches out a hand and touches the knitted hat she's wearing, teasing her. My heart is pounding in my chest as I follow them three blocks to the dog park. I watch them cavorting with the small white dog, taking pictures on Elsie's phone. What the hell is happening? I sit down on a bench to think. I take out my phone to see what's changed, but then, suddenly, they're coming toward me, walking with the stupid white mutt. I can't stop myself from staring at her. I've got to talk to her, I have to talk to her, before —

She sees me and links her arm through his, lowering her eyes. She passes me as if I am nothing. 'There's that guy again,' I hear her say in a stage whisper. 'Do you ever feel like...' But they move out of earshot. I watch them walk away, holding hands. I wait until they're far along the street before I get up. I walk back to my building, across the street from hers. I press the button for the elevator, watch the number change above the doors as it rises from the basement. The doors part and there is the woman with the orange flowers. I step inside and she offers me a polite smile. I stand a little behind her in the elevator, close enough to smell her perfume, and she presses the button again. The doors meet. The number five glows.

GREEN BOOTS' CAVE

1.

As night falls on May 14th 2006, David Sharp reaches Green Boots' Cave, a shallow overhang of rock on the north-east face of Everest, 450 metres below the summit. It's known as Green Boots' Cave because the body of Indian mountaineer Tsewang Paljor lies very prominently here, face-down in the snow: his legs, in lime-green climbing boots, splayed at the entrance, among discarded oxygen bottles.

This is David's third attempt. He's twice before turned back within a few hundred metres of the summit – conceding to weather, and to depleted oxygen. This time he's climbing alone, with no Sherpa assistance, no radio, and only two small bottles of oxygen for emergency use. The night is closing in and he must decide what to do.

Perhaps he halts now at Green Boots' Cave, in the hope of getting through the night on what oxygen he has, and making a summit bid in the morning. Or maybe he pushes on and gains the summit, then descends to the cave to shelter as the temperature drops. Let's say he does, because we cannot know, and why deny him this? Let's say he makes it and then climbs back down to huddle beside Green Boots. It's here, sitting with his hands clasped around his knees, his hood up over his head, that David freezes to death.

This is where you come in. As he freezes, David begins to dream, and he dreams that he is you. It's not like the dreams people have when asleep – those lurid, anxious, magic-lantern shows of things just out of reach. This is a vivid and complex dream of your whole life, in real-time, from your birth, right up until where you are now – whatever circumstances led to you read this story. Consider the following:

The tiny worlds you made, playing on the floor as an infant. The first time you realised you were clever. When it felt as though the world was revealing its secrets to you. When the chasm between who you hoped to be and who you are began to open. The foolish things you said. When you lay awake trying to rewrite them. When you told yourself 'I will change' and did not change. When you looked in the mirror and thought 'you again'. The accommodations you've made with yourself. How you've kept going, and what it required of you. How boring it has been, and how quickly it has passed.

Contemplate these things, then return to the story at section 3 (below). If you don't wish to participate in this way, please continue reading section 2 (directly below).

2.

Once, when I was a teenager, my parents went away for the weekend, and I had a party in our family home. The usual stuff happened, including breakages and people being sick, and a fair amount of drug taking. In the early evening, before the party had really got going, me and some friends got very stoned in my parents' living room, or the front room, as we called it. Maybe we had a bong or a bucket.

80

Someone there suggested I try this trick, which they, in turn, had been shown by someone else. It was one of those tricks to make you faint. Perhaps you know the kind – you make yourself hyperventilate, then stand up (or crouch down?) while clasping your arms around your chest. The type of thing that runs through schoolyards for a few months, and then some asthmatic kid dies somewhere, and you have a school assembly warning you not to do it.

I tried it, not expecting it to work, but it did work. I was on my parents' couch, with everybody looking on, my older sister too, concerned. I did the hyperventilation thing, then the standing or crouching, and then I was out.

I dreamed the longest dream I've ever dreamed. It lasted years. It was a dream of my own life, from birth. It was every bit as detailed as my life had been, though of course, in the dream, I had no knowledge that I was dreaming, nor of my life outside the dream: that I was passed out on the couch at my parents' house, with my friends looking on.

In this way, I lived the first seventeen years of my life twice over. Finally the dream caught up to where my life actually was. I had the party, I had the friends round, and the bong, and the fainting game. I came round on the couch.

I felt as weary as someone who has not used their muscles for seventeen years. My body ached and I found it difficult to speak. I asked my friends how long I was out for. It worked? they said. I thought you were just pretending. You were out for, like, a few seconds, at most.

3.

The circumstances of David Sharp's death are the cause of much debate and ill-feeling among mountaineers, because over the night and into the next morning, more than forty other climbers will pass within several feet of him on their way to the summit, and again on their return. There is a fixed rope running past Green Boots' Cave, and David is clipped to it. To pass him, they must unclip their own ropes, and reattach them beyond him.

Afterwards, these people will argue about whether he was dead or alive, or alive but beyond help, when they passed. Some will say his face was charred by frostbite, that they assumed he was long dead. Others will report that they were astonished to see tiny puffs of mist forming at the nostrils of this corpse – that somewhere inside his frozen body an ember of life still burned – but, unable to move by himself, he was beyond help. Some will say he was mute and insensible. Others will claim, or admit, that he was able to speak to them. It will be rumoured that he came to for a moment, that he awoke to his circumstances and said, 'My name is David Sharp and I am with Asian Trekking.' It will be rumoured that a team of mountaineers wearing helmet cameras, making a documentary for the Discovery Channel, capture this on film, but the footage, if it exists, will not be released.

Before the film crew passes, David Sharp dreams he is you. You, with your grooved habits, your memories, your worries, your contentment, your hope; the entire morass of you that's impossible to grasp at once but is there, surely, just as you know your reflection would be there if you were to look in the mirror. This is what fills his mind, 450 metres below the summit of Everest, his eyes open but unseeing, insensible to cold or wind or pain, or to the body of Green Boots beside him, as the forty climbers pass by on their ascent, and again on their way down, the lights of their head-torches flickering across his eyes, one after the other.

He is you entirely. Except that, he realises, something about being you doesn't feel right. Something is haunting you. A sense that there is something else. Something lurking behind every thought and feeling you have. Something going on that you will realise if you can only wake up to the fact.

USCHI GATWARD

THE CLINIC

IT'S SET UP to look like a home, with sofas and a coffee table, but nobody's fooled. I haven't been here since she was a newborn. Stupid of me.

'She's a bit tired today,' I say. 'Busy day yesterday. We went to the park. She didn't want to get up this morning.'

The clinician smiles briefly, a little wanly. Her assistant sets out cubes on a mat on the floor. At the touch of a keypad a mounted camera in the corner swivels towards us. Behind a glass screen another clinician watches.

Cara's spotlessly dressed in her smartest clothes. I'm wearing my dumbest outfit, complete with slogan.

Dean clears his throat. 'She might not be at her best,' he says.

'Put her down on the mat,' says the clinician.

I put Cara down and she reaches immediately for the shapes. She looks at them. Starts to put them together, clumsily. She piles them up but they fall down.

'This is normal,' says the assistant. 'By eighteen months she'll be able to do it.'

'Does she babble?' says the clinician.

'Babble?' says Dean. 'Oh yes – she talks.'

She sure as hell didn't get her brains from him.

'Talks?'

'Gabber-gabber-gabber,' says Dean. 'Mum-mum-mum.'

The assistant smiles.

'Is she walking yet?' says the clinician.

I shake my head. 'She crawls a lot more than this normally,' I say, as the assistant holds out a toy to her, arm's length away. 'She's a bit tired from yesterday is all.'

Cara crawls towards the toy. The clinician seems satisfied and touches the screen on her device. 'We don't record brain activity this time,' she says. 'Just run basic checks.'

She taps her keypad and a Perspex box to our right emits a high-frequency sound. Cara turns towards it and a puppet waves at her. She laughs. The clinician repeats the task several times, different frequencies and different directions. Then with no sound, just the puppets waving.

The assistant passes Cara a pen. Cara pincers her fingers. 'Good.' Into her device she says: 'T33. NA.'

'We'll see you again at fifteen months,' says the clinician. She consults her screen. 'Which will be some time in June.'

Cara stares at my T-shirt and starts to form a shape with her mouth. I scrunch up the shirt and zip up my jacket.

Back in the anteroom she's weighed and measured, her stats plotted on a graph – reassuringly unexceptional for her age – and then we are free to go.

We walk home. From her buggy Cara says, 'I liked the puppets.' And then she falls asleep.

We take the path by the nature reserve. The daffodils are out.

'We got away with it,' says Dean. 'For how much longer, though?'

At home, I put Cara to bed to sleep off the cough syrup.

Over dinner I say, 'I wonder if we just don't talk in front of her.'

'We can't keep her with us for ever,' he says.

~

At Wednesday baby group she's spotted. By one of the other mums, newish. Her child's well dressed. New spring trousers already, rolled up at the cuff. Woollen waistcoat and brown leather boots, though he's hardly walking. One of those.

Cara's sitting in the toy kitchen, stirring some play food round and round in a pan.

'She's a clever little thing, isn't she?' Harsh-eyed.

I laugh. 'Is she? Saves it all up for when we go out then.'

'What you got there, Cara?' says the woman.

'Egg,' says Cara.

The woman purses her mouth and says nothing more, eyes hard with satisfaction. Cara abandons her saucepan and crawls to the bookcase, clambering up it and pulling down picture books much too old for her. I read them to her to quieten her down but I know that the woman can see me, peering over from her place at the sand-table.

After the session the manager catches me. She wants to make a film of me reading to Cara. She's never seen a baby that likes books so much. I laugh uneasily.

'Think about it,' she says.

I stop taking her to the groups so regularly. I tell people she's had a cold. I tell them we're going to the park more often now that the weather's better.

'I hope she'll be walking by summer,' I say. 'I can't wait.'

And I get people to give me tips about trikes and trousers and surfaces to try her on. I go to the more active groups, leave the quieter ones alone. But a week or two later I lift Cara onto the top of a slide and she says, 'One, two, three – go!' quietly, but I look around and there's the new woman, watching me.

'Go!' I say, and push Cara down the slide.

I look up again and she's still looking. She holds my gaze for a moment and then slowly turns away.

At lunch that day, Cara counts out her beans onto her high-chair, one to twenty.

'If I eat one, it will be nineteen,' she says.

'That's right,' I say.

'If I eat two, it will be eighteen.'

I don't reply.

'Mummy? It will be eighteen.'

'Eat your beans,' I say.

After lunch she wants me to read to her. I say no – no more books now, I'm tired. While I load the dishwasher she crawls to the pile and pulls one out, then sits on the floor and studies it, turning the pages delicately. She furrows her brow. I take it from her, gently, and switch on the TV.

I'd heard of this before, on the internet. Archived chats. Coded suggestions. Always accompanied by post deletions. And then posters who just stop posting. It doesn't end well.

I start to overbuy, little by little, in my grocery order – small, cheap things that won't be noticed by the software; things that are easy to pack and that don't require cooking. Flat tins of sardines are the best, but I have to be careful – too many will raise a flag, so I get one extra every week – just enough to look like the baby's eating more and likes tinned fish, I reckon. I vary the other items – one week hot dogs, another baked beans. In this way I collect twelve tins within six weeks.

We eat a bit less, and save what else we can. We run through everything in the store cupboard – anything we can't take – and eat that instead. Pasta, rice, noodles, dried pulses, instead of valuable tins and vacuum packs.

I go to a shop in the next district and spend some of next month's tokens there, filling my basket with party foods and a small birthday cake. I buy birthday candles too, and a birthday banner, and household candles, and a cigarette lighter. In another shop on the way home I buy another lighter.

At baby group, I sow the seeds. I give out that we'll be staying with my sister for the summer, with a view to moving there. I tell them she's got an allotment.

'It won't feed all of you, though,' says the new woman, sharply.

'Maybe not, but we're going to learn how to work on it,' I say, mildly. 'My sister doesn't have the energy to make the most of it, she's not in good health. And we'll pool our tokens. Anyway, it's not definite – we'll see how we get along over the summer and then think about it.' I smile.

'I didn't know you had a sister,' says one.

'No . . . we haven't seen much of each other in recent years. She's not in good health.'

'What about Dean's job?' says someone else.

I sigh. 'That's part of it really. We always worry about him being laid off, things never look good. He can pick up some work with my brother-in-law over the summer, and then his boss'll take him back on afterwards if it doesn't work out. We won't need much money out there. They've got a generator.'

I wish I had a sister. With an allotment and a generator. Some safe place where Cara could be well, and we'd just be country bumpkins, not worthy of notice. The clinic appointment comes through, and I open it with a lurch.

Cara needs a pox jab. She's not quite old enough for it, but we'll have to be gone before she is. I could take her and tell them that we know someone who's got it, but we might be caught out, and we can't risk that. I could go to the walk-in centre in a panic and say I saw a boy with spots, and act a bit stupid when they ask for details, but it's still a risk. But then we'll come up on the records anyway when we miss the jab in half a year's time.

I take the risk, at the walk-in centre, and they agree to do her. Cara knows what's up. When she sees the needle she screams. 'No, mummy! Hurts!' The nurse doesn't bat an eyelid. I realise that she hasn't looked at Cara's date of birth.

On Dean's day off I leave him with Cara and head out to pick up the last supplies. The camping shop is in the next district but one, in a row of specialist traders. I've passed it before but never had any call to go in. As I push the door, a bell ting-tings. Proper old school. A skinny old man comes out of the back of the shop, newspaper in hand, and nods 'Morning' to me before taking a seat on a stool behind the counter and settling back down to read. I take out my phone and scroll down my list, brushing through the racks of cagoules, examining elasticated inner cuffs and breathable linings. I look at map protectors and whistles and torches, and then at thermal underwear.

'Looking for anything in particular?' says the man, eyes still fixed on his newspaper.

'I've got a list,' I say, going over to him.

He looks at it, then up at me. 'Where you going?'

'Spending the summer at my sister's in Suffolk.'

'And you'll need a tent there, will you?'

'We might do some camping while we're there. Explore the countryside.'

'Might you. Nothing firmly planned then?'

'I'll see what the prices are.' I shrug and move away. 'We'll need the clothes anyway, got nothing suitable.'

I wander over to the small bookshelf and run my hands idly over the spines. Birdwatching ... wildlife ... birdwatching ... birdwatching for children ... angling ... geology. I pick up a secondhand paperback, *Foraging*, and flip through the pages, stopping to read. I sense him watching me and snap it shut. It puffs up a cloud of dust.

'When I was younger a lot of people used to do it.' He smiles and looks at me intently.

The bell ting-tings and a middle-aged man comes in, asking for waterproof trousers in a Large. He buys them and leaves.

The owner watches me for a while as I try out binoculars, then eases himself up off his stool and beckons me to follow, round the L of the shop, through an archway.

In the inner room recess, three mannequins dressed head to toe in waterproofs – a man, a woman, and a child a little older than Cara, her dark hair cut into a bob with a blunt fringe – crouch round a campfire, in attitudes of rigor mortis. The mother, skin a waxy yellow, eyes full and staring, whistle dangling from a lanyard round her neck, clutches the cup from a thermal flask. Three silver sleeping bags – one junior-sized – sit neatly rolled in the pop-up tent behind them. Kendal mint cake and firelighters litter the groundsheet. A square of tinfoil lines the portable grill.

I inspect the tent, shiny green nylon, just big enough for one person, or one person and a child. 'I'll take the lot,' I say, turning to him.

'Sizes?' he says, going to his stockroom, and I tell him, giving Cara's next size up.

He piles the bagged-up clothes and boxed-up boots and gear on the counter, then comes out from behind it with a packet in his open palm.

'Sterilising tablets, in case you can't boil your water.' He shows me and chucks them on the pile.

He pulls things off the shelves and out of drawers. 'A flask – when you do boil water, put some in a flask. Then you have it even when your fire's gone out.

'Medical kit – essential.

'Thick winter gloves – also good for picking nettles. You can eat nettles, you know. Yes – once you cook them they don't sting. That's where your flask of hot water comes in handy.' His thin mouth stretches over his teeth in a smile. 'They also make good tea, for when you've drunk all the real stuff.'

Has he been questioned before, I wonder, about branded goods on people found (alive?) in the woods, in caves? I'd love to ask him whether they were found alive. I wonder if he ever hears back from anyone. How he knows what works.

'Do you sell anything else?' I ask, looking at him directly. He looks away. And then goes to the door of his backroom. I wonder if it's an invitation to follow.

I make another circuit of the shop. I choose a large water-proof camper bag, maps, torches, penknives, and binoculars. I pick up the *Foraging* book and *Birdwatching for Children*.

'Oh, and I might take these,' I say carelessly, dropping them onto the counter. Then I hand over the equivalent of three weeks' pay.

As he packs up my purchases into the camper bag, he passes me a card. 'Do come back,' he says. 'We do mail order too.' And he smiles again, revealing a false crown.

At home I pack the dried foodstuffs into the camper bag – cheesy biscuits, packets of small cakes, raisins, and chocolate – and all the tins. Candles. Cutlery. Vitamins. Toiletries. Jewellery. Cash. Nothing electronic. A few warm clothes, mostly things for Cara. Wellies in two child sizes. We'll wear the rest. Dean collects up all his lighters from when he used to smoke, before the pollution got too bad. I used to tease him for being a hoarder. I stuff in a couple of print books for Cara. We eat the birthday cake.

Late at night, in the kitchen, with the washer on, I read about foraging, committing to memory the properties and seasons of fungi, berries, leaves, bulbs, roots, flowers, nuts, and seeds. I make Dean learn about them too, in case we get split up. One day I'll teach Cara, if we last that long.

I re-draw the maps on paper, using codewords for the

names of places and marking in South as North. I make copies for both of us. We've got an old compass that belonged to Dean's granddad. I don't know how to use it but I'll figure it out. I know how to use the sun.

It's hard to leave all of Cara's baby things, but if we hang onto the past we lose the future. Nothing to keep them for anyway: no chance of having another one now. I don't want anyone else to have them, so I burn them in a metal waste bin on the balcony, one box at a time, one Sunday afternoon.

I tell our neighbours on both sides and down the walkway that we'll be gone for the summer. Dean tells his boss that we might not be back.

We're lucky the weather's still cool when we leave in June. No-one will comment on our anoraks. We dress as holiday-makers, in light hiking gear, Dean in shorts.

At our local shop I use some more of next month's tokens for picnic food. Some of it will keep for another day – and the tokens are no good to us now. I tell the shopkeeper we're away for the summer. He knows us. 'Sister's got an allotment!' I say. And 'Dean's got a holiday job!'

The last thing I do is tell the clinic we'll be on holiday when the check is due – gone for the whole summer. No, we don't have time to reschedule: we're leaving today. The reception-ist huffs with frustration, especially when I say I don't know exactly when we'll be back.

'She's hitting all her milestones . . .' I say.

'That's not the point!' she snaps, and huffs a bit more as she types something. 'Just call for an appointment as soon as you're home,' she says. 'I'll make a note to contact you in September, just in case.'

My heart gives a little leap.

I know that if they want to find us they will. I just have to hope that they don't care enough. We're nothing valuable to them – at least, they don't know that we are.

~

When we get to the forest, we look for an area with good cover, not too far from a stream. We find a small place surrounded by bushes. We can stay here for a while, and maybe come back here too. Some of the bushes are evergreens, so they'll shield us in the winter. I mark the place on our maps. We use branches and a picnic blanket, and cover them with ferns to build a bivouac. I set out bowls to catch rainwater. We take off our layers of clothes and pack them away, back in the waterproof bag. We make a light camp; we might need to move quickly.

We build our first fire, just for the practice: dry leaves and twigs, one match, one candle, smiling in the glow of it. We eat sardines and madeleines. I read Cara her book and brush her nine teeth. While she sleeps in the tent, I leave the camp and scrape the dirty nappies with leaves, then wash them in the stream. When I get back I curl against her. A fine rain patters on the bivouac, but in our sleeping bags we are warm, and it will only get warmer this summer. We should be hardened enough when October comes round.

In the morning I wash myself, upstream of the nappies. I find some field mushrooms on the banks, and cut them with my penknife: they smell fresh and mouldy, damp with dew or rain. I walk back jubilant, a longer way, so as not to make a path between our camp and the stream. Nettles grow everywhere. I'll pick some later, to stew with the mushrooms.

As I cross a clearing, a huge auburn fox, the biggest I've seen, as big as a pig, pounds past me, a hare in its jaws. Another, younger fox chases it. I watch them hurtle through the wet trees, flashing tawny and white.

When I return to the camp, Cara is standing outside. She is barefoot. She fixes me with her eyes and takes two tiny steps on the forest floor, then a pause, then one more. I run to her and scoop her up, then show her the mushrooms, which she wants to eat immediately. I wipe them on a cloth, slice them and put them in the pan.

'Dean, I'm going back for nettles,' I shout, and I grab my winter gloves.

I wonder about the foxes, and the other things. Will we be their prey, when the weather turns, when the ice sets in?

I wonder about loneliness.

Maybe we'll find some of the others? There must be others.

TRACEY S ROSENBERG

MAY THE BELL BE RUNG FOR HARRIET

I WAS ALWAYS a slight girl, but I had a way with strange children, and so from the age of eight or nine I was sent out into the neighbourhood whenever the nursery maids became capless with frustration over their charges. The clergyman's youngest son, who curled beneath the dining room table and gnawed on hazelnuts, shuffled over to lay his head on my knee as I sat on the hearthrug and knit him a pair of long woollen socks, without either of us speaking a word. The orphaned niece of the barrister's third wife, in contrast, tore through the forests like a bewildered fox, and I trailed her until I was rife with scratches.

But any neighbourhood can hold only so many interesting children. The girls who dutifully rocked their dolls, the boys who could not pass a stone without kicking it – they stupefied me to the point where I was prepared to thrust my own hand (or anyone else's) into the fire, simply for something to do.

Thankfully, just as I was starting to wonder whether the governess's canary might not be happier if I brought its cage into the kitchen gardens and unhinged the door, I was summoned and told that I was being sent to another household – in another neighbourhood – before sunrise.

'Her deceased mother was a butterfly.' I could tell from the curl of the lip that this was considered an unimpressive state of existence. I rather liked the idea, though, of a girl who was daughter to a butterfly; perhaps she had inherited iridescent wings, and spent her time bumping gently against the trim of the upper walls, so that before every mealtime I would have to capture her with a net.

'She is likely to be sent to relations very soon, but in the meantime you will look after her.' A glance over my form, as if gauging my substance. 'Though you are not many years older than she.'

I felt positively ancient when I took my seat in the coach. I imagined that I would spend my whole life in this manner, shuttling between positions, possibly gaining a few inches more in stature (for my parents had been tall people, and my early childhood was spent in constant amazement that I could not reach objects on the table, unless I jumped). The children in my care would soon cease to want me; they would no longer shout my name nor ring the nursery bell to summon me, instead walking away to marriage or boarding schools or lives at sea. Meanwhile, I would travel onwards by coach, finding less and less to cheer me, becoming inured to the most outrageous behaviours. 'Yes,' I imagined myself croaking to the governess, 'little Flora shimmied up one of the Doric columns, clad in the Young Master's second-best cravat, and devoured three newly hatched swallows, beaks and all. I only wish she were *interesting*.'

I did not wish to leave the coach. If I were to spend my life shuttling from one deranged child to the next, I deserved more time between them to remain as myself. But a lantern waited for me, held by a man who collected my small bag and grunted as if I were less important than that bag, so I trudged down a road comprised solely of mud, through several doorways each leading to a room colder and worse lit than the last, to find myself in a nursery.

As I removed my cloak, I wondered that my hands had not shrivelled with age.

The man and his lantern were replaced by a woman I instantly recognised as the housemaid who had been assigned to look after the girl, but who desperately wanted to return below stairs. I could barely keep her long enough to tell me the child's name – Paulina Mary, known as Polly or Missy. (I vowed to refer to her only as the latter, as I had a loathing of children called by the same name as animals.) Another maid brought a bowl of soup, and before I could do more than ask her where I could freshen myself after the journey, and confirm that I was to sleep in the same room as my charge, the two scurried away as if freed from an unbearable bondage.

I settled down before a fire which was not worth stirring. My back ached and the soup contained celeriac, which I detested. I would have to enter a darkened room and feel my way to bed, and my mattress would probably contain things that would nip me as I slept.

I had only forced down a few spoonfuls of soup when a girl appeared in the bedroom doorway. She was delicately shaped, and her nightdress hung in perfect folds. Were it not for her eyes creasing in distaste, I might have thought her a doll which had swelled into perfect little-girl proportions.

She said, in a cold voice, 'Are you neat, Harriet?'

I glanced at my rumpled dress and its mud-stained hem, and regretted that I was meeting my new charge while looking so ill-used. I might never recover my advantage. 'I'm afraid not, Missy. I have only just arrived from the coach.'

'I did not mean this moment. I can see you are not tidy. Will you be able to tie my sash properly, and comb my hair so the line is perfectly straight? The maids care only about their tea.

If you cannot make me look the way Papa wishes me to appear, you may leave on the next coach.'

A child less like a butterfly I could not imagine – not even a butterfly stiffened with pins and posed under glass. I glanced with longing at the ceiling. The maids had, at least, kept cobwebs at bay.

'I am entirely capable of keeping you as your father wishes.'

A flash of distrust appeared on her face. 'You may prove that tomorrow.'

With scarcely a flick of her nightdress, she departed.

I left the hateful soup to congeal and retrieved my bag, wishing I could sleep in the pools of mud outside. I had a little money, enough to make my way to the cesspool that was London, where I could gain a new situation or find a different sort of drudgery . . . with the knowledge that I had fled a perfectly good position because a waxwork chit implied I might not be sufficiently skilled to keep her hair in place.

I dreamed of butterflies cast from lead. They wafted just below the ceiling. I flailed ineffectually with a net, jumped until my arms ached, and despaired ever to understand how the dark and heavy things flew.

A small voice announced, 'I need you to dress me now.'

This child was neither angelic, nor dark enough to be beautiful; any attraction was in her poise.

I squinted without stirring. 'I am sure you are capable of dressing yourself, Missy. If the maid was deficient, you must have made up for her lack of care.'

A small thump greeted my words – the girl stamping her diminutive foot. 'Papa hired you to take care of me. Dress me now.'

I did not move. I felt rigid with age, or perhaps I too was turning to lead.

'I need to be downstairs by eight o'clock to pour Papa's

coffee. He cannot . . .' Her voice cracked. 'Please, Harriet, he must not be disappointed in *me*!'

I rose so quickly she jumped back, spreading her arms to balance herself.

After twitching the bedclothes into place, I cast an expert eye over her wardrobe. Of course, she wore full mourning. I easily located a black dress, sash, and hair ribbon. Every piece of clothing she owned seemed to have been set in its place with infinite care.

I spent three full minutes patting her sash into place, though it would wrinkle the moment she took her seat beside her father. When I scraped the comb across her scalp, Missy only screwed her eyes shut as if steeling herself.

As she studied herself in the mirror, I brushed the dry mud off my hem. Breakfasting in the servants' hall would be a nightmare in and of itself, though less of a trial than sitting at the same table as my employer. He had hired me unseen, and would be unlikely to let me go if his daughter was in such need of care, but I still half-wished he would change his mind.

'You are not so pretty,' I commented, finding that she continued to gaze at herself, 'that you must commit your image to memory.'

'I must be neat,' she said, and led me out of the room.

With her white face and hands, she seemed to have no substance but the black dress. The corridors were dim, and I heard no voices. It was like being shut up in a tomb, with my only companion a tiny ghost obsessed with her appearance.

I would speak to her father and insist he paid my coach fare to London. If he protested, I would thrust my hand into the fire.

We had not yet reached the staircase, but Missy paused before a door. I waited a moment, listening for chimes from the downstairs clock. 'Does your father breakfast here, Missy?'

Her hand crept to her heart. 'How could Mamma die? She was so pretty and good.'

I wondered if she were paying obeisance to the dead as a morning ritual, but when she turned to me, her face showed fear. 'I have not been inside,' she whispered. 'Not since they told me she was gone.'

After a moment of searching my face, she turned the door handle.

The room dazzled with light. I clasped my hands over my eyes. How had the maids, or the doctors, or the grieving widower, allowed the curtains to remain open?

When I finally dared look, I found my little charge sprawled on the floor, blossoming into a butterfly.

She glowed scarlet and green. With a twitch of her arm, blue skies poured across her radiant face. Ropes of gold shone between her fingers.

I grasped silks and scarves, enveloping her without care for creases. With every thread I added, she shimmered more brightly, growing iridescent under my hands.

'Mamma,' she choked.

I caught an artificial rose, but tossed it away as being too stiff, and reached for a skirt of shot silk, deep blue but containing the silver of stars. I wished to place her on this skirt and raise her, so she could flutter past the cornices as I laughed and chased her with a net. But I would only pretend. I would never catch her.

A clock downstairs began to chime.

In an instant, Missy was upright, her legs still bound in scarves. 'Help me!'

I stripped her of colour, bundling armfuls of fripperies under the bed. As she plucked anxiously at her skirt, I hastily arranged the curtains so that the room was as shadowed as the rest of the house.

'Papa will be angry,' she muttered as she fled.

I could barely keep pace with her down the stairs. The clock had faded into silence. Would I be blamed for my inability to keep to time? Could I lose my position when I had only been led to the house scarcely twelve hours earlier?

Missy halted outside another door. I heard the clink of cutlery against a plate.

'Papa will finish breakfast at half-past.'

Then she was in the room, greeting her father and closing the door in my face.

I found my way to the servants' hall. Although I was gratified to be treated with respect by the housekeeper, who also revealed an admirable ability to cow the maids, I could barely remain civil as I conversed with her, for I kept twisting to look at the clock. Was Missy revealing to her father how utterly unsuitable I was? Was he looking reproachfully at her untidiness, and determining that I was clearly not fit to uphold the standard he expected of his daughter?

Ignoring the housekeeper's amazement that I should leave my comfortable place before being summoned, I hurried upstairs and lurked outside the breakfast room. I heard clattering, and a man's grave voice, but no hint of my name. Had they already made their decision?

Soon I would be sitting in the coach. When I reached London, I would totter along with my bag in my shrivelled hand, begging for a position. I would scrub chamber pots and teach infants how to rock their dolls. There would be no more rainbows, no outbursts of light, not a single girl who concealed a butterfly within wax and mourning garb.

I steeled myself to push through the door and jump higher than I ever had in my life. If only I had a net . . .

Then Missy cried: 'May the bell be rung for Harriet! I wish to tell her all about Mamma. She will keep me tidy, Papa. Do not worry about me. Harriet will take care of me now.'

STRONG MAN

GET MY KNEE fixed then get the fridge-freezer fixed, that was the plan. I'd set everything up for a couple of days off on the basis that the medics had suggested a week. Might as well make myself useful, I thought; for once be the one to wait in for the repairman. God knows Michael has had more than his fair share of it over the years – waiting in.

Don't run on it for six weeks, don't do this, don't do that; then the nurse was making me practise going up and down stairs with a stick for a good half-hour before the op. Waste of time! I was fine. The bruising was fairly dramatic, mustard-coloured below the knee – English mustard too, not French – and purple-black above. But it really didn't hurt that much.

The freezer man arrived right on time, which I wasn't expecting, Michael having warned me there was a less than fifty-fifty chance of this happening in his experience. Plain black T-shirt and jeans, close-cropped hair, he was rather short and very strongly built. Martial arts? I thought to myself.

'Water's dripping into the top salad drawer from some-where and freezing hard,' I told him. 'Then it melts and freezes again.'

I'd have gone away at this point and put in a few calls to work if it hadn't been for Michael instructing me to stick with the process throughout. His reasoning was that it helped if you were able to explain to them what had gone wrong next time it happened, and the only way to understand what the problem was, was to go through the whole boring process with them in the first place and ask questions and try to understand it. He himself took notes, dated, before he forgot; he had a special file for them. Michael's an academic, he likes writing things down. His last published article was 'Islamic Historians in Eighth- and Ninth-Century Mesopotamia and their Approach to Historical Truth'. I haven't read it yet but I know it'll be brilliant, like all his work. Anyway I resigned myself to doing things his way this time, seeing it was once in a blue moon that I was the one hanging around.

The man refused coffee when I offered but asked for a glass of water instead. All a bit of a novelty for me, this. I couldn't quite place his accent: east European, but not Polish.

He opened the door to the freezer compartment and our eating habits were laid bare. Sliced bread, because you can toast it from frozen; litre cartons of skimmed milk so we didn't ever run out; several tubs of ice cream (Cookie Dough for Georgia, Mango and Passion Fruit for Verity, Raspberry Sorbet for weight-conscious Clio). Not much else except frozen peas and a bottle of vodka. Not much actual food. Oh well, everyone seemed healthy enough. The vodka was officially Georgia's now she was eighteen, for pre-drinking with her friends; better here where we could keep an eye on how fast it goes down, we'd reasoned, than hidden in her bedroom.

'So where are you from?' I asked, setting the glass of water down beside him.

He looked up from the fridge drawer for a moment. He had very dark eyes, like a watchful bird.

'Russia,' he said.

Snow and ice, I thought.

'Where in Russia?'

'Nearest city Moscow,' he said; then, with fleeting mockery, 'Three hundred kilometres.'

'So you're from the country?'

He nodded.

'I've been to Moscow,' I said, but he'd turned back to the freezer.

That time I thought we might get into emerging markets, invest in commodities, get a piece of the action, I couldn't believe how long it took to get there. Not the flight but the actual drive from the airport into Moscow. The roads were atrocious, it took almost three hours in the cab for what should have been a forty-five-minute journey. The crawl through the gridlocked suburbs was teeth-grindingly slow. Then when I visited Mr Petrossian in his office there were a couple of security guys with sub-machine guns in reception. The secretaries and support staff, all female of course, were trussed up in pencil skirts, tottering round on stilettos. It was like a surly version of the Fifties. Embarrassing.

The man was lying spreadeagled on the floor now, shining a little torch into the gap beneath the freezer from which he'd neatly wrenched the grille. Seen from this angle it was obvious he worked out. I found myself wondering what sport he played and at what level.

I was going to go ballistic if I couldn't play tennis for six weeks. But of course that's what had done the damage in the first place – cartilage, wear and tear, fragments of cartilage which had broken off and were floating round in the synovial fluid. We'll just have a root around, clear out the gunge, said the surgeon. He'd already done half a dozen that afternoon by the time he got to me, the nurse told me afterwards; a light general anaesthetic, just enough to put me under the surface for twenty minutes, then in at a nick beside the kneecap with his keyhole gizmo. I was all done by eight; I hadn't needed to drag Michael out after all but had gone down in the lift and straight to the cab rank outside.

The cabbie asked me whether I had any children as we set off over the bridge and I said, as I always do when I'm asked this question, yes, three lovely daughters. If I say 'stepdaughters' I find I get quizzed about whether I want my 'own' children – and by complete strangers too. I adore the girls, and that's been enough for me. Broody? Phases of it, in passing, like lust, and dealt with in the same way. Listen to your brain as well as the other stuff. Now, at fifty, I think I'm probably safe as well as fully occupied with running the business. It was shortlisted for the Dynamo Prize for Entrepreneurial Initiative last year.

Michael was so sad when I met him. It *was* sad, being left a widower with three small children. Then after a while he wasn't sad any more! He thinks I'm wonderful. He even loves my wonky nose, he says it's Roman; cartilage problems there too, that's next on the list. He thinks I'm beautiful though. He can't believe his luck, even now, twelve years on, bless him. Neither can I. The recipe for a happy marriage!

My mind was wandering all over the place. This was not like me; I was usually so focused. It must be some floaty post-anaesthetic thing, I thought. Or maybe it was the unaccustomed feeling of having to do something that didn't interest me. I made an effort.

'What do you think the matter is then?' I asked, as the man sprang back noiselessly from a one-handed press-up. Impressive!

'First I check condenser coils,' he said, selecting one from among his twenty or so screwdrivers.

'OK,' I said, then added, 'So do you miss Russia? The Russian countryside? Not much country near London.'

'*Good* country near London,' he said, turning to look at me.

'Really? Where's that, then?'

'Brentwood.'

'Brentwood?'

'Very good country,' he repeated.

A smile flashed across his face before he could suppress it.

'Very good paintballing in Brentwood,' he added.

That figured. I could just see him dodging from tree to tree with his paintball gun.

The one time I'd been inveigled into paintballing, while I was still at Renfrew's, it had been as part of some corporate team-bonding exercise. There were unflattering padded overalls to climb into, and a claustrophobic 360-degree helmet; also an uncomfortable neck guard to stop you getting shot in the throat. Paintball guns fire at surprisingly high velocity.

The objective had been to steal the other team's flag in a raid and bring it back to camp. At one point I'd been in possession of the flag. Returning to base, zigzagging to avoid the bullets as we'd been taught, gave me a weirdly nasty jacked-up feeling. I was running and I could see sudden blooms of colour bursting on the obstacles and trees in my sight line, turquoise and lime green and fluorescent yellow; every colour of the rainbow, except red of course. I got the flag back to our camp, we won the game, but I was still glad when it was over.

'It hurts,' I said. 'Paintballing.'

'Some people shoot close range,' he said, fiddling with his phone now. 'Not good.'

He showed me the phone screen and there was an anonymous torso sporting several big indigo bruises like starbursts.

'Ouch,' I said, handing the phone back quickly. It felt like looking at porn. I didn't ask who it was; I didn't want to know.

Clio had brought back a paintballing invitation from school that term and I hadn't been sorry when it turned out a clash of dates meant she couldn't go.

Being a stepmother has been good in all sorts of ways. You're close, you love them but there isn't quite the same cauldron of emotion. No, you can afford to get on with your work like anyone else.

I do earn more than Michael of course. Considerably more. My business has gone from strength to strength in the last decade, while the terms of his university employment, his tenure and so on, have become increasingly insecure and ill-paid. He hasn't got as far up the academic greasy pole as he might have, either, though he doesn't seem to mind. Maybe he'll write a surprise bestseller once he's retired, I tell him.

You're not supposed to say so but I'm very careful about employing women. This means in practical terms that I won't take on a woman who earns less than her partner. I need to be a hundred per cent sure it's true of everyone on my payroll that their job comes first in the pecking order at home. No women with alpha-male husbands! I simply can't afford them.

Back to the freezer and apparently it wasn't the condenser coils after all.

'Next thing I test evaporator fan mechanism,' he said, rooting round in his tool-box again.

'OK,' I said, and started to make myself a coffee. 'Another glass of water?'

He gave a quick nod.

Yes, funny the way that Russian trip worked out. Mr Petrossian himself had been as clever and persuasive as when I'd met him at the trade fair in London, but there in Moscow he couldn't show me anything useful on paper about his business. He had to keep all the facts and figures in his head, he explained, as it wasn't a good idea to write things down. In the end we weren't able to strike a deal and I'm not particularly sorry, looking back. Russia hasn't woken up yet. It's still only good for raw materials; it isn't actually making anything worth buying. No thanks, I thought, I'll stick with fibre optics.

Georgia locks horns with me about wicked capitalism now and then; she's doing politics, history, maths and economics

A-levels, clever girl, so it's good to hear the arguments. Liberal capitalism in the UK and the States has produced shocking inequality, she rages; regulation is toothless and it's getting worse not better. Correct, I say. Germany is the way to go, she says, corporate capitalism, more equality and a workforce which moves in tandem with management rather than automatically against it. And of course that sounds very attractive.

Yes, Germany is a more equal society, I say to Georgia, but in order to be that way it's also a more traditional and less diverse society. Swings and roundabouts. Did you know they have a special word for mothers who work over there? *Rabenmutter*, or raven-mothers. *That's* how conservative they are! And so we go, to and fro. We're making history as we go along of course and that's the truth of it; we live in time.

'So what's that wire for?' I asked the man as he took another piece of kit out of his toolbox.

'I push it through drain tube,' he said, feeding it into a small hole in the wall joining fridge to freezer. 'See. Maybe blockage. Small pieces of food.'

'Like my knee!' I said, and told him about the keyhole business.

'Many footballers have this operation,' he said, frowning into the fridge. 'Cartilage problem.'

My brothers stayed put in Middlesbrough and they don't speak to me these days. Earning more than them has done nothing for family relations. All part of the increasingly bitter civil war that's been pitting families against each other up and down the country for some time now: north against south, brother against sister, London against the rest. I moved to London at the right time, I was lucky. This year I've got twenty-eight people on my books.

The man had been here for the best part of an hour now and I started to get a sinking feeling that this was all a waste of time, he'd say he needed to order a spare part or that we'd be better off buying a new fridge-freezer despite the fact this one was only three years old. When I voiced my doubt, though, he assured me he would be able to mend it. Great, I thought.

Even so it was taking a while.

I asked him what he thought of the current Russian president.

'Strong man,' he said, with a nod of approval, adjusting a dial behind the vodka bottle.

Strong man? I thought. What, *another* one?

Hadn't they had enough?

A blast from the past: '*What* did you say? What did you say?' Beat. Then – 'You asked for it!'

Which was what happened if you challenged anything; and, after a while, if you said anything at all. I got up. I got out. I got away. The classic thing is to go for another bully in the future. You don't have to, though.

'Russia needs strong man,' he said, going over to the sink to wash his hands.

I looked at his broad shoulders and the way his body tapered at the hips, the elegant triangle of his torso, and this brought to mind the contrasting hunched back view of the cab driver who'd driven me home from hospital the night before. He'd wanted to tell me about *his* children; *he'd* had a tale of machismo to tell all right.

He had a grown-up daughter who'd become a hedge-fund manager, he said, and she had just come out of a bad relationship.

'Yeah, he was in insurance, the boyfriend. He was all right the first year then he got jealous, obsessive jealous if you know what I mean. He started raising his hand to her.'

'Nasty,' I said.

'My son went round, they had words, then my son he raised his hand to *him* and gave him a bloody good hiding. Lucky it wasn't me, I'd have sent him through the window.'

'Yes,' I said.

'My son, he got beaten up in Tottenham fifteen years ago. Yeah, Tottenham, funny that' – this said with deep sarcasm – 'Then after that, after getting beaten up he went to the gym, he trained in something with a funny name. Like karate but not karate. Anyway, now he can look after himself. And him and his sister, they've always been close.'

Sometimes it's hard to know what to say. The last time I heard that expression was when the man I was sitting next to at the Dynamo gala dinner told me, 'I have never raised my hand to my wife. To be honest, I've never felt the need to.' I think he was expecting me to congratulate him. Well done, sir!

The truth is. The truth is, no one would believe you back then. 'A bit heavy- handed' was how it was described if you had to visit A&E. Nothing happened when you told a teacher. The police had a good laugh. 'Making a fuss about nothing,' was what they used to say; or, if it showed, 'Making a fuss.'

He was still tinkering with the freezer controls. I started to tidy the kitchen, put some mugs in the dishwasher, straightened the pile of books and papers on the dresser.

'My daughter's doing Russian coursework now at school,' I told him. 'Would you like to see her textbook?'

I held it out to show him. He had turned from the freezer to sip his water. He glanced over his shoulder and shook his head.

'But it's about Russia,' I said, puzzled.

'Lies,' he said.

I blinked. I gave a little laugh before I realised he wasn't joking.

'No honestly,' I said. 'It's history.'

'Lies,' he repeated, compressing his lips, shoving his head back inside the fridge.

Wow, I thought. Bloody hell.

Wait till I tell Michael he's been barking up the wrong tree all these years, I thought; that he's been wasting his time on Mesopotamia et cetera. Lies! I put the book back in the pile of Georgia's coursework on the dresser.

I felt quite winded.

On the evening of my overnight business trip to Moscow, Mr Petrossian had booked a table at a giant marble-clad sushi restaurant. I'd arrived early and was shown to a balcony table from where I could take in the sheer girth of the chandeliers shining light on the men at dinner all around me. The table nearest was occupied by two heavies growling stuff at each other when they weren't growling into their mobiles; opposite them, ignored by them, sat two teenagers in thick make-up, immobile as captive princesses, and completely silent.

I never lied about it but I did stay silent. Secrets aren't the same as lies. It's not something I'm proud of. I told the girls someone got me in the face during a doubles match when they asked about my wavy nose. So it's not true I never lied; I have lied!

Of course, it was another time, the Seventies. An earlier stratum of history altogether. And he was plausible, my dad.

I'd had enough. My knee had started to throb and I realised I ought to rest it.

'I have fixed it,' said the man triumphantly, closing the freezer door.

He glanced at his watch and scribbled something on his timesheet. I watched him as he started to pack his tools away.

'Well done,' I said.

I felt weirdly wiped out.

I knew I ought to ask him what it was that had gone wrong in the first place. I hadn't forgotten about Michael's file of domestic notes; for some reason though, I'd temporarily lost confidence in it. It can't be that useful, I thought, otherwise we'd have got everything sorted ages ago. What if it's not the condenser coils or the evaporator fan next time round? What if it's a different part of the freezer altogether? And even if, thanks to the notes, we do find out what's gone wrong, that won't alter the fact that it's gone wrong again.

I still did ask him though, and I carefully wrote down what he said and dated it. After all, Michael hadn't once let me down in all the time I'd known him and I had no reason to doubt his way of going about things now. I certainly wasn't going to be the one to foul up his scrupulously recorded dossier.

MATTHEW SPERLING

VOICE OVER

A: Hi, I'm Marlie Prince, and I played the character of Shawna in *Forever a Stranger*.

B: And this is Baxter Fields, I was producer on *Forever a Stranger*, and can I just say how glad I am to see this anniversary edition being released now. It took a long time to make it possible, but really I'm incredibly proud and glad of the work we did to make the movie happen, all those years ago. It was a magical few months that we all worked on it together, and not least because I think I'm right in saying that it was a first film for a lot of us, and that's the case for you, isn't it, Marlie?

A: It is. I was so young, just seeing me on the opening credits there!

B: And that was actually sort of old-fashioned already when we did it, to have opening credits with the actors appearing in stills. But that was just one part of the whole look that Dieter wanted it to have, and he was very clear on things like that. An amazing capacity for attention to detail he had. And . . . well, there's nothing happening on screen really now, we can just see that wonderful landscape being established . . . so maybe we can talk a bit more about what it was like to work under this amazing director, especially as a young actress, Marlie?

A: Oh, amazing, yes . . .

B: And you'd mainly done modelling before this, am I right? . . . Well, I guess that's a —

A: Sorry, I'm just seeing Robin there, and it's still a shock to see him, you know? Still a shock. He was such a, well, such a beautiful man, and when I say that I don't mean at all in a feminine way, and yet there really was a terrific delicacy to him, which I think this movie brings out. And maybe after this it got lost a little, you know, he did a lot of movies which didn't bring out that side of him, and I think maybe in a sad way that side of him actually died out. It was never . . . nourished. Yes, I was a model before this, but really just a catalogue model, and I was just a girl, I'd never imagined this whole glamorous, you know, world.

B: And is it true, just for, uhh, getting the record straight, it's often said but is it true that Robin scouted you at the mall?

A: He scouted me at the mall, yes. But I already had an agent who was putting my name around, so in a funny way when Robin went back to the studio and said, I've got this great girl, they already had me on file.

B: That's so funny.

A: Isn't it funny? I guess that's the kind of town it was back then, it was a lot smaller, so I guess if there was a beautiful girl then probably you would know about her, she'd be on the books in some way already.

B: And Robin, of course, can't be with us today for this commentary, I've spoken to him and he regrets that —

A: You spoke to him?

B: Just very briefly, a very brief, uhh, talk —

A: Amazing. It must be ten years that I didn't speak to him.

B: Well, uhh, as I say, very briefly we spoke about, you know, this release, which he's very excited about.

A: Robin's excited?

B: Maybe *excited* isn't . . . He's certainly aware that this release is happening . . .

A: Okay. We should tell them about the movie anyway, Baxter. Look, it's this sequence, what's this shot again? You all spent so long on it?

B: The smash-zoom. This is, I guess, a thing for the real enthusiasts, and I remember that Dieter and I spent almost a whole afternoon getting this shot right, with Paul Baker, our wonderful cinematographer, who sadly died. So it's, well, it's gone now, it's a very fleeting effect, can we go back? Can we . . . ? No? Well, okay, you can't see it now, but it's where the camera zooms out, from the focus on their two hands, the lovers' hands, resting next to each other on the gate, it zooms out from there to a position behind their two backs, with all of the valley in front of them in focus, and at the same time it tracks left, to move the shot towards Robin in the centre of the frame, and Shawna is there on the edge. Which is pretty, you know, prophetic in terms of the movie. And that all sounds sort of technical, but the whole thing takes, it must be less than ten seconds, and we shot that forty or fifty times to get it right, and now I believe they teach that moment in film schools —

A: No way!

B: Yes, well, I don't know, someone sent me a book, it was a whole book about Dieter and his movies, and in it there was a whole two pages about this one shot —

A: No way.

B: It's lovely to think, isn't it? It was just something we worked out one afternoon, when we were all kids, and now there's kids in college writing term papers about it.

A: I'd love to read those papers.

B: Yeah, certainly, as I say, there's this one book on Dieter at least . . . And I remember you were wonderfully patient with us, while we made you stand by that gate with your hand there for hours, repeating this shot, and doing the lighting, and always having to clear the valleys in the background. And those pic-nickers showed up . . .

A: I don't remember that. Really I was just so grateful for the opportunity to be in the movie, I wasn't going to ask Dieter to hurry it up! Later, I would have.

B: I know you would! Well, I worked with you on *The Mighty Challenge*, uhh what is it, ten, twelve years later, and I was amazed how much more confident you'd become.

A: Well, by that stage, you know, I was a mother, and I'd been married to Robin, and I wasn't going to take crap any more really, pardon my French.

B: Well, you know, we're now up to a pretty advanced point in the courtship between Robin's character David, and your character Shawna, and it's sometimes said that the way we cut it, the story moves along too quickly, whereby, you know, they meet and then they seem to be a regular couple so quickly —

A: But Robin was a very seductive man!

B: He was that, yes. And I think we made a decision, as a team, I remember there was an ice skating sequence that we shot and then cut out, because we thought to establish them as, not just lovers, but really a couple, we thought we could do that rather . . . by a sort of short-hand, I suppose, and within the grammar of the montage people would gather that more time had passed than we had really shown. And I think that works pretty well.

A: But what's the season here? I can never remember.

B: That's another funny thing, you know, to prepare for doing this commentary I went to the IMDb and I read what people say about this movie, and there's a long list of the continuity errors we made, and the season . . . Finally the weather was so unpredictable, and the schedule for location work was so tight, we figured we had to fudge the question a little. So it's sort of spring into early summer? But there were a very small number of re-shoots —

A: I don't remember re-shoots —

B: No, you weren't there, I think you were working on your

next project already. We did a small number of re-shoots later that year with a double, so sometimes, I don't even remember which shots they are, but sometimes when it's your back or your hand, it's actually someone else's hand.

A: Oh, that's so weird. I hope she was pretty.

B: You know, I don't remember, I'm sure . . . But the thing was, the re-shoots mean that you really shouldn't pay too much attention to the state of the leaves on the trees, or the length of the grass, even though these people on the IMDb database have a long list of every time we made a mistake . . . Now, where are we? This shot looks like it was done in a studio but this is actually a real house we borrowed, do you remember that house?

A: Uhh, not so much . . .

B: This is another celebrated shot, anyway, because this whole scene is done in one long take, and it's almost four minutes long —

A: That was a real challenge.

B: And you were wonderful in it, and Robin too. You see he's making an omelette here while you two deliver the dialogue, and he's just got so much to think about, because we used a dolly for this, even though the kitchen is not enormous by any means, so Robin had to think about his lines, and his perfor-mance, and hitting his marks, and all the while he's actually making a real omelette from scratch —

A: Hey! You remember what he said?

B: He said . . . well, why don't you tell it?

A: So we did this scene maybe five or six times, and in between each take there was a woman who came and washed up the whisk and the jug and the frying pan, and I don't know, maybe she even ate the omelettes too. And Robin was just being a sweetie, an absolute darling . . . because, you know, the funny thing is, even though he was this heart-throb and this supposedly famous lover, actually he was one of the least physically well co-ordinated people I ever met! He could hardly place one foot in front of the other. Dieter used to tease him that he walked like a cripple, perhaps I shouldn't say that word these days . . . But it meant that he found this omelette incredibly challenging, because he never cooked for himself, and he's also supposed to be drunk in this scene, we've come from the bar —

B: I have a story to tell about that bar, but I'll save it —

A: — and he had this incredible task, of trying to look like someone who's a comfortable cook, whisking up this omelette without having to think about it, but also to look like he's drunk, and then to deliver the lines in this scene . . . So by the time he'd made two or three omelettes, Dieter wanted to go again, and Robin was just pouring with sweat, he was concentrating so hard. And we had this joke on set, you know there was this thing Jack Lemmon used to do where before every take he would get himself into the zone by saying out loud, *It's magic time, it's magic time, it's magic time*, he would say this ten times, and apparently when they did *Some Like It Hot*, this just drove Tony Curtis insane. But what Robin would do is he would say this, as a sort of joke, but then it became a superstition, because he did it before the final take on that great monologue that comes later in the film, even though we shot it earlier, and he totally nailed it that time, this really involved monologue, so then he started saying it for real, *It's magic time* . . . But then with this scene, he'd made this omelette three or four times already, and Dieter asked us to go again, and he said, *It's omelette time, it's omelette time, it's omelette time*, and he did it just exactly in Jack Lemmon's voice.

B: And what was the thing he said?

A: That was the thing, he said, *It's omelette time*, and we just collapsed laughing.

B: Right, right, because I remember a different line, where he turned to me and for some reason he said it in a British accent, maybe he was doing Gielgud, who he'd just worked with, he turned to me and he said, *I don't even fucking like omelettes*, in this British accent.

A: Oh, that's wonderful. That's so Robin.

B: He really was the most wonderfully funny man, in those days. Now, where are we . . . It's in this central movement of the film, in the early stages of this final movement that the theme of love, which was the theme in the opening, where they meet, but here the theme really returns and becomes the main theme. Because, you know, some people think that the disgrace of the David character is the over-riding theme, but I always thought that really the theme was love.

A: And it's a kind of redemption for the character.

B: Maybe, yeah, it's, uhh, the redemptive power of love. And that's where Dieter was so clever, I think, in putting together a script where you can hardly tell between disgrace and redemption ... because really, when you look past the surface, maybe they're the same thing really?

A: And that, for me, is very poignant, and very true, and especially in light of what happened to Robin in the, you know, in later years.

B: Yes ... I don't know if we want to go —

A: But it's hard not to mention it, because it's a part of my life now too ... I mean after I'd been married to Robin, and we had Jamie, and even though he was the most wonderful father, there was still a real danger about him. He still had dangerous tastes, and that was part of why he was exciting, like David in the film, but also, I suppose, it was his flaw, I wouldn't say tragic flaw, but clearly it got him in a lot of trouble later on.

B: In those days, of course, we were all a bit more wild. I mean, the Seventies ... It's worth pointing out that when we were shooting, Robin was a total professional. And Dieter, who's a little older than the rest of us, he had his teenage daughters on set a lot of the time, they were thirteen, fifteen, and I don't think he ever felt there was any risk in that. Robin was a gentleman with them. He was debonair, if anything, always paying them compliments, paying them attention.

A: Of course. It was a different time. It was a very ... free, very liberated sort of era really. And don't forget that I was introduced to this world, this world of heated whirlpools and mansions in the hills, and all of these wonderfully charismatic, witty men, surrounded by young girls, and I was just a young girl myself. So in a way it could have been me, that he ... In a way it was me, I mean if I'd been a few years younger, I'm sure I still would have found him equally attractive. And clearly the girl that came forward first did find him attractive, I mean she admitted to that much. She wanted to be a model herself, and you don't go back to the home of this famous so-called lothario, I mean, knowing that he's married and so much older . . .

B: Yes, really the . . . uhh, the circumstances . . .

A: Well, Baxter, I do want to talk about it, just a little, because really it's been part of my healing, part of the healing I've found in my life, after a period when I had really lost my way, to face up to that aspect of the past. It was in that lost period of my later life that these things, these allegations about Robin came out, with what I still see as a persecution, I mean rounding up old men for things they're said to have done forty years ago, of course they can't remember any of it. So it affected my life too. It made me look back at all the past, and for a while I guess there was a time when all I could see in the past was a sort of disgrace, like everything had been tainted by what they said Robin had done to these girls. And the things that were said in the deposition, you know, with the Quaaludes and the merlot, I do recognise that lifestyle . . .

B: Yes, uhh . . . In the movie here, the David character is now under arrest, and awaiting trial, and it's a really tense part of the film, where David and Shawna are separated after her father has intervened, and we can see that the sheriff here, who was wonderfully played by Carl Liebling, is sort of caught between who to believe —

A: You know, Baxter, I was never really satisfied by this part of the movie. I think that once the romance had been established, with that really kind of brooding, atmospheric, uhh, atmosphere, I think after that, the transition to a more thriller-like movement doesn't really work for me. Maybe it just becomes too much of a boy's movie, with all this business with the sheriff.

B: It's interesting you should say that, Marlie, because I really think that part of the great appeal of Dieter's movies is the way they appeal to everyone —

A: I'm not saying the movie doesn't appeal to me, it's just that, for me, I find something lacking in this part of the film.

B: I wonder if it's because your character has a much smaller role in this part?

A: No, Baxter.

B: Okay, uhh ... Well, we now have this courtroom scene which is really pretty dialogue-heavy, and again this was all filmed in the studio, so everything you see here, all the benches and the gallery and everything had to be especially constructed by the very talented set design crew we had, who really did a wonderful job. Do you have any memories of the studio work we did for this, or about life on the set, Marlie?

A: You know, not really. I was really just taking everything in, and trying not to screw up my big break as an actress, you know?

B: Well, maybe we can talk about, you mentioned your healing, then, your journey of healing?

A: Yes, that was what I called it, and when I called my book *Journey of Healing*, which has just been published, I wanted the word journey to work on two levels, because on one level

I was making an actual journey, and in another way it was a sort of metaphorical journey. So the journey was a metaphor for a different sort of journey, a journey into myself, I guess.

B: And this is with the Amazon, the tribespeople there?

A: Yes. So, I'd always wanted to go up the Amazon, in fact I'd talked about it with Robin years ago, and we never did it. And then I found myself not getting hired so much, when I got to a certain age, and I suppose also with the stigma of the whole Robin case getting dug up. I had time on my hands, anyway. And I knew someone who was taking some people up the Amazon, to go and meet with this shaman and just to be with him, in the jungle. And I was pretty sceptical, you know, but the more he told me about it, the more I became interested. So I went, and we went up the river in this little tiny boat, and it's the most amazing place, because you're going along, and there's the monkeys, and the vines and stuff on all sides, and when the little motor cuts out, you can hear just silence and nature for miles around. And after a few days we landed at this village, and we walked deeper into the jungle.

B: And that was where you had your, uhh, experiences?

A: That's where I discovered the Ayahuasca experience, yeah. Ayahuasca is a plant, a vine. But it's also a psychedelic, like mushrooms, and it's really a medicine. We met this shaman who you knew was the most wonderful kind man just from looking into his eyes, you knew you could trust this man. And the shaman is really the doctor for the whole community. The healer. But unlike our modern doctors, there the shaman takes the medicine along with the patient, and they have this experience together. And the Ayahuasca is the major tool of the shaman. We're losing track of the film here!

B: Yeah, no, David has been released now, and he and Shawna are back together again, and they're sort of wondering what to do . . . But this is interesting, let's keep on this. You really think of it as being like a medicine?

A: I was sick, yes. I was sick not in my body, but in my soul, and for the shaman, for these people, who are primitive in some ways, but in other ways infinitely more wise than us, for them that's just as real a sickness. The shaman brews the Ayahuasca for three days, and it's mixed up with another plant which activates its kind of properties, and it's a real involved process, and you drink it down, and it's a pretty strong thing to drink and to hold it down. I can taste it in my throat if I just think of it. Then it lasts for about six hours, and it's like mushrooms, but it feels a lot more pure, if that makes sense. After we drank, the shaman walked us further into the jungle, we walked to this sort of temple he had built, and as it came on, it was clear that we were journeying towards the god within. You know? It was a great emptying of the self, a purgative effect, and then a great journey towards silence, away from the senses, and just a drifting inward, where you discover the most wonderful visions. I wrote about all this in my book, which has just come out. And it's part of a whole cleansing ritual, you drink these things — the shaman gives you other things to drink — and then it's really, you know, coming out both ends, excuse my vulgarity! And he boils these roots, and you rub the liquid on your skin, and pretty soon your skin and your nails go blue. All incredibly blue, like a smurf.

B: So the dye is a symbolic, uhh, representation of the changes that are happening inside of you?

A: Well, Baxter, you have a tendency to take things to all these extraordinary levels of analysis, but for me, it was just a detox.

I don't like to complicate things. It was just a cleansing, inside and outside. Altogether I stayed with the shaman for around two weeks, and I used the Ayahuasca I think six times in that period. And each time, I felt myself looking deeper into the god inside myself. But the funny thing is, after a certain time in that environment, you hardly need to take a drug any more, you're freed into this wonderfully exalted and sort of euphoric and pure state of mind where you can just be, you can just sort of reside in your own being.

B: It's a wonderful story, Marlie.

A: Thank you. It was a wonderful thing.

B: And we can see now, we're almost right at the end of the film, where Robin walks off into the sort of sunset on his own, in that famous ending that seems so full of ambiguity and potential ...

A: And Shawna is left on her own.

B: Is that your understanding, that the characters won't see each other again?

A: Yeah, I think it is, and certainly that was how I played it, in these final scenes, as if she wasn't going to see him again, even though it's not stated in the script. But ... seeing Robin here really at his most beautiful, you know, I want to mourn for him. Not that he's dead, but that so much has been taken from him, with all these allegations and charges. And I just feel so sad that in all his life he's never known the sort of quietness of being that I experienced on the Ayahuasca.

B: Well, here come the credits... Thank you, Marlie, this has been a lot of fun, and I hope the audience has learnt something. I've been Baxter Fields.

A: And I'm Marlie Prince.

K J ORR

THE LAKE SHORE
LIMITED

'TALK ABOUT A view,' the woman said. 'Will you look at that view?'

He acknowledged her comment with a nod, but did not speak.

'Will you look at those clouds?' she said.

He was looking. He didn't have much choice. The train was crowded and he was standing shoulder to shoulder with this woman and a line of others, their backs pressed flat against the wall of a sleeper compartment, leaving just enough space for people to squeeze past along the corridor. He was facing the windows, as they all were, by default, bags tucked behind legs. The woman was to his right. Conversation might have seemed more natural to her than silence, but he didn't want to talk. He wanted to be curled up in a seat by himself in a corner somewhere, asleep.

The rail tracks ran so close to the river that he felt they were skimming the surface of the water and that any moment they would all be sucked into a chaos of water and air. The river reflected a mass of high clouds – great puffs, cotton balls, blinding white, a spumous procession.

'When I see weather like this,' the woman said – she spoke slowly, giving each word weight – 'when I see clouds like this, you know, I think of my husband, my George.'

She shifted beside him. Cramped as they were it was a small adjustment of weight on feet. He sensed her looking at him – and so she was, her head tilted awkwardly against the wall. There were tears in her eyes, but she was smiling and had a guileless expression on her face.

'He passed three years ago, almost to the day, and it was just like this. So very beautiful. I couldn't help feeling it was a sign.'

The way he was standing he could feel his toes pressed hard against the ends of his shoes. He moved his feet a fraction. He fixed his gaze on them.

She kept talking.

'And when my grandson asks where his Papa has gone, and what he should do when he wants to talk to him, my son says —,' and here she paused for a moment, swallowed, 'my son says, "Anytime you want to talk to him you just look up at the clouds. Look up at the clouds."'

The young woman to his left was deep in her book. Intermittently, depending on the play of light, he saw her reflected in the window. She had a smile on her face, which could have been the book, or the situation; either way she didn't seem inclined to help him out.

He could turn to her, a plea in his eyes.

He could lower himself down the wall, slowly; in his bag, propped behind his legs, there were things he could fetch. He could take a step forward, towards the window, and turn around to pick the bag up.

But it was beyond him. He let his head fall back against the compartment wall.

'You look tired,' he heard the older woman say. 'Are you tired?' He could feel the pressure of her arm where it rested against his. 'But you have lovely skin. You must have been told that. You must have been told that many times.'

He had closed his eyes and now he opened them a fraction, but he didn't respond. His stomach was furious with acid. He wished he had food.

'Do you have a regime?' she said. 'For your skin?'

He shifted his head without lifting it from the compartment wall. She wasn't looking at him, he found, she was staring out of the window at the view, but when she sensed the movement she turned once more and beamed straight up at him, her eyes still damp.

'No,' she said. 'Silly question. You're too young for a regime.'

He thought to make his way to a washroom. He thought perhaps he could shake her off. But an attendant, now, was making her way down the corridor, taking reservations for the restaurant car. She was substantial. Her progress was slow. People were adjusting bodies and legs as best they could.

'I got five, a quarter after, five-thirty, a quarter of, six,' the attendant said, at volume, nasal, as she arrived in front of them. She had a buzz cut and pale, peeping eyes. She was so wide she seemed to be addressing both of them at once.

'I'd like to eat early,' the woman beside him said. She turned to him. 'Do you mind eating early?'

'I'm not eating,' he said.

'Come now. Young man, I would like to buy you dinner. It would be a pleasure. What time shall we say?'

'I'm putting you down for five, okay? For two,' the attendant said. 'What name? Gotta move on. Got a lot of folks.'

'Joanie,' the woman said. 'And five is just perfect.'

Maybe she was getting off the train, he thought. She was so keen to eat early. It would be surprising if a woman of her age were going any great distance without a seat.

The train was working its way up the river. They passed a string of small stations, platforms only a few metres long, hovering close to the water. They passed the old prison, its walls worked over with barbed wire and weeds. Nearer to Manhattan he had seen a flotilla of white sails on the far side of the Hudson, the New Jersey side, but nothing since. The towns they passed seemed emptied out – parking lots with no cars, deserted streets dividing rows of neat, quiet houses.

Joanie had fallen silent. For the moment she was watching the world coursing past. Now and then, an intake of air as she braced herself against the motion of the train, the jolting back and forth.

A change in the land beyond the river, to wooded hills.

When the train slowed and they pulled into a station, the carriage juddering and becoming still, he remained a long moment, palms flat behind him, pressed against the wall.

'You have a half hour, folks. Half an hour.'

People were manoeuvring past, filing along, bags hugged to chests. And then the corridor was clear, and they were gone. Joanie, too.

On the platform he gratefully breathed the fresh air.

He made his way up a flight of steps towards the facilities, following the throng from the train. There was a water fountain outside the washroom and he drank from that, splashed his face. Heading back to the platform he was following his hand, skimming his palm along the smooth rail that ran beside the steps: Joanie.

'It sure is a long way up!' she said. She was hauling herself one step at a time with the help of the rail. He took her in: the roomy, low-cost, middle-American clothing. The hair, which must be grey or even white, dyed caramel and coaxed into a wave.

'Do you want a hand?' he asked. He was unable to stop himself. The words just came out.

'Oh no! You are a very lovely young man, but this is good for me, this is necessary. Look around at our nation, won't you?'

She pulled herself up another step so she was level with him. 'Fatties!' she said, bugging her eyes and raising her brows knowingly. 'Look around.'

He didn't look around, and neither did she. He waited until she started moving again, and then continued down to the platform, leaving her on a slow upward trajectory.

Passengers were standing alongside the train, stretching their limbs, sipping coffee or sugary drinks. There wasn't much to see. On one side the view was blocked by the carriages, and on the other there were railings, another empty lot, a thin row of trees.

A flurry in the leaves of the trees and it started to rain. It didn't matter. They were all under the cover of a walkway. He watched the rain fall, soft and thick and wet, adding a slick sheen to the expanse of asphalt opposite.

'Would you see that!' Joanie was at his elbow, face angled to the sky. 'Oh I knew it!' She was jubilant. She was actually clapping her hands.

He could see what she saw: just visible in the rheumy air, faint above the gunmetal parking bays, a rainbow. Joanie was gripping the railings with both hands. 'Isn't that something?' she said.

It wasn't much of a rainbow. He had seen better.

'When we buried my George,' she said, clapping one hand to her chest and spreading her fingers wide, 'when we buried my George, a rainbow just appeared in the sky.' With her free hand she reached out and touched his arm. 'A perfect rainbow. Perfect. Right. Over. His. Grave. I had been waiting for a sign and there it was.' She was looking into his eyes as she spoke and when she had finished speaking she kept on looking. Tears were coming. She was trying to smile but the smile turned into a grimace and then she let out a series of sobs. Suddenly she pulled herself in towards him and pressed her face into his chest. People were watching. He couldn't do anything about that. He brought up his hands and saw them stop, poised, just above her head.

When it was time to board the train once more, the carriage guard – who had also been watching – came forward and, assuming they were together, offered them seats in the compartment he used.

Joanie nodded her head, attempting a smile and wiping her eyes with the edge of one hand, still clinging to him with the other: her weight on his forearm, his bag slipping from his shoulder, a trail of warmth on his skin from the pull of the strap as it slid down the length of his arm.

Caught up as he was – a seat, perhaps, even so, he thought.

The guard showed them the way, leading them along the cramped corridor where they had been standing to the sleeper where he had set himself up – the fold-down table top laid over with neat rows of Amtrak ticket stubs, and brochures, and timetables.

'You are a nice man,' Joanie said.

She was sniffing but seemed to be over the worst. As if to confirm it, she flashed her teeth in an approximation of a smile, took a sharp breath, sighed, and settled into a seat.

'Well,' she said. 'Would you look at this.'

He had found himself in Times Square that morning, had stood bathed in colour, had closed his eyes.

When he opened them, there it was: a vast animated hoarding with a moving image of a woman. She was looking down – at the street it seemed – and holding one finger to her lips. She was deciding.

He hadn't slept and it had taken him a moment to understand what was going on. Those people looking up at her were being filmed, so they appeared on the screen somehow, in miniature, like minions at her feet.

The giant woman held her finger and thumb like a pincer,

suspended. She would move her hand so these jaws would rove and stop, rove and stop. They would be poised of a sudden above a person's head like a threat. A smile on her lips.

It was random, pre-recorded, but it looked like intent. A cluster of tourists close by were tracking her hand, moving about so that it might be them standing beneath. The camera zoomed in to pick out faces. Each time: a cheer from the street.

And there he was. He was suspicious-looking, shifty. This look he now had.

The giant woman above him, scattered laughter, he had tried to cover his face with his hands.

The sleeping compartment was smaller than he would have guessed. The seat backs and curtains were blue, and everything else was grey. Everywhere there were levers and tilts and multi-level sections of surfaces serving different purposes. There were buttons to be pressed in yellow and blue and red. There were arrows up and arrows down. There were signs of warning – Caution! – and a row of stubby red lights, alerts of various kinds related to the sink, mirror and toilet. A bed suspended from the ceiling blocked the upper half of the window. The second bed, he thought, must be made up somehow from the seats, with the table pushed back. The two seats faced each other. Joanie was in the one facing forwards. He was watching the world slip away behind the train.

The guard's handiwork was laid out on the table between them like a hybrid of Monopoly and Patience, careful lines of overlapping counterfoils with route stops stamped out in caps: BUFFALO, NY; ERIE, PA; SOUTH BEND, IN.

Joanie opened a route guide. It was large enough to obscure her face. 'Henry Hudson,' he heard her murmuring behind it, 'The Wonder Years. General William Jenkins Worth.'

Putting the guide down, she inspected their surroundings. She pointed out a narrow post-box slit that sat between them underneath the window. 'That,' she said, 'is where the table folds into.' She nodded to herself. She looked past his head to the compartment wall. 'See all those lights?' she said. 'They have a light for everything.' She squinted. 'They have a reading light. They have a main light. And they have a mirror light.' She turned her attention to her own seat, glancing down and about, animated, like a snuffling creature of some sort on a hunt. She had been resting her arm on what appeared to be a step to the top bunk, but with a little encouragement it flipped up and she found herself looking at a metal funnel. 'Oh my, it's the john!' She let the lid drop and sat back.

He wished she would wash her hands. From where he was sitting he could see that a sink was hidden just above her head – flagged by hand towels and wrapped bars of soap – but she hadn't seen it.

He tried to focus on the magazine that he found in his hands, that he must have picked up somewhere. The feel of it: the gloss tacky against his palms. He saw her looking. He rolled it into itself, made a tube of it. It was a women's magazine.

As the train lurched, the door to their compartment slid open and shut, open and shut. Across the corridor, in the compartment opposite, a pair of legs was visible from the knees down – pale chinos, buffed brogues.

'He did not!' a woman's voice exclaimed, loudly.

'I swear to God,' came the dry response.

'He did not!' the woman exclaimed again.

Back and forth the door went, back and forth. Across the way the pair of legs uncrossed and re-crossed – fingers drummed on one knee.

The door opened and shut. He started counting it: gave it numbers.

1, 2; he counted.

1, 2.

1, 2.

'Okay,' Joanie said, making a face, swiping an invisible something from the air with one hand. 'Would you mind? Would you mind latching that?'

There was a hook you could slip over a nub of metal to secure the door. He was able to lean from his seat and flick it into place. Now the legs were obscured. The voices were faint. It was just the two of them.

It had started a couple of months in. He hadn't noticed at first. He had been aware instead of changes in his hands. His fingers developed blistered patches – tiny, swollen, liquid puffs. He noticed these before the counting. He bothered them. He broke the surface of the skin to let the liquid out. It became a thing – and then the counting. Once he had noticed the counting he watched himself doing it with an awareness that seemed to offer nothing in the way of helping him stop.

1, 2.

1, 2.

Like breathing.

Joanie's head fell back against the seat, and in a short time she was snoring softly.

Through the window he watched the rail tracks multiply and diminish, the telephone wires running overhead. He looked beyond the tracks to the water, and beyond the water to the land opposite, the dense woodland hills.

Joanie's breathing had changed. It was heavy and slow. With the door shut the sound was amplified. It seemed to him that the whole compartment was breathing with her, that he was locked in the humid cavern of her chest.

Looking up, he was surprised to see she was awake and studying him.

'Why have you locked the door?' she asked. Her voice was

querulous. Her eyes were small and scared. She was pushing her hands downwards on her legs in a rhythmic way, like a cat working the edge of a couch. And she was looking again at the magazine he was holding tight in his hands.

'The noise,' he said.

She kept kneading at her thighs with her hands.

'You asked me,' he said. 'You asked me to. And then you slept.' He put the magazine along with the guide in the slot between window and table.

'Oh.' She remembered now. 'So I did. So I did.'

Rain started to beat down – pellets of water strumming the top of the carriage like hoof beats. The sky dimmed.

'My,' Joanie said, taking it all in. 'My-oh-my-oh-my.' She propped her elbows on the table, clasping her hands in a gesture of pleasure. 'Oh! I love the rain when I'm tucked up,' she said.

She kept talking. The rain was so loud that he could not hear what she was saying, but he could see her mouth working.

He counted her face:

eye, eye;

eye, eye, nose.

When the rain eased off a little Joanie settled back in her seat. 'Where are you headed?' she asked. 'Are you going all the way?'

Lately, when he dreams – if he gets to dreaming – vast clouds bank on the horizon. Waves gather, scraping the pitch-black belly of the sky. He wakes, knowing the clouds must spill, the waters must break. Dreaming, he manages to make it all stop, and wait.

Give me time, he asks. Just give me time to work this out.

At home, in the kitchen, he counts the mugs above the sink, and in the bathroom the tiles on the wall. In the hallway, he counts the line of boxes for mail. In the subway, he counts the pillars on the platform, and once on the train he counts the lights that appear in the darkness of the tunnels.

When he counts he tends towards multiples of 2, never goes past 6. Mostly he sticks to 1, 2.

Beads of water were being pulled, one by one, backwards, across the window pane.

'You don't say much,' Joanie said.

They passed an old-fashioned station – lampposts with elegant lampshades, the roof of the building bordered with filigreed woodwork.

'I'm really very easy to get along with,' she said.

They passed a bridge, a criss-cross of girders. They passed a stationary freight train, the wagons a deep green, here and there bursting into blossoms of white graffiti. In the narrow spaces between the wagons he saw, at intervals, a momentary flash of gravel, rail tracks, grass, water, hills, and sky.

'Utica,' said Joanie.

She leaned forward, putting both hands flat on the edge of the table, like a contestant in a game show. She held her face in a crush of concentration, and then let it relax.

'Erie!' she said. 'Sandusky!' Her eyes were all lit up. 'I'm guessing where you're going.'

Lately, when he sleeps, he loses his bearings, can't remember where he is: at the hospital, in the chair bedside his wife's bed, or alone at home, where he tries to fall asleep on the daybed, watching television, listening to the radio.

When in his dreams he becomes aware of his bladder, he mentally traces two routes to the bathroom before attempting to get to his feet. Route one takes him out of the chair, across the slumbering ward, across the corridor glossed with night lighting, past the nurses' station, past the drinks machine, to the left, or to the right, either one will do. Route two, at home, he kicks the sheet off and pads in his boxers in a beeline. He doesn't need a light. He knows the way. He wipes his hands at the sink – thoroughly – a habit he can't shake, reaching all the while for water, paper towels, antiseptic gel.

The restaurant car's booths had the same blue upholstery as the sleeping compartment. There were groups of people already seated, but the car was not yet full.

'They run a tight ship,' Joanie said. 'You see if they don't.'

A woman seated them – pale, and skinny, and drawn. She hovered beside an empty table a moment but then sidestepped to seat them at the one opposite, where a young couple were already deep in their menus, side by side.

'You go,' Joanie said, and he slid on in to take the seat closest to the window. She edged herself down then, on to the end of the couch, beside him. They were facing backwards. He was facing the girl, and Joanie facing the boy. It was an arrangement better suited to old friends, or a double date. The couple didn't acknowledge their arrival at all.

'You ready?' the attendant asked, turning her attention to the couple.

Only the girl looked up. 'Yes,' she said. Her hair was cut in a neat bob. She was maybe in her early twenties.

The attendant waited, pen hanging mid-air over a pad.

'Number 28,' the girl said. 'Thank you.'

'Both of you?'

'Yes. Thank you,' the girl said, tucking her hair behind her ears; first the right, then the left.

1, 2.

The boy was still immersed in the menu.

Sometimes they get muddled – routes one and two – sometimes he'll be halfway to the hospital bathroom and he'll panic, believing, suddenly, that he is in his boxers, for all the world to

139

see, or maybe, worse, his fly is unbuttoned, or maybe, worse still, he has a hard-on. It is not possible, of course. He never falls asleep in the chair beside her bed dressed only in his boxers, and even at home, alone, it is a long while since he has woken up hard. Some switch has flipped. He's not even sorry.

'No drinks?' the attendant asked.

'Can we have water?' the girl said.

'You can have water.' The attendant's hand hovered over the pad as she cast a glance at the boy. 'Both of you?' she asked. The boy didn't move, didn't acknowledge her at all.

'Please. Thanks,' the girl said. She tucked her hair behind her right ear; once, twice. It was just the gesture. There was no hair needing to be tucked.

The attendant shifted her feet side to side as she ticked off the boxes on her sheet. 'You sleeper or coach?' she asked.

'Sleeper,' the girl said.

'Number?'

'Nine.'

'Car?'

'4911.'

'Both of you?'

'Yes,' the girl said.

The only other thing to say about routes one and two is this: he cares about them inasmuch as they get him from here to there, from bladder-full to bladder-empty. These are essentials. Energy expended on anything else is wasted. In the versions he imagines, asleep, as in the versions when he is awake, he walks with tunnel-vision – everything else, everything around the edges, he shuts out.

'I need you to sign,' the attendant said.

She leaned forward and handed one sheet to the girl and

put another one down on the table with the pen in front of the boy. 'Both of you,' she said. The boy didn't look up. He tilted his head towards the girl, who nodded, and pointed at the bottom of the sheet. He took up the pen now. When he was done the girl signed hers and took both sheets and handed them back.

The attendant tore the customer copies from her own copies, deposited them on the table, and left.

At the hospital, he shuts out the other patients, the nurses, their sympathetic smiles, their chat. He shuts out the people who mill around by the drinks machine, and those sitting on the endless rows of plastic chairs.

At home, he shuts out the postcards they have been sent by friends, family, that over time they have stuck to the cupboard above the sink. He shuts out the picture that she painted, badly, in Corsica – rocks, sea, sky – that he had framed and hung in the middle of their living room wall. He shuts out all the bits and pieces they found together on day trips, museum trips, foreign trips.

From the restaurant car, with windows on both sides, facing backwards, he could see the whole panorama. On his right, the river; on his left, salt marsh, weatherboard houses, porches bearing the ubiquitous national flag.

The menu was a yellow oblong. Non-Egg Entrée, he read. Egg Substitute. Dinner Special. The list of numbers ran to 79, but some of the numbers did not have options alongside. He wondered what would happen if you ordered 31 when there was no option listed.

'Grits. Oh my,' Joanie said. 'I have not had grits since . . . I don't know when.'

He was watching the couple opposite. He kept expecting

141

one of them to make eye contact, to say something, but neither of them did.

At home he shuts out things other people wouldn't see if they walked with him on his short route: her reading on the daybed with a look of the deepest, most peaceful concentration; or banging pots together in their kitchen in the morning to wake him up; or in the bath sloshing the water, chattering – him, stationed on the toilet lid close by, elbows on knees, eyes on her, listening. No. They wouldn't see any of that. He would rather not see it himself. He shuts it out.

'Where are you all from?' Joanie asked.

The girl gave Joanie a wary smile that did not extend to her eyes. The boy no longer had a menu, but kept his gaze down nonetheless.

'DC,' the girl said.

'Do you like it?' Joanie asked. 'Have you always lived there?'

'We like it,' the girl said. 'Not always. No.'

'Where are you from originally?'

'Michigan.'

'What about you?' Joanie asked the boy, but still he didn't look up.

The girl nudged the boy's hand gently where it lay on the table top, and he did look up, a question in his eyes, his head turned to her. The girl leaned in and said right into his ear, 'Where are you from, the lady is asking.' He frowned, moved closer, studying her lips, as if all the answers were there. She tried again, gesturing at Joanie, and finally then he took their companions in.

'I don't hear well,' he said, loudly, so that people nearby were twisting in their seats to look. There was a small distortion in the way he spoke, but the words were clear.

He turned back to the girl then. He nodded, very slightly, just once.

She did the same. And she smiled at him.

It was the briefest exchange.

The sleeping ward, early that morning, had brought him back to night flights they had taken together. Cabin lights off and shutters down. Air hostesses – attentive like nurses – drifting up the darkened passageways, shadowy moths in the half light, now and then summoned by a lone glow.

He had enjoyed being lodged for those hours in the purring heart of the jet, while beside him his wife, who could never sleep on a plane, talked quietly, non-stop, spinning tales to keep her mind off the fact they were in a tin can, too high, trawling her memory bank for odd fragments, sending a stream of offerings to him through the fuggy cabin air – a picnic in Maine, a school trip to the city, the particular challenge of a long-forgotten ballet pose. Their heads would be resting close, and as he listened he would feel her breath on his ear, across his cheek, his nose.

It was so stealthy, the memory, that it had taken him by surprise. He was tired. His defences were down. He had tried to make it stop, but something had already taken hold – vice-like at the back of his neck, reaching deep into his chest.

He had left the hospital. It was still early. The streets were almost empty.

He walked in Central Park where the trees were black-barked and lacquered in the rain, the ground studded with fragments – foliage frayed and cast down by the wind. He bought a coffee in a coffee bar in a mall at Columbus Circle. He walked on south towards the glint and flare of lights in Times Square, which he tracked from several blocks up, great swatches of colour against the buildings, pulsing towards the leached sky.

At Madison Square Garden, instead of continuing to his office, he followed the stream of bodies heading for Penn Station.

A normal interaction: something to bring her with him into the world. At Hudson News: a bottle of water and a magazine. A conversation with the woman at the counter.

But as she gave him change – the woman's skin against his.

And then staring at the hoarding for Amtrak, choosing at random, buying a ticket. Waking from his daze on board the Lake Shore Limited.

TAMAR HODES

THE FIRST DAY

HELENA LOOKED OVER to the tiny figure sitting next to her in the car. Betsy barely took up half the seat. Her little face was tight with anxiety.

'You'll be fine,' said Helena, reassuringly. 'Everyone feels nervous on their first day.'

She moved her hand off the steering wheel to touch and comfort Betsy. She squeezed her tiny hand for an instant; then returned it to the wheel. She needed to concentrate. Here in the New Forest, three horses were heaving their suede bodies slowly at the side of the road. One walked nonchalantly in front of the car and seemed in no hurry. Helena braked. She had heard of accidents caused by wandering animals here and she didn't want an unfortunate incident, today of all days. Betsy needed her to be calm.

'Look at the horses. Aren't they lovely?'

Betsy nodded.

They waited a minute and the animal edged slowly away.

They drove on. Betsy was very quiet. Helena glanced over at her little face, tight with terror. She wanted to stop the car and just hug her, hold her tiny body close to her own and kiss her. But she knew that they both had to be brave and move on.

The horses were behind them now and they were surrounded by green bushes and trees. A few rabbits nibbled the grass on the verge.

'Look, bunny rabbits. You like rabbits.'

No response.

'You know, you're going to be fine. It will feel a bit strange at the beginning but you'll soon settle. Everyone there is very nice.'

'But what happens if they don't like me?'

'Of course they'll like you.' Helena laughed to show how ridiculous that idea was. 'Everyone is new at the beginning. And then they settle.'

'Will I have any friends?'

Helena felt tears prick her eyes. Would she ever stop feeling protective of her?

'Of course you will. Wherever you go, people like you. You're so friendly.'

'What will we do there?' Betsy's voice was small and slightly squeaky.

'Oh, all sorts of lovely things. Maybe some painting or drawing. Baking. Singing. All things you enjoy and you're good at.'

Outside, Helena saw the first signs of early blossom sprigging the trees. Maybe they were a good omen. Was that even a bit of blue in the otherwise granite sky?

'Will I have lunch there?'

'Yes. You'll enjoy that. I've told them that you don't have a huge appetite.'

'Will I have to eat all of it?'

'No. Just leave what you don't want. Okay?'

Betsy nodded.

'And then I'll pick you up at three and see how you've got on.'

Helena sighed. She was pleased that there were no other cars on the forest road today. She needed as much calm as she could get. Why was life so hard? Why did she find leaving Betsy so difficult? Would she settle? Would it improve as time went on?

She had to admit that her devotion to Betsy had probably destroyed her relationship with Miles. He had felt excluded from the tight bond that the two of them had and he could not break in. He had pleaded with Helena to let Betsy make her own decisions, to stop mollycoddling her.

'She has to look after herself,' he would say. 'Think for herself. She's too reliant on you.'

'She needs me,' would be Helena's response and then she would storm out. Except that on one occasion Miles did the storming out and he hadn't returned.

A ray of sunlight broke through the trees now. More blossom. The trees were bushier here, as if they were bursting with life and freshness. The foliage was the green of hope and new beginnings.

They left the forest now and entered the outskirts of Lyndhurst. Betsy was playing with the toggles of her coat, twiddling them in her tiny hands.

'I'd like to stay at home with you.'

'I know,' said Helena, 'but I have to go work and you'd be lonely and bored all day on your own.'

Betsy shook her head in disagreement. She could be stubborn although at times she seemed rather defeated.

Helena thought now of Betsy's belongings, pink with prettiness everywhere: white linen hearts; floral bags; trays and boxes full of shiny brooches and tinny trinkets. How they belied this vulnerability.

They drove up to the gate which was open onto the drive.

'Here we are,' said Helena as cheerfully as she could.

The red brick building was solid and smart. There was an attractive garden in the front with picnic benches where lunch could be eaten on sunny days. A neat pattern of gravel paths and trimmed bushes edging them; a buddleia attracting butterflies; feeders filled with nuts for the birds.

Helena got out of the car and went round to help Betsy undo her seatbelt. She came tentatively out. They walked together, hand in hand, to the front door, Betsy clutching her pretty floral bag.

There was a sign, letters engraved into a gold plaque: Lyndhurst Care Home for the Elderly.

She rang the bell and a petite Chinese lady in a pale blue uniform answered.

'Hello,' she said warmly, 'you must be Betsy.'

Betsy didn't answer. She looked to Helena for reassurance.

'Yes,' said Helena for her, 'my mother has come for her trial day.'

She let go of Betsy's hand and passed it to the lady. 'Come with me, then,' said the woman to Betsy. 'I'll look after you. We'll see you at three,' she said to Helena.

'See you later, Mum,' said Helena, as she left them, and went back to her car. 'Have a lovely day.'

She looked up.

The door was firmly closed.

ALAN McCORMICK

GO WILD IN THE COUNTRY

As Nadine walks slowly towards the entrance to the Villa, she ties her dressing gown tight around her waist and slides the palms of her hands down from her thighs as if she's rubbing away something. Renzo sits casually on the brow of the hill smoking a cigarette, not caring if anyone sees him, the sleeves of his grey porter's jacket rolled up his arms, the collar up around his neck as if he's an extra in *Grease*. When he exhales it looks like he's whistling. As Nadine comes up the entrance stairs she sees me and gives me the finger.

Since qualifying, I've been running writing sessions for the Villa's younger patients. Nadine is a disruptive influence when she bothers to turn up, her snaking moods, sometimes enchanting, but more often sullen, brooding something within. Today she's the first to arrive, and, after shedding her anger outside the nurses' office – what are you fucking looking at? I can talk to the porters if I want to, and I can fuck them if I want to! – she seems different, the hormonal blush of anger on her neck already fading into blotchy pink and white, calmer, ready to be open . . . opened.

'I saw you looking, Tom.'

'Renzo is not a good guy.'

Nadine pretends to be surprised and then stares at me, holding her gaze a little too long, then suddenly laughs.

'I like his cock, Tom, I don't like him.'

'Okay, Nadine, I get it.'

She mimics what I say with a heavy, breathy accent: *'Okay, Nadine, I get it*. Do you get it, Tom?' she adds lightly in her own voice.

'You could express your thoughts on the page.'

She stifles a laugh and tries the same trick, mimicking what I say, but her eyes soften a little when repeating the phrase 'thoughts on the page' as if it were suggesting something quaint, safe to dive into.

'I still have the poem you wrote when you came the first time.'

'Poor you.'

'It was honest.'

'It was bollocks.'

'You said the marks on your wrists were the "blade's curse", your "flesh tattoos", I remember those phrases.'

'Poetry bollocks, Tom, I said it so you'd like me.'

'I like the words, Nadine.'

'Not me? Or these?'

She pulls up the sleeves on her dressing gown and stretches out her arms, palms up to the ceiling. The cuts look surprisingly deep and purpling, and a few are fresh, red and angry, jagged at the edges like wild bite marks.

She steps closer. 'You can touch them if you want.'

'Do the nurses know?'

'Tom, it's okay.'

The surfaces of the old cuts feel hard and knobbly like reptile skin but the new cuts are too real.

'You know they can get infected?'

'So?'

'Well, you'd get sick.'

'Duh, Tom! I'm already sick.' She smiles. 'You can press harder, you won't hurt me, nothing really hurts me.'

Nadine would never show the nurses her cuts, and I would never tell them. Elaine, their leader, likes to sit on the table in the staffroom and address the other nurses as if she were giving a sermon. In their tank tops, cheesecloth shirts and pale blue jeans, they look like the Manson family, a joke I would share if everyone weren't part of the cult.

I first talked to Elaine at the social club at the end of my first week at work. She came up to me as I chose a song on the jukebox: Bow Wow Wow's 'Go Wild in the Country'.

'It's Tom, isn't it? I love the singer, so cute. What's her name?'

'Annabella.'

'I've been observing you at work so I thought you'd know her name. She's really pretty, don't you think?'

'She's got a great voice.'

'Good tits too though, eh, Tom? But she's only fourteen. Makes me feel a little uneasy, that Manet painting on the cover of the single with her in the nude, it's not right, is it?'

'No, I suppose it isn't.'

'I'm joking, Tom, she's beautiful. Why shouldn't she be naked?'

She watches me closely, waiting for a response.

'But if I weren't joking, I'd be saying she shouldn't be naked on the cover of a single that sad little men are going to take into their bedrooms to fondle and drool over. But am I joking or not joking?'

'I don't know.'

One of the gang called Steve came over: 'Are you playing with the mind of our new member of staff, Lane?'

'I'm not playing with your mind, am I, Tom? I'm too old to

be playing with Tom's mind. I think he'd prefer younger girls to play with . . . his mind. Wouldn't you, Tom?'

'Come on, Lane, that's enough.' And then Steve looked at me with a sympathetic smile. 'Sorry, old chap, Lane makes her mind up pretty quickly about people. If I was you I'd lie low.'

I started to walk away.

'Heh, Largactyl boy, keep moving because I've got you in my sights,' Elaine said and shaped her hand like a pistol, one eye cocked like Travis Bickle, and pretended to shoot.

When I started at the Villa, Nadine was thick with a boy called Gavin. During workshops I'd often find myself looking out into the grounds. One afternoon I saw them walking hand in hand towards the sheep fields on the asylum farm. One of the patients said they were going to pick magic mushrooms.

When they came back later they were laughing like coyotes, running up and down the paths in purposeful patterns as if creating a topographic maze together, one only seen by them or by an imaginary bird hovering overhead.

A nurse ambled out and talked to them, shared a toke on a cigarette and brought them inside.

One night Gavin walked out of the Villa without telling anyone. He went home to see his mother who hadn't been answering his letters. His mother was a paranoid schizophrenic and didn't let him in the house because she was scared what he might do. Gavin smashed the lounge window and then hung himself from the rope swing under the tree at the bottom of their garden.

When Nadine was told, she said nothing for weeks. She was taken to the main hospital for special treatment. Six ECT sessions were prescribed and when she returned, she'd chopped her hair, smudged raven's lipstick on her lips like a charred clown and talked slowly and deeply as if she were underwater. She came silently into a writing session and wrote on the wall:

'The angel boy that flew down to peck out my eyes made me see.
I dream of him still and he touches me, holds me,
Smiles as he tightens his grip on my heart, carries it into the
sky, and then lets go.'

Lola, my girlfriend, likes to call Nadine 'Crazy Cat'.

Funny that, because cats have taken over the intimacy of our relationship: bromide in our tea. We stare at the television in dead-eyed awe, empty mugs collecting in front of us on the table; Roger, the tabby on my lap, Tabatha, the mottled sphinx, purring into Lola's thigh. The cats speak for us or rather we speak through them. My voice is a bass growl for Roger: 'Daddy would like to watch *The Professionals* now.'

'Tell Daddy to earn some more money and buy a video recorder. Otherwise he'll have to wait for *All Creatures Great and Small* to finish.' I have grown to hate Lola's soft velvet kitten tone for Tabatha: rejection with a cartoon Aristocats girly voice when the voice, like its message, should be spiky and cold.

When I slide my hand across the sofa I have to go under Tabatha's purring belly to reach Lola's skirt. As I attempt a lift I feel a claw and hear Lola's Tabatha voice: 'When Daddy stops behaving like The Son of Sam he may have a kiss. Until then he can relieve himself in the bathroom.'

When I stand up, Roger rolls casually onto the floor and lies on his back waiting for his tummy to be stroked. I fall on him as if enacting the rug scene in *Sons and Lovers*; Roger is Oliver Reed.

After I finish the workshop I find Renzo and Nadine sitting on the steps by the Villa entrance. She has a huge red love bite on her neck, and Renzo gives me a wink.

'Did you just wink at me, Renzo?'

'Yeah, and I can give you a kiss too if you want.' He squeezes his lips grotesquely together for an imaginary snog and Nadine laughs.

'You're an animal!'

He growls and Nadine tilts her head back and howls.

'And you're a pussy boy.'

'Why don't you leave her alone?'

'So you can have your taste, pussy boy?'

Nadine laughs at this.

'Fuck off, Renzo!'

'Pussy words! I fuck, you fuck off!'

Elaine throws open the entrance door. 'No, you can both fuck off. Nadine, leave your little fan club and get inside, now!'

I'm left with Renzo at the top of the steps. He squeezes out two cigarettes from the top pocket of his porter's jacket, lights both, and then offers me one.

'Women are cunts,' he says and spits his gum over my shoulder.

In *Taxi Driver*, Robert De Niro shoots the pimp, Harvey Keitel, in the belly. I take his cigarette, inhale, and block him out and fantasise about how I can save her and save myself.

I find a bench at the back of the Villa. It's mid October and the grass has been full of damp and dew for weeks but there hasn't been a frost yet. A mist hangs over the sheep fields at the edge of the asylum grounds. I was told earlier by Jonny, one of the porters who looks a little too much like Jim Davidson, that today is perfect for picking mushrooms. He told me to what to look for: a small white pointed dome with a kink half way down a tall spindly stalk. He told how to dry and prepare them and warned me not to eat too many the first time.

Nadine appears from around the building and joins me. 'You were right about the wop,' she says. 'He's fucking another nutcase now.'

'He'll get his comeuppance.'

'I doubt it, Tom. That sort get to rule the world, don't they? But you're not like that, are you?'

'Not normally.'

'Fancy a stroll?' she says.

We walk out towards the sheep fields. When we get there we find that the sheep have been moved from the farthest field.

'Perfect!' she says. 'I'm going to get out of it. Will you keep watch?'

'I'm not one of the patients, Nadine.'

'Are you sure about that, Tom?'

'Anyway, I'm partial to a magic mushroom now and then.'

'Fuck off, you're way too straight.'

'It's the silent ones you should look out for, Nadine.'

'If you say so. Here, be useful for once and take my hand.'

I help her over the stile into the empty field, and we start picking.

'You need to wipe them clean to get off any sheep shit. Then eat a few at a time,' she says.

I have maybe forty in my hand and eat them in front of her.

'You stupid bastard, that's way too many in one go.'

I eat another handful – they taste rank, putrid – and then sit on the grass and watch her get her measure. She is careful, artful, bent over so she can examine them as she picks, rejecting some and discarding them back onto the ground, keeping the good ones and dropping them onto the curled hem of her skirt. She wipes away the dirt and eats a few at a time, sipping from a bottle of water between each mouthful. As I watch her my nausea starts, takes me in a tidal wash so that I suddenly tip forward, my gut twisting, falling hard and wrenching tufts of grass out from the earth with my hands and my teeth. I lie there for what seems like ages and fight to let the poison out.

My stomach quietens for a moment. Looking up, it is as if the earth is lying on its side, the asylum tipped up like a drowning Titanic, the clouds disappearing into the earth.

Nadine looks at me from an angle and smiles and it's the smile of the ancients in the here and now, at once wizened and wise but also pixotic and mischievous. I am crying and when I rub my eyes, dirty salty rainwater spits up and dribbles into my mouth. The nausea is overwhelming again and I want to be sick but can't. I want Mum. Nadine is by my hot head, a curious monkey girl flicking ticks from my hair and rubbing my head. But her hand is cool porcelain; a shop dummy girl in a Victorian dress shop and I start laughing, the Victorian asylum, her Victorian doll-like face, a Victorian clockwork monkey beating a drum, Keith Moon gurning on snare, the pale moon a cymbal, the ley lines that travel beneath me and through the grounds and out onto the Downs, a secret swirling snake . . . wild, go wild in the country . . .

'Where snakes in the grass are free?' Nadine asks.

Her face changes, cheekbones heightening and sharpening, and she's Annabella, her voice like the cooling breeze tingling my skin. I want to shit and it makes sense to do it here on the earth, shit to shit, dust to dust, ashes to ashes, my brain hot-wiring connections as a greater awareness keeps promising to emerge. I try to take my trousers off but my fingers are weak and I can't unclasp the belt. And then I feel her arms around me like warm insulating wings. I want her to hold me like this forever but things never stay still for a single moment.

'Tom, don't do that. Just relax and let it happen but promise you'll keep your clothes on.'

She drops a handful of mushrooms and I swear I can see them pop like golden sherbet in her mouth.

'You look like you need company,' she says.

That sounds exciting but somehow worrying too. I feel an overwhelming panic taking me over and I want to shit again. I go inside, burrowing. I see Lola and our cats mouthing along to an advert on the television, *Cats would buy Whiskas*, and I feel a blanket, my jacket over my head. It's the saddest feeling

I've ever had and I start crying again. It seems like I'm crying for ages. When I take the jacket off my head it's raining and Nadine is dancing like a maniac at the top of a slope.

'Stop moaning about your girlfriend and your cats, just leave them!' she shouts.

I didn't know I'd been talking.

'We don't make love any more,' I say.

'Well, you shouldn't be fucking your cats anyway, it's illegal!'

'Lola isn't a cat!'

And suddenly we're both laughing. Nadine stands tall on a burial mound braying like a donkey, her huge toothy mouth turned up to the sky. I'm chattering and guffawing like monkeys and I can't stop.

Nadine runs over, still laughing I think, and taps me with a knuckle on my forehead.

'You're making my brain hurt, Tom, stop talking about her.'

'Do you miss Gavin?' I ask and I see her face change, a landslide after an earthquake so all the features melt and drop, her mouth softening and caving in, water running down her cheeks and across her lips.

'You fucking bastard, Tom! You're trying to do my head in.'

I try and grab her but touch her breasts by mistake.

She screams in my face and pulls off her top and throws her bra onto the ground.

'Just like all the other fuckers, Tom! Come on, cop a feel, that's what you want, isn't it?'

She pulls my hands towards her breasts and I struggle to stop them touching. They're scarred red, small slash marks, yellow burns across the breasts and over her nipples.

'Come on!' she screams.

'Nadine, stop, please.'

I am trying to climb out, sober up . . . rescue.

I grab her in a bear hug and start making reassuring animal

noises, it's what comes naturally, 'grrr grr' slowly becoming 'there there'. After a while she stops struggling, stops crying. I repeat the 'there there' mantra, squeezing tighter and tighter until she jabs me in the ribs.

'For fuck's sake, Tom, I'd rather you touch my tits than suffocate me.'

I let go and she puts her top back on.

'Come on then,' she says, taking my hand, 'I'm soaking and it's not working here. Let's go back and find somewhere dry to sit and ride it out.'

'Not inside, I like it out here,' I say. 'There's something about being outside, the earth.'

'Oh, I can tell you like the earth, you kept trying to cultivate it with your shit.'

'I didn't, did I?'

'You did so.' And she points to a crap, shaped like a giant mushroom dome, a few feet away.

'Clever, that one,' she says and we start laughing again, and we keep on laughing until we find a bench under a large oak tree in a quiet part of the hospital grounds to shelter from the rain. There we sit together barely speaking, my brain slowing, settling, but still flickering connections, wondering if hers are making the same ones but somehow knowing she wants to have her thoughts to herself and not hear mine, watching the leaves dance and spin before settling on the grass, the giant October sun dropping below the hills, the sky grey and blackening, the stars, the stars . . . and when I wake up Nadine is gone.

HELEN MARSHALL

SECONDHAND MAGIC

A BAD THING is going to happen at the end of this story. This is a story about bad things happening, but I won't tell you what the bad thing is until you get there. Don't flip ahead to the end of the story. Stories like this only work if you don't know what the bad thing is until you get there. Wait for it to happen, don't try to look ahead, don't try to stop it from happening. Because you know how magic works? When you try to cheat it, it just gets worse and worse and worse. That's the way of it. So, please. Just wait for it. I'll ask nothing else from you. Cross my heart.

Sayer Sandifer had very few of the ingredients necessary to be a true magician. His patter? Weak and forced on account of a childhood stutter he got when he turned four. His fingers? Short, stumpy things that couldn't make a silver dollar disappear no matter how long he practised. His sense of timing? Awful. And worse yet – crime of all crimes! – he had no assistant. The fact of the matter is that lacking any of these things might not have been enough to sink him, but all of them? What chance did the poor boy have? And at twelve years old he was just learning the first and only real lesson of being grown-up: that wanting a thing so bad it hurt didn't mean getting a thing, not by a long shot.

The only thing Sayer *did* have going for him was the prettiest set of baby blues you ever saw. That wasn't nothing. Not for a magician. And those eyes were only useful for one thing: getting an audience. When Sayer put on his star-spattered cloak and the chimney-pot hat he had swiped from Missus Felder's snowman the winter before; when with utter seriousness and intent he knocked on your door at eight in the morning while the coffee brewed and the scent of fresh-mown grass drifted through the Hollow; when you had just kicked up your heels to browse the paper in search of discount hanger steak and sausages, then Sayer would be there.

'Missus S-S-Sabatelli,' he would stutter. Or if he was having a particularly bad day then he might not get that far, you might see him swallowing the word like a stone and searching out a new one. The first name instead, 'Marianne,' he might say and bless him for being so formal. 'I require your attendance this afternoon at the house of my mother and father. Please bring gingersnaps.'

And maybe you'd fall in love with him just a little bit right then, the way you could tell just by looking that he knew he didn't have the right stuff in him yet for magic, but he wanted it, oh, he wanted it. He'd chase it even if it meant looking a fool in front of all his mother's friends. He'd stand there, trembling, waiting for you to deliberate. Waiting for you to make some sort of pronouncement upon him. And you'd know how badly you could hurt him, that was the thing, you'd know you could crush him right there if you were of a mind to do so.

'Whatever for?' you might ask, hoping to surprise him, hoping to give him a moment to deliver a staggering statement of pomp and circumstance of the kind you knew he ought to have rattling around inside his head, because, *God*, you just wanted this kid to have it in him. Have that special something, even if it was just a flair for the dramatic. But, no, Sayer didn't know the turns of phrase yet, he didn't know that a magician was supposed to do something besides magic. You couldn't expect him to, not at twelve years old, not even if he had studied the masters like Maskelyne, Thurston, Houdini and Carter. Which he hadn't. All he had was a 'Magic for Beginners' tin set an uncle had gotten him for Christmas – the same Christmas Missus Felder's snowman had lost its chimney-pot hat and knitted scarf.

What Sayer didn't know was that magic was never at the heart of being a magician. There was supposed to be something else. Something kinder.

But, as I said, what Sayer did have – what made you say 'Yes, sir, gingersnaps it is!' – were those wide baby blues of his. Eyes a kind of blue I never saw before, blue like a buried vein. His father's eyes.

Joe Sandifer had all the things that Sayer lacked: clean and polished patter; his fingers long and grateful like he'd filched them off a piano man; a near perfect sense of when to come and when to go; and you can bet your bottom dollar that he was never without a partner. Us girls, married though we were, still resented Lillian Sandifer a little for managing to grab hold of good old Joe. Handsome Joe. Joe who could lie like it was easy and beautiful.

Sayer might have had the beginnings of what Joe had, and would surely have discovered more as he passed the five-foot mark, but for now he was too much of a kiddie. A little lamb. All he had was his dignity, which he tugged as tight about him as that star-spattered cloak. And that dignity was the one thing that we in the Hollow were scared to death to take away from him.

Thus, we dreaded that Tuesday morning knock.

Thus, we dreaded that chimney-pot hat.

We dreaded the hungry eyes of Sayer the Magnificent.

~

Maybe it seems cruel to you that I'm talking like this about a poor runt of a kid with his heart stitched onto the red-and-black satin handkerchief he tugged out of his sleeve – courtesy, again, of that 'Magic for Beginners' tin box. I swear I'm not trying to be cruel. It's the world that's wild and woolly. The world that cursed a stutterer – who couldn't holler 'sunshine' or 'salamander' – with a name like Sayer Sandifer.

You want to know I'm not cruel? Shall I prove it to you? Let's make him a Milo. Milo's a good name for a kid his age. Milo Sandifer. Easier with that 'M'. At least for a little while. Until he grows out of it. We can do that much for the little guy, can't we? The poor duckling?

When the time came, and we all knew it without really having to look, we went over as late as we possibly could. We being the women of the Hollow, me with my plate of gingersnaps. Just as the boy asked.

Lillian had set up the backyard with lawn chairs. An old red-striped beach umbrella in the northeast corner, just past the rhododendrons. Card tables covered with plastic cups and lemonade for the parents. Nothing is quite so apologetic as homemade lemonade in these circumstances.

'Thanks for coming, Minnie,' Lillian whispered as I laid down a plateful of gingersnaps like the boy asked.

'It's nothing worth mentioning,' I told her. 'I need me some magic today, you hear? Must be he's got a sense for these kind of things after all.' I let her smile at that. 'It's a good day for it too.'

'Some kind of good day,' Cheryl Felder muttered. She scowled at the top of her chimney-pot hat poking out from behind the stage and curtains that Joe constructed special. Poor Milo. He never quite figured out that of all the women in the Hollow, Cheryl was the one you didn't want to mess with. Most kids know this sort of thing; they can sense a real witch with a bee in her bonnet if you catch my drift. Or maybe he was just bolder than we gave him credit for.

The other women were coming in then. They laid out licorice strands and tuna fish sandwiches with trimmed corners, whatever the boy asked for. Lillian didn't meet our eyes at first, but then she all of a moment did and, you know what? – give her credit, her eyes were just blazing with pride for little Milo. That buttered us up some. You could see it changing people. Missus Felder's face, well, her face was the kind of face you might associate with sucking lemons, but even it got a little bit of sugar into it.

And the rest of us? Well, I'd always liked the boy. He had a proper kind of respect and reverence, and if there's two things a magician ought to fluff his hat with, it's respect and reverence, magic being no easy business, magic being a thing that ought to be done carefully. Not that I ever suspected poor Milo could mend a cut rope or pull the secret card, but there you have it. He would try, and we, the ladies of the Hollow, we kept company mostly by Hoovers and the *Watchtower* babble and crap society; we would smile those husband-stealing smiles of ours come Hell or high water.

And so the show began.

'And now for the Lost Suh-suh-suh . . .'

Milo's face screwed up with concentration so hard you could see a flush of red on his neck. Lillian was saying the word alongside him in the audience, but he wouldn't look at her. Missus Felder shifted in her chair.

'And now for the . . .'

His hands palsied and twitched as he shuffled the oversized Bicycle deck, patterned blue flashing in front of our eyes. But no one was watching the cards. We were all watching his mouth. We were all clenching the edges of the Sandifers' lawn chairs.

'For the Lost Suh-s-s . . .'

He paused again. That moment stretched on and on like putty. Just when we thought it was about to snap. Just when we thought *he* was about to snap – you could see Missus Felder leaning forward now, *she* might've said something, none of us would've dared, we knew you didn't speak for a stutterer, not ever, but she would've, she had the word on her lips and she was going to give it to him – that was when Milo swallowed, pushed up the brim of the chimney-pot hat with his wrist.

'Beg pardon, ladies,' he murmured ruefully, but it was out and the words were solid. 'And now for the Lost . . . Sisters.'

The applause was bigger than it had been for any of the other tricks. Milo took it as his due.

'For this I need a volunteer. Anyone?'

No one budged. We couldn't, not yet. We weren't ready for it.

'Anyone? Ladies, please. Ah, good. You there. The . . . missus in the blue dress.'

It was Ellie Hawley from across the street in the blue cotton frock with the raglan sleeves her husband brought back from Boston. We were all a bit thankful. She was a good sort. The type who knew to bring licorice strands to a boy's magic show.

'I'm hard of hearing, boy,' Missus Felder said. 'Which was that?'

God, we were thinking together, do not make him say it again.

It was no good though. She was smiling. Her words were sweetness and light, and she was smiling like she was some sort of old biddy about to offer him tea and biscuits. You couldn't trust a smile like that. Oh, boy, not ever.

'I, uh, suh-suh-s-sorry, folks.' The hat tilted forward again. Milo pushed it up, and licked his lips. 'I meant . . .' He paused.

Why was he pausing? Don't pause here, boy, we were thinking. Stick with Ellie Hawley. She's already getting up. She's halfway to the stage now, boy. Stick with her.

But we could see the look coming over his face. It was a proud look ... and something else, something I couldn't quite tell yet. A look older than he was. He knew that Ellie was the easy choice. He knew it the same way we knew it. He knew this was a trap, but there was something in him that wouldn't let it go. We were watching. We were waiting. Milo was fighting with this thing, and we let him do it.

' ... you there, in the front. Missus Felder. Puh-puh-please. Come on up here. Ma'am.'

No, we were thinking together, do not ask for her. Do not do it, boy. Do not call on her, boy. Can't you see the Devil has come to your garden party? Can't you see the Devil has gotten into Missus Felder, and there ain't no way to cheat the Devil if you let her up on stage with you?

Missus Felder, she just smiled.

She took her time getting there, walked almost like an old woman even though she didn't look forty yet. Passed Ellie Hawley along the way, just swished past her blue dress with the raglan sleeves.

'Well, boy,' said Missus Felder.

'Thank you, Missus Felder,' Milo said like he meant it. He shuffled the cards again, each of those big, blue Bicycles. Missus Felder watched primly, patiently, hips swaying slightly as she shifted her weight from side to side. As he was shuffling, you could see Milo starting to look for the words, starting to line them up in his mind like bowling pins so they'd fall down easily once he got going.

Just as he opened his mouth to start the patter, Missus Felder piped up:

'Aren't you going to ask me my name?'

Milo paused at this, chewed back those words he had all

lined up for the show. 'Nuh-no, Missus Felder. They all nuh-know it already.'

She nodded at this, like it was what she had been expecting all along. We all breathed a sigh of relief, but half of us were saying something pretty foul with that breath, let me tell you. Milo smiled a little wobbly smile and got with the shuffling again until he was all good and ready.

This time he got three words into the patter – three perfect words, three flawless, ordinary, magical words –

Then: 'Aren't you going to ask me where I'm from?'

Milo shook his head, and his Adam's apple bobbed up and down. His hands missed the cards and three of them went flying out: an eight of spades, a red jack, and the two of diamonds. Milo tried snatching them out of the air, but he missed with those little hands of his and they fluttered like white doves to the grass.

He placed the deck down steadily on the card table, and all the while Missus Felder was watching him with a look as wide and innocent as his own. There was a hush. We all knew something was coming. The kid knew something was coming. The kid was the kind of kid born with enough sense to know when something was coming but not enough to figure how to get out of the way. We could see the poor kid's hands were trembling. He stooped to grab the cards, and as he was stooping, off slid that the black magician's hat.

Missus Felder was faster than a rattler. Like lightning striking or tragedy.

The hat was in her hand then. She was holding it up to the audience. She was squinting at the inside of the brim of it.

'My boy,' she said, squinting away, 'my boy, it seems as if you've dropped this.'

Milo straightened up right away with only the red jack in his hands. He was staring at the hat. He was staring at Missus Felder.

'Aww, c'mon,' someone whispered in the audience; we didn't know who, but we loved that person.

'Come now, Milo, we can't have the magician without his hat, can we?'

Milo didn't move. No one moved. No one dared to. Only the breeze tickling at the edges of his star-spattered cape.

'Come here, boy. Now.' Her voice cracked like a whip. Milo couldn't ignore it. None of us could ignore it, our feet itched to stand. Ellie Hawley went so far as taking that first step forward before she caught hold of herself and paused.

Milo, though, he was too young to know better. He had been trained to obey voices like Missus Felder's. He was stepping forward, he was stepping forward, and there – he was forward, he was just in front of her, and she was putting down the hat, she was resting it gently on his head, and she was tugging just so at the brim to set it straight.

And she was tugging at it.

And she was tugging at it.

And down came the hat an inch farther.

And down came the hat another inch.

She was still tugging at it, still smiling like she was doing a favour for Milo, but none of us could see his face any more. The hat was past his nose. The hat was past his mouth. The hat was past his chin, but Missus Felder just kept tugging it down and down and down. Now his shoulders were gone, and it was taking the boy up into it, Milo, he was just disappearing into the hat, disappearing to his knees and his shin and his ankles until the hat was resting on the ground.

Missus Felder blinked as if she was confused. She blinked as if she didn't understand what had happened. Then she picked up the hat. Quizzical. She held it out to the audience, showed us all the inside and it was empty. Perfectly empty.

'Well,' she said, almost apologetically. 'I guess that's that, then.'

And she stepped off the stage.

The thing about magic is it only works when you let it. It only works when you believe in it entirely, when you give yourself over to it entirely. Magic can only give you a thing you want that badly, that desperately. No one can work magic over you. You can only work magic over yourself.

Cheryl Felder knew something about magic.

There were stories about Cheryl Felder, stories that poor Sandifer kid ought to have known the way that all kids know whose trees not to filch apples from and which backyards shouldn't be ventured for Frisbees and baseballs. Some might say that these sorts of stories were nonsense and spoke only to the curmudgeonly tendencies of the grumbles who reside in any town block.

But those people would be dead wrong.

After Sayer disappeared not a single soul spoke, not a bird twittered, not a skirt fluttered in the breeze. You could see those faces, each of them white as snow, white as a snow-woman caught in a melt.

Lillian trembled, but she said nothing.

She watched Missus Felder pluck a crustless tuna fish sandwich off the platter and vanish it with three remorseless bites.

'Could use some cayenne,' she said with a sprung smile, 'but all around, fine work, Lillian. Thanks for the show.'

Cheryl Felder knew something about magic, and the biggest trick she knew was that people don't like messing with it. Messing with magic was like sticking your hand down a blind hole, you never knew if there might be treasure at the bottom or if it might be some rattler's hole. And all those women, they had something to lose, they had sons of their own, they had husbands, they had pretty hair or blue cotton frocks – something they didn't want vanished. So after a while each of them stood up and collected leftover plates still piled high with uneaten licorice strands or oatmeal-raisin cookies and then each of them filed silently past Lillian Sandifer with neither a glance nor a touch nor a whisper of comfort.

Don't be too hard on them.

They had loved that boy. We had all loved that boy.

They tried to make up for it over the next couple of months, knowing as we all did what a bad time Lillian would be having with that empty room at the top of the stairs, the room filled with arithmetic workbooks and bottle rockets and adventure paperbacks. They dropped off casseroles. Their sons took over the raking of the lawn and the watering of the flowerbeds. Ellie Hawley brought over a fresh-baked apple pie every Sunday. But it was never spoken of, why this neighbourly hospitality was due.

And Missus Felder, she did the same as she had always done. She shopped at the grocery store, squeezing peaches and plums to be sure they were ripe. She got her hair done once a week at the salon at the corner of Broad and Vine.

The missuses of the neighbourhood never spoke to her of it. None could manage it. I wanted to. I did. That little boy had a way of being loved that seemed a brand of magic all his own, but if there was one thing I knew it was that I couldn't meddle in this.

Once I saw Lillian try, but only once.

This was about three weeks after it had happened. Poor Lillian was looking wasted and fat at the same time, her cheekbones sharp as fishhooks but her chin sagging like a net. Joe had gone on one of his business trips out of town, leaving her by her lonesome for the big old holiday weekend. All the ladies of the Hollow were bringing out bowls of punch and wobbling gelatine towers filled with fruit and marshmallows, while the children lit up Burning Schoolhouses and Big Bertha firecrackers. There was a fizzy feeling to the air on those kinds

169

of days, as it exploded with pops and whistles and sparks and the smell of hamburger sizzling on the grill.

Missus Felder, she came out too for the block party and she brought with her a bowl of plump, red strawberries. She set them up at the end of her driveway on a little wooden table with a lace cloth thrown over, and she handed them out to kiddies as they whizzed by.

Now she was trimming the hats off them, one by one. *Snip!* A little stalk and a flourish of leaves went skidding onto the sidewalk. *Snip!*

And there was Lillian standing in front of her, trembling, thin-boned, in a yellow print dress that made her skin seem old as last year's newspaper.

'Please,' Lillian said. Just that. Just that word.

'Careful,' said Missus Felder, never looking up, her fingers dusted white to the knuckle as she pinched strawberries out and laid on the confectionary sugar. 'You'll spoil your makeup if you keep up with that. You've too pretty a face for tears and if I'm not wrong there's others around here that'd be willing to hook that husband of yours. A nice man, Joe. A handsome man. He deserves a pretty wife.'

Lillian didn't say anything. Her lips trembled. They were chapped and unrouged, and maybe she was wondering why she hadn't put a touch of red on them. Missus Felder plucked up another strawberry and she looked at it carefully.

'You're a beautiful woman, Lillian, and children wear you out. They trample the roses of youth, leave a woman like some tattered thing hanging out on the clothesline. Let the boy go. He was ungrateful, selfish. Have another one if it's in your heart to do so, but let that one go.'

'But he's my son, Cheryl. Please.'

'Son or no son.' Now Missus Felder sighed a worn-out, old sigh as if the weather had gotten into her bones and really, she was just an old woman, why was she being troubled with this?

'Do as you like, Lillian. But I'll tell you for nothing that some children are best let go.'

And that was that.

The last flickers of September's heat burned out in the flood of a ravenous, wet November that shuttered the windows and played havoc with the shingles; by the time December whispered in, we were all thankful for it. All of us except for Lillian Sandifer.

There were some women who could take a loss and find their own way through, but Lillian, bless her, had had an easy life. Joe was everything you ought to have in a husband. He treated her gently. He brought her back fine cotton sheets from Boston, dresses and trinkets, a music box, a tiny wind-up carousel. Lillian loved all beautiful things. She had come as close to a life without loss as one can. But when December blew in – an easy December, full of light snows and bright silver days – it was like she took all the harshness, the cold, the cutting, fractured freeze into herself, and she let it break her.

And then we all saw the snowman in Missus Felder's yard.

The snows had been light, as I said, barely enough for a footprint, really, but there it was: round as a turnip at the bottom; a thin, tapering carrot for a nose; two silver dollars for eyes; and a fresh knitted scarf in green and gold hung beneath its hawkish, polar jowls. It was a king snowman, the kind of snowman that children dream about making before their arms give out from pushing the ball around the yard, the kind of snowman that wouldn't melt until halfway through May.

And on its head was a black chimney-pot hat, creased somewhat at the brim with a red silk ribbon drawn around it to set off its colouring.

A beauty, that hat; gorgeous to the eyes of a child and pure pain to his mother.

I could never do a big thing with magic, and that has always been both a blessing and a curse to me. Oh, there are ways and there are ways, and I know this is true, but the ways have never worked for me. It's an easy thing to change a boy's name. It's a little thing, particularly if it is a thing done kindly, if it is a thing that might be wanted. Then the change comes easily. But I cannot get blood from a stone, nor flesh from bread, nor make healthy a woman who wishes she were sick.

That is the province of my sister. And if it is none of mine to meddle with that greater magic, then it is at least something of mine to meddle with her.

It was a month into the hard end of winter I finally broke my silence.

'You must let the boy go,' I told Cheryl, stepping in out of the cold, stamping my boots off to shed them of the slush that had begun to freeze around the edges. Winter always followed the two of us, winter and spring, summer and autumn, they had their own way about us whether we willed it or no.

'I will not, Minnie . . .' She paused like the name was bitter to her. 'Minnie, they call you. Ha. They have a way with names, don't they? Marianne. No, Marianne, I cannot.' She closed the door quickly. She hated the cold, kept a thin blanket wrapped around her in the winter. I could see her curved fingers clutching at the edges. Winter turned her into an old woman as surely as summer made her a young one.

I gave her a look. It was not the dark and hooked scowl that came so easily to *her* face, no, it was a look entirely my own.

'It's time. It is long past time.'

'Too skinny, and what has that husband of yours got you doing with your hair? I could never abide him, you know.' Her mouth twisted as she looked me up and down

'I know. You could never abide any of them.'

'I abided my own well enough,' she said. 'The poor duckling. The little lamb. Let me fetch you some cake.' She did. Tea, as

172

well, the heat of it warming through the bone china cup. Her movements were quick and sharp as a bird's.

She settled us at the kitchen table. I remembered this house, I knew the ins and outs of it. The gold December light filtered softly through the window, touching a lace cloth, a badly polished silver candle holder. She never had an eye for the details, no, and this was what came of it.

'Where is the boy, Cheryl?'

She touched her tongue to her lip, scowled something fierce. 'You know as well as I do.'

'Let him out.'

'No.'

'They will come to hate us.' I knew she knew this. I could see it in her eyes, in the way she twisted at the lace cloth, but she could be a stubborn old biddy sometimes. 'He was a good boy, and it was a small thing,' I said.

'It was not a small thing!' she cried so harshly it took me by surprise, that her voice could go so ugly. So sad. I looked at my sister, and I saw then the thing that they all saw. That missus of nightmares and twisted stories, the hooked woman, the crone; she who devoured baseballs and Frisbees and footballs; she who stole the bright heart of summer and cursed the strawberries to wither on the vine; the son-stealer, the child-killer.

'It was,' I said gently. 'You know as well as I do that it was, and it is only spite and pride that keeps you from letting him go.'

'You are a meddler too, Marianne, so mind your tongue,' she muttered but the words stung nonetheless. 'No,' Cheryl whispered, chin curved down, and she was retreating, drawing in upon herself. 'I know it as well. It was a mistake, all of it, nothing more than that.' She cupped the bone china in her hand and blew on the tea to cool it. 'I did not mean for it to happen, you know I did not, I would not do such a thing to a child. To his mother.' She paused, took a sip, eyes hooded, lips

173

twisting. 'I know that the woman is dying. I know she will not live through the winter, but I cannot touch her, don't you see that? Don't you see, sister? I cannot heal the mother, I cannot summon the child. I cannot force a thing that is not wanted, and the boy *will not come out!*'

I could see the truth of it written on her face.

She was not a monster, she had never been a monster, and how I wished I could take her in my arms, her frail bones sharp and splintering as a porcupine; how I wished I could whisper the words of comfort to her. But she did not wish to be comforted. Her spine was made of sprung steel. She would not break herself upon this, for she knew what loss was and what mistakes were and the hardness of carrying on anyway. My sister knew this. She had buried a husband she loved. She had cried tears for her own lost boy, and knitted a scarf for him in green and gold, and hung it upon the cold reminder of his body in the yard.

Her fingers twitched, knuckling the bone china cup. I wanted to take her hand, but I knew something of her pride, the pride and the grief and the love of all of us missuses of the Hollow.

'Let us do something,' I say. 'Even if it is a small thing.'

It is an easy thing to take a handful of snow and fashion it into a boy, easier than most anyone would believe. Snow longs to be something else. Bread does not wish to be flesh, water does not wish to be wine, stones do not wish to bleed – but snow, snow wishes always to be the thing that is not, a thing that might survive the spring thaw and live out its days whole and untouched. And a boy, a boy who is loved, well, what finer shape is there?

And so we two fashioned it into a shape, and we set the silver dollars for its eyes and we wrote its name upon its forehead. Then, of course, it was not a thing of snow any longer but a thing of flesh: a thing with Milo Sandifer's bright blue eyes, barely nudging five-feet, and still as tongue-tied as any boy ever was.

'Missus Suh-s-sabatelli,' he whispered, trying out that fresh new mouth of his.

'Yes, boy,' I allowed with a sigh. 'That I am. Now get you home to your mother, she's been calling after you, and don't you bother her with what you've been getting up to. Just give her a kiss, you hear?'

'Right,' the boy said, 'Yes, of course. I'll do that. Thank you, ma'am.'

Already his tongue was working better than poor Milo's ever did. But it wouldn't matter none, I reckoned. Missus Felder unwound the scarf from around the king snowman's neck. The hole in its chest where we had dug out the boy yawned like a chasm. Like Adam's unknit ribcage.

'Here,' she said, and she wrapped the scarf around Milo. 'You ought to keep warm now. Little boys catch cold so easily.'

He blinked at her as if trying to remember something, but then he shrugged the way that little boys do. Then he was off, scampering across lawns and driveways, home to his mother. I looked on after him, staring at the places where his feet had touched the ground, barely making a dent in the dusting of white over the grass.

'What do you reckon?' I asked Cheryl. She'd gone to patting away at her snowman and sealing him up again, eyeless, blinded, a naked thing without that scarf, only the hat on him now, only that gorgeous silk thing to make him a man and not just a lump.

'He'll last as long as he lasts,' she said with a sniff. 'Snow is snow. Even if it wants to be a boy.'

'And Lillian?'

She didn't speak for a time, and I had to rub at my arms for warmth. For me it had already gone February and the little snowflakes that landed upon my cheeks were crueller things than the ones the other missuses would be feeling as they took their sons and daughters to church.

'Maybe it's a kindness you've done here, and maybe it isn't.' She wasn't looking at me. Cheryl couldn't ever look at you when she was speaking truths. She smoothed the freeze over the place where she drew out the boy, and her fingers were like twigs, black and brittle, against the white of it. 'You can't ever know the thing a person truly wants, but you keep on trying, don't you? I hope your husband is a happy man, I hope you give him children of your own one day.'

'Well,' I said, but I didn't know what more to add to that.

She was right, of course, she always was about such things: maybe it was a blessing and maybe it wasn't, but the boy came home to find his mother curled up in his bed surrounded by arithmetic workbooks and bottle rockets and adventure paperbacks. And he kissed her gently on the forehead, and she looked at him and smiled, her heart giving out, just like that, at the joy of seeing him once again. But the boy had been made good and sweet, and so he wrapped himself in her arms, and he lay next to her until the heat of her had faded away entirely.

That heat.

Poor thing didn't know any better. But snow is snow, even when it is flesh. A thing always remembers what it was first. When Joe Sandifer came home it was to find his wife had passed on, and from the dampness of the sheets he knew she must have been crying an ocean.

Joe was a good man and a strong man; his fingers were long and graceful. He pulled up the sheet around his wife, and he kissed her gently, and he buried her the following Tuesday. Perhaps it was hard for him for a time; it must have been, for he had loved his wife dearly, and he had lived only to see her smile, but the spring came and went, and then a year, and then another year, and he was not the kind of man who needed wait long for a partner. It was Ellie Hawley in the end, childlike and sweet, whose husband had brought her the blue dress with the raglan sleeves, whose husband had left her behind when he found a Boston widow with a dress that didn't make it past the knees and legs that went all the way to the floor. Ellie was the one who managed to bring a smile to Joe's face and to teach him that there were still beautiful things left in the world for a man who had lost both wife and son.

And so it goes.

And it goes and it goes and it goes.

Until one day Milo came back.

'Missus Sabatelli,' he said when I opened the door to him, that bright June Tuesday with the scent of fresh-mown grass drifting through the neighbourhood, nine in the morning, just like he used to.

He was a grown man then, the height of his father, with his father's good looks and easy smile. A handsome man. The kind of man you'd fall in love with, easy, but the kind of man you'd never know if he loved you back.

'Milo,' I said, and I had to hold on to the doorframe. I was half expecting him to be wearing that star-spattered cloak of his, to chew on his words as if they were gristle in his mouth. But he didn't.

'Thank you for that kindness,' he said, 'but I'm not Milo any longer. I've learned a thing or two since then.' I saw then that he was right. Whoever he was, he wasn't little Milo Sandifer.

'You've come back,' I said. I shivered. For him it was June, but for me the wind was already blowing crisp and cool, carrying the smoky scent of September with it. Time was running faster and faster ahead of me.

'Yes,' Sayer said, lingering on that 's' with a lazy smile as if to show me he could do it now and easily at that. 'I've come home again. Would you mind if I stepped inside, Marianne? I'm not one to gab on porches, and if it's not too impertinent I could use a cup of coffee something fierce.'

'Of course, boy.'

He chuckled, and the sound was rich and deep and expansive. I stepped aside, and he took off his hat as he came in. Not *the* hat, of course. The one he wore was an expensive, grey trilby that matched his expensive, grey suit and his expensive, leather shoes. He followed me into the kitchen: I regretted that I hadn't had time to clear up properly that morning, but he didn't seem to mind so much. He said nice, polite things about the colour of the curtains and about the state of things in general, and when he sat it seemed as if he were too big for the chair, as if that chair wanted to hold a small boy in it but had now discovered a man instead. The coffee's aroma was thick in the air, and I found I could use a cup myself so I poured for both of us, and served it plain. He seemed the sort to take his coffee black.

I was nervous. It had been some time since there had been a man in my house.

'You found your way then?' I asked him.

'I did, ma'am. I surely did.'

'And you know about your mother?'

He smiled, but this time there was something else to the smile. 'I do,' he said. 'Missus Felder told me of all that, and I'm sorry for it, I suppose. She whispered it to me while I was gone. She cajoled, she begged, and she pleaded. She has a tongue on her could scald boiling water, Missus Felder does, could strip paint off a fence.'

His eyes were bright blue, and surprisingly clear. I wondered if he was lying to me. I could see he had learned how to lie. Like lying was easy and beautiful.

'You didn't come back for her,' I said.

'I did not.' He paused, and breathed in deep, like he never

smelled coffee before and found it the finest thing in the world. 'I could say that I was unable.' He glanced at me underneath a fan of handsome eyelashes, quick as a bird. 'But you know that's not true, you know that's not how magic works, don't you? I wanted to stay. I wanted to stay, and it didn't matter. What Missus Felder did – your sister, yes, I know about that – what she did was cruel in its own way, sure, but not in the way you'd think—'

'No, boy,' I cut him off. He looked surprised at that, like he was not used to people cutting him off. I wondered who this new boy was, this boy that Cheryl and I had made. 'We figured it out, of course, though it was too late for anything to be done. You were always a boy who was looking for magic, even then, even then you were, and we knew it, Cheryl and I both knew it, but we had hoped it might be a different sort of magic. A kinder sort.'

'But it wasn't,' he said.

'No, it wasn't. You found something in there, didn't you?'

'I did.'

'And you stayed for it.'

'I did.'

'And now?'

'Now I have taken what I need from it,' he said, and he flexed his fingers, long and graceful. They were not the fingers he had when he was a boy, those poor stubby things that couldn't palm a quarter or pull off a faro shuffle. These were magician's fingers.

'So I see you have, my boy. Has it done ill for you or aught?'

At this he paused. I could see he wanted to get into his patter now, and it was not the same kind of pause as when he was young, when he knew the word but still it tripped him up; this was a different beast.

'I don't know,' he said at last. 'I want you to tell me. That's why I'm here, I suppose, Marianne.'

'No one can tell you that, Sayer.'

He took to studying his fingernails. Maybe he learned that trick from Cheryl, not looking at a person. 'I think you can. I think you are afraid to tell me.'

A shiver ran down my spine like ice melting. I tried to shake the feeling though.

'No, boy.' He looked up at that word. 'Your sense of timing was always characteristically awful. You never learned how to wait for a thing. Don't you know that? When you try to cheat magic, it just gets worse and worse and worse. What you found in that hat – some sort of secondhand magic I'm reckoning, that piece of truth you were looking for all that time – it's yours now. It ain't your daddy's magic. It ain't Lillian's either. Poor, sweet Lillian. You've suffered for it, and you've caused suffering for it, so it's yours to own, yours to do with as you will.'

'There is a bad thing coming at the end of this,' Sayer told me. He reached out that long-fingered hand of his, and he touched me on the wrist.

'I know, boy,' I said. 'We always know these things. Time's always racing on for us; even if most other folk can't see it properly, you can. But, God, the thing we never learned right, Cheryl and I, is that magic is about waiting, it's about letting the bad things happen. It's about letting the children pass on into adults, and the mothers grieve, and the fathers lose their way, or find it, and the sons come home again when they are ready to come home. That is the thing you will not have learned in that place you went to, because that is only a thing you can learn out here. What are you going to be, Sayer Sandifer? Why, whatever it is you choose to be. You saw what was coming that day when you invited her up on the stage with you. Boy, there were twenty people out in the audience who loved you, who would have waited with you, who would have helped you get there on your own, but you wanted what she had and so you took it.'

The words were hard stones in my own mouth, but I had chewed them over so long that I had made them round and smooth and true.

'Where is my sister?' I asked him.

'She's gone now,' Sayer told me, and this time I could tell that he wasn't lying. I didn't know what kind of a thing he was, this man drinking his coffee in front of me, this man who had taken power into himself but not knowledge, not wisdom, not the patience of a boy who learns to speak for himself.

'Well,' I said, and the word hung between us.

I felt old. I felt the weight of every summer and winter hanging upon me.

I knew it would only happen if I let it. I knew it would only happen if I wanted it to happen. I knew this just as my sister knew it.

Then Sayer laid down his grey trilby on the table, and, lo and behold, it was the thing I'd been looking for after all. The hat, the chimney-pot hat. That little piece of secondhand magic. He turned it over so that I could see that yawning chasm inside – the pure blackness of it, deep and terrifying. The place he disappeared to. The place he found his way out of.

'You could marry me,' he said. 'You always loved me, and I can see there's no man about now. Living like that can be awful lonely.'

The words pulled at something inside me. He was right. I was lonely. This life of mine felt old, misshapen, stretched out by the years. But I did not want him. I did not want that stranger. 'No,' I said.

He sighed and shook his head like it was my tragedy. My funeral.

'I'm not cruel,' he said to me in that handsome, grown-up voice of his. And he looked at me with eyes wide as two silver dollars, but flat-edged and dull as if the shine had been worn off them by residence in too many dirty pockets. 'I swear I'm not trying to be cruel. It's the world that's wild and woolly.'

And I knew that magic only worked if you let it. I knew that magic only worked on a thing that wanted it. But I was tired, and I was tired, and I had lost my husband, and I had lost my sister, and I had lost that little boy I loved.

Sayer pushed the hat toward me.

I took it up carefully, studied the dilapidated brim, fingered the soft black silk of it.

And Sayer smiled. Just once.

And then the bad thing happened.

CHARLES WILKINSON

FRESH WATER

WHATEVER THE BOY was holding was a little too pale, and perhaps a little too pink, the Headmaster now realised, to have been extracted from a living body, but there was nevertheless something *arterial* about it that reminded him of the aftermath of open heart surgery. And why on earth was Tanfield, normally one of his more tractable pupils, standing outside the front entrance of the school accompanied by a bemused, middle-aged woman whom the Headmaster had never seen before?

A few minutes earlier the Headmaster had been sitting securely in front of the computer in his study working on a new line-management policy. It was one of the hottest days of a particularly hot summer, and the blinds were drawn. The lake was at its lowest level for many years and now so shallow that even the junior boys were being allowed to take the boat out unsupervised. In a glassy haze, a desultory cricket match was taking place on the main field, but the majority of the school had decamped to the swimming pool, and a distant splashing provided a soothing soundtrack to his administrative meditations. When the bell rang the Headmaster waited for the clatter of high heels on parquet flooring before recalling that he had given his secretary the day off. In many ways, it was, he thought, greatly to be regretted that it had become necessary to lock the front door during the day, but a series of thefts and acts of petty vandalism, not the least of which had been the disappearance of his wife's handbag from the hall, had resulted in a review of the school's security arrangements; and the dismal fact was that he was now sometimes obliged to answer the door himself. Although the school was located in a patch of countryside, London and its Home Counties outriders were now well over the horizon, colonising the spaces between once isolated villages, tearing down the big old houses and building fifteen properties where one had stood before. Transport links had improved and on the main road outside the school gates the traffic was grid-locked by three in the afternoon. When the wind was in the right direction, you could just hear the trains carrying commuters to and from Kings Cross.

Dreading another incident, the Headmaster got up with a sigh and made his way to the door. The previous Saturday evening, whilst the school was in the Assembly Hall listening to the Summer Concert, one of the highlights of a crammed calendar of events, a gang of youths on bicycles had swept down the main drive, breaking the windows of parental cars parked on the verge, before escaping with a collection of mobile phones that police were still attempting to trace. As he opened the door, apprehension was rapidly followed by bewilderment, that was in turn succeeded by something like the beginning of process that would lead to an understanding of the significance of the extraordinary tableau before him: the unknown woman, whose expression seemed to echo his own perplexity; his pupil, Tanfield, paler and larger eyed than usual, cradling the third member of the trinity, as if it were all that remained of a once much-loved infant: a little flayed torso, a dull blue-pink heart, a tangle of veins and ribs like tiny claws. But the fact that Tanfield was dressed in the cross-country running team strip, now a dirty medicinal white, suggested that whatever bizarre concatenation of events had culminated in the scene before him could not be unconnected with Mr Vengelo

➔

who, some thirty-five minutes previously, was to be seen running down a narrow gravel track enclosed by tall hedges that led to a wooden bridge. A hundred yards behind him, the first of his pursers, a tall boy with lank blond hair whose sun-reddened skin clashed with an orange and maroon T-shirt that had been bought at Camden Town market, clambered over the five-barred gate at the top of the hill. In the early '80s, when Mr Angus Vengelo had first joined the school it would not have been unusual to see him at the head of the field, or at least keeping comfortably abreast of some of the more athletic boys, but at the age of forty-nine his longstanding habit of drinking three pints of Benskins Best Bitter every night after work, combined with a penchant for a late-night single malts, had finally undermined whatever claims to athleticism he might once have had. During his eighteen years as master in charge of the cross-country team, Vengelo had come to know every road, lane, path, hill, style, bridge, gate and stream within running distance of the school, and so when his fitness had first started to fade, it had been a simple matter to send the boys on a long route whilst he took a short cut that enabled him to emerge, much to their chagrin, triumphantly in front of them. Since the arrival of the new headmaster, whose fertile awareness of health and safety issues proliferated in the form of a multitude of memos, emails, notices, and letters to parents and colleagues, Vengelo had thought it prudent to stick to the same course as the boys, even though he had been reduced to the humiliating expedient of awarding himself a start of five to ten minutes. When even this ruse failed to keep him ahead of the pack for long, he had instructed them to wait at certain agreed points on the course: the bridge over the river Ver, the stile at the entrance to the park, the old oak tree, the entrance to the neo-Gothic pile, once the home of an American banker now a training college for teachers. Every year he got a little slower and arrived at the meeting points to increasingly ironic applause. But for once lassitude had infected even the keenest runners, and Mr Vengelo was able to enjoy the rare sensation of being in the lead, although strictly speaking the summer training sessions were not competitive.

As the ground dipped slightly, the weight of Mr Vengelo's stomach impelled him forward, giving him the pleasant sensation of having accelerated effortlessly. A decade ago he had been stones lighter; now although his legs and arms were still slim, his great belly, encased in a white, skin-tight top, peered over the rim of his black tracksuit bottom like a boiled egg jammed into a cup that was too small for it. In deference to the hot weather, and partly as a belated acknowledgement that the side parting was irrevocably out of fashion, Mr Vengelo, who already had a small head, had instructed his barber to cut his unruly, yolk-yellow hair close to his scalp, so that now, only faintly conscious of the absurdity of his appearance, as he half rolled, half ran down the hill, he appeared to be all stomach. Once he had reached the bottom of the hill, and the first bridge was in sight, Mr Vengelo gave himself an approbatory pat on his right thigh and smiled, a smile that soon dissolved in a pink pool of dismay as he realised that he had once again forgotten the mobile phone that he was supposed to take whenever he went running with the boys outside the school grounds. Then he remembered what had distracted him: he had been on his way to get changed when he had met his colleague

→

the Head of English, John Craft, perhaps Vengelo's only ally in the Staff Common Room and the longest serving member of staff, who was making his way with a martyred expression to a session of the Curriculum Development Committee, one of the most influential of the many committees that had replaced traditional staff meetings.

'It's virtually impossible to sit down in this place. There isn't even time for a cup of coffee.'

'Would you rather go running with the boys?'

'I think I'm a bit old for that.'

'I think I'm a bit old for it too!'

At the moment that Vengelo met his cross-country group, which had been augmented by two Hong Kong Chinese, under the wellingtonia on the front lawn, John Craft arrived five minutes late for the Curriculum Development meeting. The Headmaster looked up from the document he was reading, but did not acknowledge him. Possibly in order to prevent people from getting up to make cups of coffee, the session, the fifth in under a fortnight, was taking place not in the comparative comfort of the staff room, but in the newest classroom block, a building that was principally noted for its tall glass windows, which could only be opened very slightly and with great difficulty, apparently a clever, post-modernist nod to Hardwick Hall. Everyone had taken off their jackets, and the Head of Science had even removed his tie. When Craft sat down in the empty chair next to him, his colleague leant over and whispered something about 'conical-shaped line-management structures'. Resisting the temptation to point out that 'conical-shaped' was tautological, Craft made an attempt to understand what the headmaster was saying. Apparently it had once been thought that line-management structures should be linear; subsequently a case had been made for a triangular model, but now the most advanced educational theorists favoured 'the conical-shaped option'.

At some point in the year Craft had been told who his line-manager was. Since the arrival of the new headmaster, most of the colleagues with whom he had worked for years had been replaced by vigorous young South Africans or Australians, broad-shouldered games players with well-laundered hair, small moustaches and a freshly acquired determination to deliver their host country's National Curriculum; they were soon awarded 'positions of responsibility'. No doubt one of them was his 'line-manager', whatever that meant. But which one? Craft pretended to make notes on a sheet of A4 paper. He had only three more years to go before retirement. There had been a time when he had contributed freely, perhaps even volubly, to staff discussions, but under the new dispensation his views had been poorly received. The thing to do, he had decided, was say as little as possible and try to avoid annoying anyone who might be important.

'Yes, but we must allocate at least one period a week for it. It's one of the main criteria for entry that schools in our local-ity are looking at. It's only right that all of our pupils should have the opportunity to practise these vital skills.'

The Director of Studies was talking about next year's time-table, one of the few topics of genuine importance and inter-est. Craft put down his pencil.

'How are we going to fit these extra lessons in? The school day is quite long enough as it is, Todd.'

'No one is suggesting that the school day should be any longer. As I have made clear these lessons are already in place in the Junior School. What I am proposing is that the number of Classics periods should be reduced from three to two. I have discussed this with the Headmaster.'

'You have my support on this one, Todd.'

With dismay, Craft realised that they were proposing yet

another reduction in the number of Latin lessons. Vengelo was the head and only member of what was still called the Department of Classics, though Greek had been abandoned long ago. In spite of himself, Craft suddenly found that he was talking.

'Do you really think that Angus is going to be able to get them through their exams on two periods a week? I know for a fact that he's finding it hard enough on three.' They were looking at him. He had made the error of mentioning someone who was not present by name, a procedural legerdemain of the very worst sort. Discussion was supposed to take place at a suitably elevated level of abstraction, and proper nouns were seldom permitted to denote people unless the intention was unimpeachably phatic. Stung, he decided to continue.

'Anyway, I thought that the whole point of these verbal and non-verbal reasoning tests is that you can't cram for them. They're supposed to give some sort of objective assessment, aren't they?'

The Headmaster was looking at him with an expression of impatience mingled with disgust.

'We would not be suggesting this change if there wasn't sound educational justification for it. Educational research has shown that children can and do improve their scores significantly. As for the Department of Classics, I'm sure they'll cope . . . John.'

With a sour shrug of the shoulders, Craft fell silent. In spite of his years of not disloyal service, his position at the school was less strong than he would have liked. One by one, the forms that he taught had ceased to understand a word that he was saying. At first incomprehension had been confined to the less able sets, but now even the scholarship streams were restless and apparently incapable of following stories and poems that had enthralled previous generations. At first, he had been able to buy a little time by jettisoning any text that had pretensions to literary merit, but now he was having difficulty finding a single book that was bad enough to command their attention. There was one form that couldn't even watch a video in silence.

The Headmaster had begun to explain how form masters would assume responsibility for marking the weekly verbal reasoning tests and giving the results to the Director of Studies. It was hard to believe, Craft reflected, that the whole business would not end in Vengelo's enforced resignation. Although they were not especially close, they had worked together for almost two decades and had recently taken to meeting for a drink once a week, a shared revulsion to the new regime having at last created a bond. Craft wondered what he should say to his friend, who was at that moment

running towards across the floodplains in the direction of the river Ver. In bad winters the field had been so wet as to have been impassable, were it not for the narrow causeway that connected the two bridges. But now the stream that had once flowed under the first bridge had disappeared and the Ver itself had been reduced to a sluggish green trickle. Nevertheless, there was something almost Japanese about the scene: the two bridges, the ancient trees, the delicate summer grasses. Vengelo stopped and turned round. The blond boy was now crossing the first bridge, but there was no sign of the others. He hoped that the Hong Kong Chinese were not lost. As he waited, he looked around and saw that a burnt-out car had been left close to the river bank; he could just see that it had no number plates. It had probably been stolen in London, driven down here and doused in petrol. Giving way to a desire, which he recognised as rather childish, to be the first one to reach the bridge, Vengelo broke into dignified trot. On the other side of the Ver was a park with mature trees and a grey

Elizabethan house. Cattle sheltered under horse chestnuts. As he approached the river bank, three anglers stood up. The tallest, a youth of about seventeen, wore a purple shell suit and a baseball cap. With him were a middle-aged woman in a track suit and a lilac top and a boy with gooseberry hair.

'Have you got a knife?'

The woman was speaking, and Vengelo noticed that she had hardly any teeth.

'Not on me.'

'It's just that we've caught this lobster.'

'A lobster?'

Vengelo was assailed by a sudden sybaritic vision: what else were they going to fish out of the river: a bottle of champagne in an ice bucket, a crisp salad and dish of buttered new potatoes?

'Yes, we've caught this lobster.'

'Congratulations!'

'No, you don't understand. We don't want it. We want to put it back, but we can't; it's stuck on the line.'

The pale blue-pink creature, which was probably some species of freshwater crayfish, lay still on the grass; the barb at the end of the line was stuck deep into its side.

'I'm sorry, I can't help you.'

As the runners arrived, they too began to look at the crayfish, and the tall youth, who had the appearance being slightly simple, questioned them in the hope that they would somehow be able to liberate the creature. Tanfield, the only boy to be correctly dressed in the official cross-country strip, had knelt down and was examining the barb carefully. Irritated, Vengelo ordered the runners to the other side of the bridge.

Once they were in the park the questions came:

'Can't we go swimming?'

'Not today.'

'Why not?'

'The river's too shallow.'

'Aren't you going to rescue those people's lobster?'

'It's not a lobster.'

'Please let us go swimming, sir; it's hot, sir.'

'Oh all right. You can splash about, but you mustn't swim. It's not deep enough. Has anyone seen Wu and Shu?'

No one had seen Wu and Shu. Perhaps they'd been left so far behind that they'd decided to make their own way back to school. If anyone from the senior management team saw them return unaccompanied . . .

'It's Tanfield, sir. He's been wounded, sir. You must come at once.' Vengelo had been dimly aware of commotion on the other side of the river. He hurriedly crossed the bridge to find an apologetic Tanfield holding the crayfish and the line of the fishing rod. It appeared that Tanfield, driven by misguided compassion and curiosity, had remained with the angler who had then persuaded him to free the creature; in doing so, he had somehow ended up with a barb in his forefinger. The only consolation was that Tanfield had remained calm and there was surprisingly little blood.

'Go on, sir. I don't mind if you just rip it out.'

Vengelo inspected the finger a little more closely and then gave an experimental tug. There was no gentle way of easing the barb out. It would just have to stay where it was.

'Can we have our rod back?'

'Be quiet. I'm thinking.'

'You can't leave with our rod.'

'You'll just have chew through the line, won't you.'

Just how many of the school's health and safety regulations had he broken? He had forgotten the mobile phone, omitted to fill in a risk assessment form, lost two members of his group and now the son of one of the most influential parents had been wounded in an encounter with some sort of lobster. At seven o'clock he was due to meet John Craft in the Cat and Fiddle. It was the one occasion of the week when he had company, the one time when he had an opportunity to exercise a little dry Scottish humour, and he had been looking forward to telling him about his meeting

→

with Murray Donoghue, the newly appointed Australian Deputy Headmaster, who had been in charge of break detention when Mr Vengelo had been to see him that morning. Two boys in the front row looked up and smirked.

'And what can I do for you, Mr Vengelo?'

A parody of the British manner. General laughter and the sound of a pencil case falling to the floor. Donoghue raised a hand for silence before turning to Mr Vengelo, who was craning confidentially towards him. It would be something to do with the running club. Not so much a disaster waiting happen as one parading itself before their very eyes, that's what he'd told the Headmaster.

'It's about my club. In this very hot weather, I've been letting the boys have a dip in the Ver. They've always been allowed to do this, but I thought I'd better just check that this is still OK.'

Donoghue looked at Mr Vengelo closely. With that belly on him and in this heat it would be a miracle if he made it round. The guy should appoint a spade monitor and tell the kids to bury him where he falls. And what was the paratrooper's haircut about?

'Well, strictly speaking, you should have a qualified swimming pool warden present. Are you sure you want to go running in this heat?'

'They're looking forward to it. It's more of a fun run than a training session. The Ver's not very deep at the moment. Frankly, it would be an achievement to drown.'

Something of the freedom of his childhood on a Queensland

farm came back to him. The kids were twelve to thirteen years old, for Christ's sake. Why couldn't they paddle in a stream that came up to their ankles?

'Well OK – but I didn't say so.'

'Sorry to bother you, but there are just so many . . .'

'You don't have to tell me. Remember to fill in a risk assessment form.'

As the door closed behind Veneglo, Donoghue sighed. Strictly speaking it would have been better to put a stop to the whole thing, but with the Curriculum Development Committee meeting in games time they were short staffed. And it was hard to know how to treat these old guys, Vengelo and the other one, the one with the white face who looked as if he was actually dying, John

Craft, who, three hours later, shifted restlessly in one of the most ergonomically unsatisfactory chairs ever to have been designed, whilst two and a half miles away from the room in which the Curriculum Development Committee was meeting, the tall youth in the purple shell suit succeeded in biting through the line, thus releasing Tanfield and regaining control of the rod, at the very moment that the Headmaster began a ten-minute speech on the ways in which he saw curriculum development developing, which concluded as Tanfield and Mr Vengelo ran-walked up the gravel drive towards the neo-Gothic mansion that had once housed a teacher training college, and where a secretary, who was just about to leave for the day, was persuaded to drive Tanfield, still holding the creature, back to school, leaving Mr Vengelo, alone on the drive and not within supervisory distance of any of his pupils, to consider the repercussions of entrusting a pupil in his care to an adult whom he had never seen before, a lady now alone with a strange child, who was holding what appeared to be a crayfish resting on a bed of spaghetti, as he gave directions to the school, where the Headmaster had left the new classroom block and was walking back into his cool dark study, whilst Mr Vengelo waited for the cross-country runners to join him and wondered what on earth had happened to Wu and Shu, who had clearly made no attempt to keep up with the others and would have to report to the study, in which the Headmaster would soon be seated in front of his computer, with just five minutes to work on his revisions to his policy document on line-management, before a red car would come down the long drive from the main road and two figures, a middle-aged woman and a boy carrying a crayfish/small freshwater lobster, would get out and walk towards the front door which is once again locked, for it seven o'clock and most of the staff and pupils have gone home. It is a little cooler and the evening light is a deeper shade of sherry-gold. A few boarders with brightly striped towels over their shoulders wander past the rose garden on their way to the swimming pool, from which a faint splashing can still be heard. An angora rabbit has escaped from the animal hutch and sits on the cricket pitch. In a bungalow at the edge of Barnet the secretary thinks about the school whose sign she has driven past for fifteen years, but whose buildings she had never seen until today; she thinks of the long drive, the boys playing croquet on the front lawn, so small beneath the ancient trees; the wisteria hanging over the porch, the sun-polished ivy. She could never have afforded a place like that for her son. Bandaged, Tanfield has returned from Accident and Emergency and is using his one good hand to access the internet. Soon he will find his creature, the one that he rescued and put in the lake. He cannot believe that it might already have been dead. He learns that crayfish can be called yabbies, ghost shrimps, crawdads, mudbugs, carmels, spoondogs and tiny creek lobsters. The study of crayfish is astacology, and they like crevices. Some are good at escaping and others, to judge from the pictures, are best served with a side salad. A few are kept as pets. He hopes his crayfish will be happy in its new home. John Craft reminds his wife that he is going to the pub and takes the car keys off the hall table. It isn't going to be a good evening. Somehow he must find a tactful way to warn Vengelo. Mind you, at this rate it looks as if they will both be for the chop. He still cannot forget the way that his colleagues were looking at him, as if he were some sort of antiquated ghost, perhaps the one with a face like 'crumpled linen' in . . . was MR James? An author he'd long ago had to stop reading to the children. Since it is the one evening when he knows he will have company, Mr Vengelo has left his edition of Horace in his bedroom. It has been a difficult day, but he is a little more cheerful now. The Tanfields were surprisingly understanding, and apparently Accident and Emergency had been extraordinarily efficient. A relief to learn that he had done the right thing in leaving the barb exactly where it was. He represses a shudder when he remembers how close he came to pulling it out. Once inside the Cat and Fiddle he is surprised to find it half empty. No doubt most of the customers are in the beer garden. He is looking forward to telling Craft about Murray Dohoghue and the risk assessment form. What these people are incapable of understanding is that the real dangers are often unforeseeable. How could he possibly have anticipated the incident with the lobster or whatever it was? Perhaps they would now ask him to write a policy document: 'Crustaceans and Cross-Country Running'. The Polish barman wonders why the man with the funny haircut is laughing. In the study, which is the coolest room in the school, the Headmaster has finished his document on line-management. Now he has just one more task before he can go home. Vengelo has become impossible. Forcing a pupil into a complete stranger's car is utterly unacceptable and flies in the face of everything that the school's child protection policy has been set up to achieve. Of course having to get rid of a member of staff at this point in the academic year is far from ideal, but the examinations are over and if a suitable replacement cannot found for September it will not be a disaster if Classics is dropped altogether. Few schools seemed to want it. Of course, some parents would object, but they would be a tiny minority. As he lifts up the phone, he is sure the Chairman of the Governors will agree. At the bottom of the lake the crayfish lies next to the wheel of an old bicycle. Even if it is still alive, it will not survive for long. No, it is lost now, along with all those who can only dream of fresh water.

REBECCA SWIRSKY

THE COMMON PEOPLE

AND THE PEOPLE-OF-THE-COMMON had a wide open, green area. They kept this area trimmed and neat and glowing, as though it were a smooth billiard table. They were good citizens, these people, whose living areas were maintained in efficient, spruced fashion. A community of roughly 500, theirs was an infrastructure of which they were proud. 'Good morning!' called the bustling widow to her neighbour who lived in the cedarwood stucture next door. And they stared up happily into the empty bowl of sky.

Slap-bang in an amber afternoon, a caravan arrived. The caravan's spoked wheels rolled, causing red and green and white flakes of paint to settle over the grass. Because the heat was so hot, and the afternoon densely still, not even the dogs of the area took notice. The caravan's awkward piebald lowered its neck towards finely trimmed grass. Two men jumped out. They wore rings in their ears, and natty red neckerchiefs with white dots. As the piebald was apt to wander, the men tethered it to a small stake. Lazily chewing stalks, the men lay on their backs and squinted at the sky, speaking in quiet undertones.

As if by direct connection to this first arrival, a pick-up truck pulled onto the grassy communal area. The engine switched off, shuddering and grumbling. The truck's dented fenders were grubby. Loud, foreign-sounding music blared from speakers. Unlike the caravan, this truck was not quaint. Women and men spilled out, children also, ranging from toddlers in nappies to almost-adult. Even the young children rubbed their backs, as if they'd been bumped or jolted as the truck drove over potholes. Directing this dazed group was an old woman, bent and powerful with age. A cherry-red scarf was tied underneath her chin. She directed the making of a fire. When the flames were merry, a brass teakettle was produced from a streaked gunny sack. Cigarettes were rolled and strolls taken around the nearby pond. The younger children played tag and chase, and stick-in-the mud. Presently, the children approached the homes adjoining the grassy communal area. Not having seen mullioned glass before, the children made faces at the swirled panes, which looked like hardened tree sap. They waggled tongues and scrawled dirty words in the mist from their breath, wheeling away with laughter.

As most of the people-of-the-common were in the fields, or on errands, the new arrivals were noticed by very few. These were either the extreme old who spoke little, or the young who spoke not at all. When these older residents spotted the flitting, starling motions in the dusk and twinkling camp fires, they drew their charges closer and lit lamps, feeling the bright glimmerings of unease. Yet the residents returning from working in the fields were relaxed. This was a travelling fair, they told each other, a raggledy-taggledy group stopping en route to some distant place, not staying long. The people-of-the-common knew themselves to be sensible. They had no business making life difficult for those passing through.

It was clear these new people were not passing through. Over the next week, hoes and blades were used, and latrines dug. Vegetable patches were marked in the fertile soil. The earth of the region was widely known to be of excellent quality, nourished by steady, temperate seasons, loamy as Christmas cake. It was said seeds could be blindly tossed, and within 24 hours plants would sprout, rich with glossy offerings. Although whether this was because of well-nourished soil or the seeds' tenacity, it was unclear.

The people-of-the-common felt the new people were a circus without the exciting, main elements of a circus. They made wheeling, haphazard journeys as they picked their way through an oil drum here, a collapsed, disposable barbecue there. Efforts at communication were met with flashing-gold grins, the new people's soil-lined palms outstretched, as if in prayer, or hope. Often, the new people would break away to duck into tents. There they would remain still as statues, silhouettes sometimes visible, leaving the people-of-the-common to shake their heads and walk away. Yet every dawn without fail, the-people-of-the-common would be woken by the sounds of their rubbish being picked over as they lay in bed. The lids were always neatly replaced afterwards.

Rumbles began. The people-of-the-common began talking. Sproutings of discontent took root. At the northernmost field of the neatly bordered land, the people-of-the-common called a meeting. The woman of these people, the residents mumured in low, soothing tones, swayed hips and wore skirts festooned with roses, and wild daisies, and looked *different*. The men of these people had flashing teeth, wore red-spotted necker-chiefs, were thin, and looked *different*. They didn't like to ques-tion, said the residents, not really. Not at all. *But.* Hadn't they been generous? Clean-living? These were half-queries, vague as the wind, and so received only half-answers. Then one old man spoke. Leaning on his walking stick, he called out that if these new people had been *familiar*, well. That would have been something. If they had shared some *common interest*. But. It was time for the people-of-the-common to take *action*. If, he added. If they didn't want to be looted in their beds, gutted from their comfortable homes. In answer, there was a rippling silence, heavy with knowledge. Then one by one, the people standing nearest began to boo, a booing which extended outward like waves. No-one, the man was told, was interested in hearing such prejudiced, mean-spirited talk. And so the man stumped home, where he vented his dissatisfaction to the hens, and blew out the lamps. Slowly, the rest of the commoners who'd gathered also began to drift home. Something big had been averted. Because of this, despite their dissatisfaction, they were proud.

At the season's peak, when every moment seemed paused in syrup before being allowed to continue, and the sun skeetered on the pond's iron surface, two extra vans arrived. Seen from the uppermost window of the tallest home, so a small boy reported, these new vans looked like neatly parked hyphens. From the first of these vans came a stream of hammers, and saws, and nails, and silver jemmies, and a quantity of other carpenter tools all oiled and winking. From the second van came plyboard sheets, flat and white and gleaming with threat as new bone.

The sinewy, teeth-flashing men of these new people began to hammer and nail and measure. They worked in lines of fours and fives, in synchronicity and in breathtaking speed, as though performing well-rehearsed movements. The original, old people-of-the-common gathered in throngs to watch and take note. Eventually, they realised that the skeleton of an outhouse was being built. With every nail driven, new life was being breathed on, flesh added to the bones. As if flint had been struck against the people-of-the-common's souls, they realised. Unless action was taken, unless they came to, soon nothing would be the same. New structures would be built, and others, their own probably, torn down.

All that had been protected over the period of their existence here would be destroyed – although no-one could remember quite when that had begun. One wizened old woman living by a brook that was now a trickle remembered *her* grandparents as they'd knitted, and smoked pipes, during a very long winter. They had often recounted stories of travelling as little children, for days, weeks, months, years even. And when they'd arrived at this spot, *their* grandparents, they'd said, had collapsed on the soil, crying with happiness.

The people-of-the-common appealed to the mayor of a nearby city. Then they appealed to the main opponent of that mayor, a grizzled, wily *politico* in a cramped, shadowy office located at the back of the city. When the residents left, they knew they had found a solution to their problem. That week, nearly all the people-of-the-common's grain was neatly bagged up and marked as donation to this wily opponent. It would be hard to survive without the grain, but the people-of-the-common understood this was a price worth paying. After the bags were left on the clean scrubbed steps of the city's Big Hall, more vehicles arrived. They slid sleekly around the common's outer grass edges. There were more than ten in number, and when they parked, their engines did not make any sound at all.

Now the common was covered. Not one inch of space was visible. Not one blade of grass. These new trucks were black. They had C.I.T.Y. stamped on them in big, shiny grey letters. Spiked claws were at their sides like clenched hands with thorns, and flat sheets of iron at their front, to sweep away plyboard and nuts and makeshift bolts as though in a tide of water. The sort of tide that would easily edge objects from their original, truer meaning.

At first the new people were still. They ran everywhere and nowhere. They wheeled about, giving great hollering shouts. They beat their chests. The response of a small number was to sing. Women and men opened their mouths, velvety tremolos tipping from their throats. But after they'd recovered, the new people fought. Sticks, fragile brooms, tent poles and even hair-brushes were collected, to beat off the masked and armoured men pouring from the trucks. Singeing palms, they hurled firewood with licking fire attached. But the masked figures' armour was barely dented. Instead the firewood bounced off and flames licked at whatever was nearest. Canisters of eye-spray were aimed at adults, children, dogs, patiently waiting mules. Nothing that could be judged as alive was excluded. Hens scattered. Boots kicked at canvas tents or latrines and the grass reddened. Recognising defeat, the new people ran, scooping up shrieking children and hurling them onto whatever pick-up truck or horse was nearest. Or they dove into fields, shivering nose-down along fox dens and badger burrows, to slip silently into the night. One by one, or in packs, they disappeared.

When the rubbish of these lives was left, a cheap-looking spangled scarf here, a ripped khaki tent there, its canvas cloth giving the appearance of a crumpled, grubby skirt, the people-of-the-common worked together. Each put in their fair share. They teamed up in pairs to cleanse the grassy area and tiny cobbled streets. Carefully, they drew out objects strewn across the surface of the pond, and plucked colourful fabric scraps from the branches of trees. They were efficient, and tireless. Not one resident stopped until all had agreed the area had been returned to its previous spotless state.

Once the rubbish bags were removed, it was clear that the grass of the common had been starved of nourishment. Where the new people's main structure and smaller tents had blocked the sun, the shoots were yellowed and pale. But, the old people-of-the-common remarked, how familiar the area now smelled! With relief, they agreed that it was once again familiar, an atmosphere stripped of scents.

For all the people-of-the-common's efforts, one object had been overlooked. Hidden by a sheaf of burdock, with its silken fringe of dangling threads and a hole gaping in the toe, was a barely recognisable maroon-and-green child's slipper. Only the old woman who lived by the brook spotted the slipper's muddied tones and fraying threads. She marked its presence, until one day she marked its absence. A mother fox had taken it, the woman decided. To be tossed and caught between the glistening milk teeth of her cubs. It wouldn't be long, the old woman nodded, before the slippers would fall apart, buried by the rich soil of the area.

For a long time, the people-of-the-common tested the width and breadth of this new silence. They completed daily chores dazed, but with care. They said good morning to each other before nodding up at the empty bowl of sky. Pails were filled with local blueberries and roseberries, and front gardens swept clean. The communal area sparkled, once more returned to its billiard-green brilliancy. Autumn was on the horizon, and the people-of-the-common prepared for the cleaner, surer months winter would bring.

For the summer's remainder, the silence of the common was golden, and the silence of the common was deafening. Autumn slid by, and as winter approached, the people-of-the-common were pinned to the cloth of this silence like tiny frozen puppets.

ALISON MOORE

EASTMOUTH

SONIA STANDS ON the slabs of the promenade, looking
out across the pebbly beach. It is like so many of the seaside
resorts from her childhood. She remembers one whose tarred
pebbles left their sticky blackness on her bare feet and legs
and the seat of her swimsuit. She had to be scrubbed red raw
in the bath at the B&B. Her hands are wrapped around the
railings, whose old paint is flaking off. When she lets go, her
palms will smell of rust.

The visibility is poor. She can't see land beyond Eastmouth.

'I've missed the sound of the gulls,' says Peter, watching
them circling overhead.

He says this, thinks Sonia, as if he has not heard them for
years, but during the time they've been at university, he got the
train home most weekends. Sonia does not think she would
have missed the gulls. She is used to the Midlands and to city
life.

She lets go of the railings and they walk on down the promenade. Sonia, in a thin, brightly coloured jacket, has dressed
for warmer weather. Shivering, she huddles into herself.
'Let's get you home,' says Peter. For the last half hour of their
journey, while the train was pulling in and all the way from the
station he's been saying things like that: 'We're almost home,'

and, 'Won't it be nice to be home?' as if this were her home too. Their suitcases, pulled on wheels behind them, are noisy on the crooked slabs. 'They'll know we're here,' says Peter.

'Who will?' asks Sonia.

'Everyone,' says Peter.

Sonia, looking around, sees a lone figure in the bay window of a retirement home, and a woman in a transparent mac sitting on a bench in a shelter. Peter nods at the woman as they pass.

'It's quiet,' says Sonia.

'It's quiet most of the year,' says Peter.

He points out a modernist, pre-war building just ahead of them. 'I've always loved coming to see the shows,' he says. 'My all-time favourite act is Cannon and Ball.' Reaching this seafront pavilion, they stop to look at the posters. 'Look,' says Peter, 'Cannon and Ball.' He is beaming, cheerful when he says, 'Nothing changes.'

Peter lets them into the house with a key that he wears on a chain around his neck. His mother comes into the hallway with her arms wide open, saying to Sonia as much as to Peter, 'You're home!' Taking Sonia's jacket, looking at its bright colours, she says to Sonia, 'Blue and green should never be seen!' and then she puts the jacket away.

As they sit down to dinner, Peter's mother says, 'Sonia, what were you planning to do with your summer?'

'I've applied for a job up north,' says Sonia. 'I had the interview yesterday, and I think it went well. I should hear tomorrow whether or not I've got it. I gave them this number – Peter said that was all right. If I get the job, I'll save up for a while and then I want to go to Las Vegas.' She mentions pictures she's seen of the place, all the lights.

'If you like that sort of thing,' says Peter's father, 'you should take an evening stroll along our prom. You'll see it all lit up.'

He chews his food for a while before saying, 'It's a lot hotter there, though. It wouldn't suit me. We stick to England, the south coast.'

A gust rattles the window and Sonia turns to see the wind stripping the last of the leaves from a potted shrub in the back yard.

'Look,' says Peter's father, 'the sun's coming out for you,' and he nods towards a patch of sunlight the colour of weak urine on a whitewashed, breeze-block wall.

Peter's mother opens the wine and says to Sonia, 'You'll be needing this.' Sonia supposes she is referring to their long train journey, or perhaps the cold weather; it isn't clear.

'It's nice to have you home,' says Peter's mother, later, when they are clearing the table.

'I think Peter's glad to be home,' says Sonia.

'And what about you?'

'I don't live here,' says Sonia. She is surprised that Peter's mother does not know this.

'You didn't grow up here,' agrees Peter's mother. Opening the back door, she throws the scraps into the yard and the seagulls appear out of nowhere, descending instantly, filling the yard with their shrieks. 'Our home is your home,' she says, as she closes the door, 'but I do remember what it's like to be young and independent. There are lots of empty flats around here and they always need people at the pavilion. The place is crying out for young blood.'

'I wasn't planning on staying long,' says Sonia.

Peter's mother nods. She looks around the kitchen and says, 'Well, I think that will do. I'll go and change the sheets on your bed.'

Their bags are side by side in the corner of Peter's bedroom. Hers has a sticker on the side saying *I ♥ Las Vegas*, even though she has never been there. His has a label giving his name – Peter Webster – and his home address, his parents' address, so that it can't get lost.

They go to bed early but Sonia lies awake in the darkness, in between the cold wall and Peter, who is fast asleep. She finally drops off in the early hours before being woken at dawn by what she thinks is the sound of babies crying, but it is only the gulls. She finds the noise depressing.

Sonia, in the bathroom, doing up the belt of her jeans, can hear Peter's mother talking on the phone at the bottom of the stairs. 'No,' she is saying, 'I don't want it. I've changed my mind. Please don't call here again.' Sonia checks her face in the mirror before coming out, finding Peter's mother on the landing now, outside the bathroom door. 'All right, dear?' says Peter's mother. 'Come down to breakfast. I've made pancakes with syrup, just like they have in America!'

Sonia stays in all day. At the end of the afternoon, at ten to five, she phones the company she had hoped would call to offer her a job. She speaks to a receptionist who says, 'Please hold.' Then she speaks to a secretary who tells her that the job has been offered to someone else. The secretary sounds impatient and terminates the conversation as soon as she can. Sonia redials – she has some questions to ask – but no one picks up; they've all gone home.

When Sonia goes up to bed that night, she finds that the sticker on her bag has been doctored with a permanent marker. 'Las' has been neatly changed to 'East' but 'Vegas' required a heavier hand, a thicker line. *I ♥ Eastmouth*.

The following day is Saturday. After breakfast, Sonia watches the dead-eyed gulls gathering on the wall of the yard. They grab at the scraps Peter's mother puts out, and if the door is not kept closed they will come inside, wanting the cat food, taking more than they have been given.

'I think I'll go for a walk,' says Sonia.

'I'll come with you,' says Peter, beginning to get to his feet.

'I'd rather go on my own,' says Sonia. Mr and Mrs Webster stop what they are doing and look at her. They watch her as she leaves the room.

She puts on her shoes and looks for her jacket but she can't find it. She asks Peter's mother if she's seen it and Peter's mother says, 'I'm washing it. Wear mine.' She takes down a heavy beige coat and helps Sonia into it. 'Yours was too thin anyway,' says Peter's mother. 'You'll need something warmer now you're here.'

Sonia walks a mile along the promenade before coming to a stop, leaning on the railings and looking out to sea, watching a yellow helicopter that is circling in the distance. As a child, she used to wave to rescue helicopters even though she knew they weren't really looking for her; she just did it for fun or for practice. She raises her hands now and waves, scissoring her arms above her head, like semaphore, as if she were someone in a high-vis jacket on a runway, although she does not know semaphore; she does not know how to say 'stop'. The helicopter turns away and leaves.

'Sonia.'

She turns around and finds Peter's parents standing behind her.

'We thought we'd walk with you,' says Peter's mother. 'What a good idea, a little leg stretch.'

They walk along with her, nodding to the woman in the transparent mac as they pass the shelter.

When they reach the end of the promenade, Peter's father says, 'We should turn back,' and as they walk Sonia home again they tell her about the evening's entertainment: a show at the pavilion and dinner at the Grand.

'I've booked you a table,' says Peter's father. 'It's a fine place. It's where I proposed to Peter's mother. We go there every year for our anniversary.'

'Have the seafood platter,' says Peter's mother.

Peter, wearing one of his father's ties, walks Sonia along the blustery promenade. The seafront is all lit up with lightbulbs strung between the lampposts. 'See?' says Peter. 'Who needs Las Vegas?' At the pavilion, they see an Elvis. Sonia finds him disappointing. When the show is over, they go on to the Grand.

They are greeted as 'Mr and Mrs Webster' and Sonia opens her mouth to correct the misapprehension but they are already being led through the restaurant towards their table in the corner, and in the end she says nothing.

When the waiter comes to take their order, Sonia asks for a pasta dish.

'Are you not going to have the seafood platter?' asks Peter.

'I don't think so,' says Sonia.

Peter looks concerned. He orders his own meal without looking at the menu.

Sonia, looking around at the decor, says to Peter, 'I doubt they've changed a thing since your parents first came here.'

Peter touches the flock wallpaper and says, 'That's a nice thought.'

The waiter returns to light their candle and pour the wine. They raise their glasses, touching the thin rims together. Sonia brings hers close to her mouth but barely wets her lips before putting it down again.

'All right?' says Peter.

Sonia nods. She has not yet told him about the test she did in his parents' bathroom, about the white plastic stick with the little window in the middle, the vertical line that proved the test was working, and the sky-blue, sea-blue flat line that made her think of a distant horizon seen through an aeroplane window. She has not told him that when she came out of the bathroom with the plastic stick still in her hand, Peter's mother was standing there, and that when, after breakfast, she looked for the stick, it had been moved.

The waiter returns with their meals. Peter, smiling down at the food on his plate, picking up his fork, begins to talk to Sonia about the possibility of a management position at the pavilion. His dad, he says, can pull a few strings.

The waiter is coming back already. He is going to ask them if everything is all right, and Sonia is going to say yes even though she has barely had a taste yet. Peter is holding his fork out across the table towards Sonia, offering her a piece of something whose fishy smell reminds her of the stony beach, the tarry pebbles, and the gulls that will wake her at dawn.

She sees, in the molten wax around the wick of the candle, an insect. Sonia picks up her fork, aiming the handle into this hot moat. She is an air-sea rescue unit arriving on the scene to lift the insect to safety. Carefully, she places the insect on a serviette to recover, as if it has only been floating in a sticky drink.

'I think that one's had it,' says Peter, and Sonia looks at it and thinks he might be right.

Peter, who had the whole bottle of wine to himself, is still sleeping the next morning when Sonia gets up, puts on the beige coat and lets herself out of the house. She walks down the promenade again, away from Peter's parents' house, heading in the direction she and Peter came from when they arrived here. She goes as far as the end of the promenade, where she stops to watch the gulls, and then she goes further, climbing up above the town until she is standing a hundred metres above sea level in the wind. She is still in Eastmouth, though. She cannot see across to the next town. When she looks at her watch, she realises that she has been gone for a while now. As she makes her way down from the cliffs, she hears the tolling of a bell; it is coming from the church that stands on top of one of the hills that surround the otherwise flat town.

On the promenade, all the shelters are empty. All the bay windows of all the retirement homes are empty. She realises that it's Sunday and wonders if everyone's at church. Peter's parents might be there, and perhaps even Peter.

She veers slightly away from the promenade now. It is the start of the summer and ought to be warmer, but it is windy and cold and she is glad of Peter's mother's coat. She has her purse in the pocket. She heads down a side street that brings her out at the train station, which is overlooked by the church.

Alone on the platform, she stands in front of the train time-table. She looks at her watch, although pointlessly, as it turns out, because when she consults the timetable she finds that no trains run on Sundays. She wanders to the edge of the platform and looks along the tracks in the direction she would go to get home, and then in the opposite direction. Is there really nothing at all on a Sunday, she wonders; does nothing even pass through?

She is still there when she notices that the woman in the transparent mac is now standing at one end of the platform. She is talking on a mobile phone but she is looking at Sonia and so Sonia nods at her. She doesn't know whether she has been recognised. The woman, putting away the phone, approaches. When she is within touching distance, she says, 'You're the Websters' girl.'

'No,' says Sonia, preparing to introduce herself, whilst at the same time noticing the locals coming down the hill, coming from church. The service is over. It seems as if the whole town is heading towards them, like an army in beige and lilac.

'Yes,' says the woman. 'You are. You're the Websters' girl.'

The crowd is nearing the foot of the hill; they are close now and one by one they look at the woman in the transparent mac and they nod.

JULIANNE PACHICO

THE TOURISTS

WHO'S COMING TO the party? A lot of people, it's going to
be a big success: the Mendozas and the Vasquezes, the Loren-
zos and the Smiths. The maids drag the white plastic chairs
into the yard, forming half-circles beneath the mango tree
and around the barbecue pit. The gardeners carry out the big
wooden table, a security guard following closely behind with
a ruler to scrape off the white globs of dried candlewax, accu-
mulated in thick layers from weeks of blackouts. The dogs yip
excitedly, nipping at people's ankles, and behind the safety of
their chickenwire cage the rabbits look on, horrified. Inside
the kitchen, staring out the window, one of the cooks says, 'We
really need to lock them up. Can you imagine Lola rolling in
her poo and then licking Mrs Montoya's hand?'

The caterers have arrived; they're getting set up. They're
carrying big metal pans, steam rising beneath the lids, filled
with white fish soaked in lemon juice, red peppers for the
grill, raw bloody steaks and chicken breasts stabbed with fork
marks. Nothing is extravagant, nothing is over the top, except
for maybe the lobster claws on ice, the tins of caviar and the
oysters that the cooks are busily prying open with their special
metal knives. That's not his style.

Here he comes. Folding the cuff of his black shirt above his wrists so that a pale strip of unburnt skin shows, like a patch of exposed land on a jungle hillside. People rarely notice, but the three middle fingers of his right hand end abruptly in smooth pink stumps, neatly aligned with the humble pinkie. 'Looking good,' he says to the blinking white Christmas lights hanging from the branches of the grapefruit tree. 'Excellent,' he says while strolling past the arts and crafts supplies set out for the children by the pool: crayons and candles and paper plates. 'Go along now,' he says to one of the many cats, sitting on the drainpipe above the jacaranda bush, a distasteful expression behind its droopy whiskers. Who knows how many pets they have at this point? Just the other week he saw a turtle lumbering under the sofa in the living room, but when he got down on his knees to check there was nothing there, not even dust balls or coffee-flavoured candy wrappers.

He wanders inside the house through the swinging patio door, scratching the back of his neck. The maids have done a good job at making everything seem presentable. The bookshelves have been dusted, the broken electric piano cleared away (a lizard got electrocuted deep inside its mechanical guts years ago and ever since it's refused to make a sound, not even when the cats frantically chase each other across the black and white keys). Considering that they only come out to this country ranch every few months, for Easter or holiday weekends, the house still feels fairly lived in: the living room fresh-smelling with the sharp scent of white laundry powder, the lampshades shiny without a single dead moth smear, no cobwebs around the chandelier or shelves of VHS tapes.

'How's it going?' he says, knocking on the door to his daughter's room at the same time that he pushes it open. The room is deserted – the only sign of her presence is a stack of CD cases spilled all over the bed, next to some shredded packets of plantain chips. It's hard to restrain himself, this rare opportunity to intrude in her bedroom – normally the door is firmly locked, American bands screaming their angst-filled rage from her stereo on the other side. So he now finds his eyes flickering greedily, taking in one new poster after another hanging on the walls. The one of a mournful-eyed American singer with shaggy blond hair holding an acoustic guitar, that's definitely new; Snoopy dancing with a balloon, that's been up since she was in kindergarten and received it as a present at one of the immense birthday parties she hosted here for all her classmates. The closet doors are half open; he can glimpse the shelves lined with stuffed animals that couldn't fit into the storage trunk in the hallway, Care Bears and shabby dogs and other beasts that were never loved enough to be guaranteed a spot at their main house in Cali. There are rows of plastic toys based on countless American cartoon shows, Transformers and ThunderCats and Ghostbusters, stiff plastic bodies randomly positioned in a messy parade, silently poised with their daggers and ray guns, ready to leap into battle with invisible enemies at a moment's notice. Everything slowly gathering dust.

From where he's standing he can clearly see that the empty packets of plantain chips have been licked clean, not a single crumb remaining. Shaking his head, he picks them up between two fingers and drops them from the bed onto the floor where it'll be easier for a maid to sweep them up. That's when he sees it – the small ziplock baggie lying on a pillow, half-filled with bright red JELL-O powder – the kind of treat you can purchase from street children at traffic lights. He picks it up and shakes it up and down, the powder accumulating at the bottom, except for the wet clumps clinging near the baggie's thin lips. He can already picture the garish stains across her front teeth and mouth, the demon red of her tongue flashing at the guests as she utters a sullen *hello*, the sticky finger smears on her shirt, running up and down the fabric as though a tiny animal with miniature bloody paws had danced all over her body. *Ave Maria*, the maids will say when they see her, closing their eyes in supplication. *Mija, what were you thinking? What will your father say when you show up looking like that for his party?*

The automatic gate rumbles at the same time that he hears car wheels crunching on the gravel driveway. He puts the JELL-O baggie in his back pocket, jammed tightly behind his cellphone. After closing the door behind him, he pulls his right shirtsleeve down as far as it'll go, almost completely covering the white scars snaking over the backs of his hands.

Here they come. Black and blue high heels clicking, jackets draped over arms, wispy strands of thinning hair combed neatly back. The chauffeurs park the mud-splattered jeeps with Bogotá licence plates under the fig trees; the bodyguards climb out and immediately cross their arms, already hovering in the background. He waits under the mango tree in the backyard. Smoke rises from the barbecue pit. The chefs grimly rotate sausages slashed with deep knife cuts over the fire, red peppers and onions impaled and sweating on wooden sticks.

'Hello, hello,' he says in greeting. Right hand hidden behind his back in a clenched fist, left hand extended and welcoming, fingers spread wide.

Everyone arrives safely, happily. Nobody's been chased by the crazed spider monkey, the one the maids have nicknamed 'Baloo' for the size of his black testicles, so impressively heavy that the housecleaners whisper amongst each other: *Now that's a real man, Linda, just what you need, someone to keep you satisfied*, before exploding into giggles. At the last big party (two years ago? Three? Was it celebrating the successful Congress run, or hosting the visiting HSBC managers?), Baloo had run back and forth over the stone wall for hours, staring hungrily at the food, the tables, and the guests most of all (this was before the shards of glass were installed along the wall's perimeter, before Uribe's successful presidential campaign based on vows to 'restore national peace and security', before he'd started hearing the clicking sounds of recording instruments every time he lifted the phone). At one point, Baloo had jumped down and stuck his head up Mrs Montoya's skirt, and her banshee screams had caused the maids in the kitchen to raise their eyebrows at each other.

Thankfully there's been no sign of Baloo for months now – the fact that the security guard has been tossing his slimy orange and banana peels inside the forest, well away from the main house, has possibly helped. As a result the party is going well, the conversation gliding along smoothly, effortlessly. No bottles of *aguardiente* or rum yet, it's still early, the sun casting hazy yellow light over the freshly mown grass, the mosquitoes blessedly absent. Instead it's green glass bottles of chilled beer for the gentlemen, tall slender glasses of champagne for the ladies. The hired waiting staff stalk silently back and forth across the patio, black and white uniforms still free from wine splatters and crumbs. Everything is under control; everything is fine.

He doesn't see us, but we're watching.

We've been doing so for a while now. We didn't get any greetings, no gentle air kiss near the cheek, no firm pumping handshake, but that's okay, we don't take it personally, we don't mind. Instead we take our time, take things slow: there's no reason to rush, no reason to make things happen before they need to. We walk in slow circles around the barbecue pit, smelling the charcoal fire and crackling chicken skin with deep inhalations. We put our hands tentatively in the glass bowls of peanuts; what a nice rattling sound they make when we stir our fingers. We take turns gently touching the beer bottles, admiring the streams of condensation running down the smooth glass bodies. No one makes eye contact; nobody invites us to sample a plate of sliced limes or a tray of roasted garlic. But we're not upset; we're not bothered. For now, we're happy, watching the hummingbirds dart nervously amongst the orange flowerpots. Everything has been so tasteful, nothing over the top – no helicopters landing in the football field, no spray-tanned models greased up and wrestling each other while the guests cheer and look on. No one's slinging their arms around each other, singing classic Mexican *corridos* at the top of their lungs; no one's pulled the gun from their holster and started shooting wildly at the darkening sky. Nothing like that. The food is delicious, and everyone is having a wonderful time.

He loves it when parties are at this stage – the post-beginning and pre-middle, when no one has gotten too drunk or noticed who's been pointedly ignoring them. It means he can sneak away to the bathroom adjoining his private bedroom, lock himself inside for up to fifteen minutes at a time, sometimes twenty. He sits on the bowl, chin resting in hands, trousers sagging around his ankles. It's moments like these when it's impossible to ignore: how all over his body there are patches of skin now drooping where they used to be firm and taut. There are brown and purple spots all over his arms that definitely weren't there twenty years ago either, and red moles on his upper shoulders he keeps mistaking for insect bites. This year, too, he suddenly found himself mentally adding secret descriptions to his friends' names: prostate-cancer Andrés; emphysema-cough-Pablo; beet-juice-diet Mauricio. More and more lately, it seems as though everyone he knows is talking to doctors instead of priests, men with stethoscopes around their necks instead of crucifixes. He can't pinpoint the exact moment when it changed, but there's a new fear now lurking beneath everyone's low-volume conversations. It's not just extradition to Miami prisons or undercover DEA agents or stash house security guards secretly wearing wires beneath their collared shirts. It's also cancer cell counts, will-drafting, uneasy conversations with mistresses, even more uneasy conversations with wives. He's started biting his nails again too – they haven't been this short since he was seventeen, doing deliveries in the hillside neighbourhoods for local bosses. His first job. He would sit in the front seat for hours, waiting for his partner's signal, and tear off every last possible shred of nail, until the cuticles were non-existent.

(His right fingers were long back then too, with deliciously bitable nails – the index finger was his favourite.)

But now's not the time to dwell on it. Not tonight. He pulls his trousers up briskly and rebuckles his belt. As usual, he flushes but doesn't wash his hands. He wanders past the bookshelves, back out to the porch. Under the drainpipe Mauricio is telling a story about his recent senatorial trip to Uruguay, how uncomfortable it made him to see all the small children at his official reception, the way they honoured his presence by saluting and marching across the basketball court, military dictatorship style.

'At least, if nothing else, we've never had that issue here,' he says, beer bottle coming dangerously close to clinking against his coffee-stained teeth. 'Long live democracy.'

By the mango tree Ravassa's wife is already drunk; he can tell by how closely she leans towards Alonso as he speaks, summarising a TV series about medieval knights in Spain that he's just finished watching. Alonso is half-Mexican, which maybe explains why he uses so many hand gestures while talking: the way he darts forward, parries, blocks, defends, you'd swear you could see the sword glowing in his land, a luminescent silver. Ravassa's wife keeps laughing and reaching out, trying to brush her maroon-coloured nails against his chest.

The Rossi brothers are sitting in the white plastic chairs by the barbecue pit, smoking red-boxed Marlboros. When they make eye contact with him they both raise their hands at the same time like choreographed puppets, crooking their fingers in a *come-here* gesture. He shakes his head; he's not in the mood to discuss business. Not at the party; not here.

He turns away and merges with the group of children, huddled by the swimming pool. It only takes a quick scan of the crowd to see that his daughter's not among them: no long black braid hanging down her back, no baggy blue T-shirt with holes in the collar from her anxious chewing. His fingers brush briefly against the slight bulge in his back pocket from the JELL-O baggie. The children are all busy, hunched with intense focus over the paper plates. They're dripping crayon wax in the centre of the plates, creating a base that will harden and keep their candles propped up. The plates are then cast away into the swimming pool, transformed into tiny fragile boats, the orange flames casting faint reflections in the dark water below.

'Oh!' he shouts when one candle topples over and extinguishes with a mournful hiss. Some of the kids jump, startled by his cry; most simply turn slowly and stare. He tries to smile, even though he knows this never looks comforting: the scar splits his upper lip so that his tooth pokes out, a pink hairless line arches over his left eyebrow.

'It's fine,' one of the older girls says to a little boy she's been helping, whose eyes are getting bigger and more watery-looking by the second. 'Just make another one. What colour crayon do you want?' She shoves some into his fist.

He turns away, shoes crunching on the gritty patio tiles. He does this all the time: he'll bang his knee against the dining room table, or drop a tangerine onto the floor immediately after peeling it, or accidentally fumble a fork, and then let out an explosive bellow of *OH!* It makes the maids come running, the bodyguards look up sharply. *Everyone keeps thinking you're having a heart attack,* his daughter once told him, *but then it turns out you just spilled some milk.*

By now he's wandered over to the mango tree, where Alonso

is still breathlessly summarising his beloved TV series to a circle of people. Alonso has the unfortunate skin type that turns as pink as strawberry juice, no matter the humidity levels or how slow he's been drinking.

'So they bring in the red-beard guy, begging and screaming,' Alonso is saying. 'But when the blade comes down, he doesn't cry out for his mother or wife or daughters. Instead he starts sobbing for his country, his army. *I did you wrong, I did you wrong*, he's shouting, and the crowd starts cheering.'

'Like the Romans,' says Ravassa's wife, lightly touching a small mark by her lower lip that she hopes nobody else has noticed – a pimple? A mole? 'The Christians and the lions.'

At the border of the group, Mrs Montoya has just finished her story about Baloo, how he chased her around the yard, tugging on her skirt and smacking his thick black lips. 'Thank God they got rid of him,' she says, gesturing towards her feet. 'There's no way I could run in these heels.' Tom Harris and Robert Smith nod in unison, even though they're in separate departments at the fruit company (agronomy and marketing respectively) and don't really know each other that well. They're both secretly glad that Mrs Montoya's incessant chatter is filling in the silence between them. When she finally heads back to the patio to refill her drink, Tom shyly asks Robert if he has a lighter. Smoking together, looking at the pool and the squat orange flowerpots, the Christmas lights dangling like fireflies stuck in the grapefruit tree, Robert will tell Tom that Amanda Quintero's husband has just joined a strange new American religion that doesn't allow you to cut your hair.

'What will he do once it's summer?' Tom asks, who's only been here for six months and still sleeps with the fan as close to his bed as possible, blasting air in his face, even when it rains.

'Be hot,' says Robert, taking another drag.

He blows the smoke right into our faces, but we don't blink, we don't move an inch. We've been listening carefully, behaving ourselves, lingering on the edges. Sometimes we lean in close, inhale the faint scents of cologne and perfume, study the sweat on men's upper lips, the base of women's collarbones. An enormous black cicada buzzes past and hits the drainpipe with a clatter.

We're still watching him, too – the way he's rocking back and forth on his heels, rubbing his shirtsleeves as though chilled. 'Excuse me,' he says abruptly to one of the passing servers, a young woman holding a bowl scraped clean of lavender-flavoured goat's cheese. She immediately freezes in her tracks. 'My daughter – have you seen her?' He pauses, trying to find the right words for a description – the tip of her black braid, permanently wet from her nervous sucking? The damp patches in her armpits, regardless of the temperature? The scowling, baby-fat cheeks, the sour curdling of her mouth when he hesitantly says something like *You know, you could invite somebody over to spend the weekend – a friend of yours, if you'd like.* The icy cold feeling oozing from her shoulder blades as she contemptuously retreats to her room?

But the young woman is nodding her head, backing away, holding the bowl close to her chest like a shield. Right before she turns around, she says in a fast voice, 'By the palm tree, sir – Ramón was bringing her shrimp.' And just like that she flees across the patio, almost bumping into a flowerpot. As she disappears through the swinging door, he thinks, *Ramón?*

He turns and starts walking into the depths of the garden. He swings his arms purposefully, wrinkles his forehead with the expression of a man on a mission, so that anyone contemplating stopping him with a *Why so nice to see you, it's been ages!* will think twice. He pauses by the palm tree, resting his hand on the scars hacked into the trunk. They're ancient relics from his daughter's kindergarten birthday parties, epic affairs in which the garden filled with screaming children, waving plastic Thunder Cat swords, their lips stained with bright blue frosting, the swimming pool transformed into a froth from their kicking legs and cannonball dives. *How about that friend of yours*, he'd said. *You used to invite him over here all the time. I don't think I've seen him in years. You know, the blond one?*

Dad, she'd said. *Why don't you shut the fuck up?*

On the ground is a solitary flip-flop, the grey ghost of her foot imprinted on the thin rubber. Nearby is a wooden stick smeared black from the grill, gnawed with teeth marks from where she scraped off every last piece of shrimp possible. He looks around, but the only eyes he meets are those of the rabbits, their trembling noses pushed up against the chicken wire, expressions the same as the young waitress moments before.

He walks ahead, leaving the flip-flop behind. He moves past the papaya trees, which have been afflicted by a mysterious disease for weeks now, the fruit stinking of rotten fish and the trunks covered in oozing sores. He passes the compost heap, filled with dry branches slashed from trees by the gardeners' sharp machetes, and kitchen scraps that the maids routinely carry out in orange plastic buckets. He walks by the abandoned birdhouse, vines hanging down the rotting wood, the lion cage with its rusty bars and leaf-covered roof. César the lion has been gone for half a decade, the peacock a few years less than that. César died convulsing, mouth filled with a thick yellow foam that the keeper nonchalantly said had come from eating 'something bad', while the peacock – what happened to the peacock? Its throat ripped open by a possum? An unexplained disappearance into thin air, leaving only glimmering blue-green feathers behind? Even five years ago he felt too exhausted to replace them, and it feels even less worth it now – it's just not the time and place for those sorts of things any more, for that kind of exhibitionism. Not the right atmosphere. He walks on, the house getting smaller in the distance, the sounds of the party getting fainter, ignoring the dampness seeping into the hems of his trousers, the midge-bites forming on his arms.

We follow him as best we can. We tread carefully over the squashed mangoes and dark green chicken turds curled up like undiscovered Easter candy among the grass. We follow him past the fenced field, the one with the steer who always looks so sad, and never bothers to flick the flies away from its thick eyelashes. We pass the outhouse with the backup electricity generator, the acacia tree where the buzzards roost. The ranch is over a thousand hectares long but he won't be going much farther.

We're just about to begin, when it happens. At first there's hardly any sound, the canopy barely rustling, trees shaking. We stand as still as possible as he turns around sharply, staring deep into the darkness around him. 'Sweetie?' he says. 'Is that you?'

The sound grows louder, leaves and twigs crashing down.

'Who's there?' His hand moves to his hip, towards the hidden holster. Fingers tensed and ready.

The monkey takes its last swing out of the tree, landing heavily on the ground. It straightens up, wet black eyes blinking. His fingers relax around the holster, but don't move away.

'Well,' he says. 'Hello there, old friend.'

Baloo doesn't even give him a glance. Instead, he stares right at us.

We stare back.

'Sorry I don't have anything for you,' he says. 'Any, ah, goodies.' He's touching his waist and back pockets, instinctively feeling for something, wishing he'd brought the flip-flop, or even the gnawed stick. His fingers suddenly detect the plastic baggie of JELL-O powder, which he immediately pulls out and throws in Baloo's direction. It flutters weakly like a translucent moth, landing near the monkey's foot. Baloo doesn't even flinch, his eyes still fixed unblinkingly on us. We shift around uncomfortably, glancing at each other, nervously crossing and uncrossing our arms. Some of us tentatively touch our cheeks and foreheads, tracing the skin with our fingertips.

It's almost like he's saying: *What's wrong with your faces?* Or even: *Wait – what did they do to you?*

'Good monkey,' he says, backing away, one slow but steady footstep at a time. 'Nice little Baloo.' In response Baloo releases a long lazy yawn, flashing a row of solid yellow teeth. His breath is warm and stinks of overripe fruit.

The cellphone rings, its high-pitched trill breaking the silence, and we can't help but jump as Baloo swiftly turns and flees into the undergrowth, bushes rattling like chattering teeth. He fumbles with the cellphone as he pulls it out, fingers clumsy, answers just before it goes to voicemail. At first he thinks it's Nicolás from the processing laboratory, speaking rapidly in muffled tones, but finally recognises prostate-cancer Andrés – he's agitated, calling long-distance from Medellín, asking repeatedly if it's safe to speak right now. He listens calmly to the update, strolling back towards the house. He interrupts with a stifled snort of laughter, after Andrés says, *My advice would be for you to take a trip abroad for a while – with your daughter especially. Why risk it? Go to Europe; take her someplace nice. Just until things blow over with these guys. Until the situation is safe again.*

'We're not going anywhere,' he says, cutting Andrés off. 'I don't care what you have to do. Just take care of it.'

The walk back to the house feels strangely short. Right as he passes the flip-flop he pauses, as if about to bend over and scoop it up, but at the last second he turns quickly away, leaving it behind in the grass. The party's now reached the point where it's either going to turn into anarchy or collapse into exhausted decay. Somebody's thrown up on the grass, a sour orange puddle. The dancers and drinkers on the patio are still mingling, eyes glassy, cheeks stiff from smiling. Somebody's turned the music up so loud that the bass hurts his eardrums.

He's heading towards the patio door when he's spotted. *Hey, there you are! Where have you been hiding?* He's reluctantly tugged away, pulled into the crowd. His shoulders are slapped, his arms are squeezed, he receives winks and smiles, shouts and whoops. A shot of *aguardiente*, miraculously still cold, is pushed into his hand, followed by delicate kisses on his cheek. *Terrific party! Amazing! Best time I've had since Carnival!*

Everybody's happy to see him; they're thrilled that he's here. He briefly scans the crowd one last time, but there are no children to be seen at this point – no small bowed heads, no hands stained with hardened candle wax, no wet chewed braid. The phone sits in his back pocket, still warm from the call.

He checks his messages one more time from the quietest corner of the patio, under the grapefruit tree by the swimming pool. There are no new voicemails. Not even a text.

He's walking past the swimming pool when he sees it: the last paper plate, bobbing up and down, half-sunken. Its candle is long gone, most likely sunk to the bottom, now rolling slowly across the tiles. The pool is completely dark; there's no longer any light to be seen. He stops and watches.

There are more packages of paper plates deep inside the pantry somewhere. He could go ask a maid to bring more out. Or even better, he could get them himself. Take the key off the chain, unlock the door, head inside. If he wanted to, he could spend some time slumped on the floor, leaning against the wall, eyes closed, hands resting calmly in lap. It could be the kind of place where he could stay for ever. Stay secret. Stay safe. A place where he could lock himself away and never, ever be found.

We'll be watching, though. We don't mind. We're not in a hurry.

We're not going anywhere.

JOANNA WALSH

WORLDS FROM THE WORD'S END

WE NEED TO talk.

I'm writing to you so you'll understand why I can't write to you any more.

I could never talk to you. We didn't exactly have a meaningful relationship. Perhaps that's why I have all these words left when so many others have none at all. The postal system's still going, so I expect you will get this letter. Bills continue to be sent by mail (figures accompany icons: an electric light bulb, a gas flame, a wave) as do postcards (wordless views). And letters do still arrive (addresses are roughly sketched maps, in case you wondered) so I'll take this opportunity to get my words in edgeways while I still can, folded into a slim envelope. When they drop through your letterbox, I hope that they don't fall flat.

It's the old story: it's not you, it's me. Or, rather, it's where we're at. We don't talk any more, not now, not round here. You know how things have changed. But I have to tell you all over again because what happened between us seemed to be part of what happened everywhere.

It was more than a language barrier. I thought we were reading from the same page, but it was really only you that ever had a way with words. Sometimes you put them into my mouth, then you took them right out again. You never minced them, made anything easier to swallow, and the words you put in for me were hardly ever good. They left a bitter taste. As for me, you twisted my words and broke my English until I was only as good as my word: good for nothing, or for saying nothing. I stopped answering and that was the way you liked it. You told me you preferred your women quiet. You wanted to increase your word power? Trouble is, you didn't know your own strength.

Communication went out of fashion about the same time as we stopped speaking. It started, as does almost everything, as a trend. Early adopters seeking something retro, as usual, looked to their grannies, their aunties: silent women in cardigans who never went out. Who knows if these women were really quiet? I doubt the hipsters knew, any more than they could tell how cheese-makers or hand-knitters really went about their business. Whether their adoption of these women's silence was a misinterpretation of the past or a genuine unearthing, it happened. Initially, gatherings – I mean parties, that sort of thing – became quieter, then entirely noiseless. Losing their raison d'être, they grew smaller and eventually ceased to exist, as people came to favour staying in, waiting at telephone tables for calls that never came.

We scarcely noticed how the silence went mainstream, but if I had to trace a pattern I'd say our nouns faded first. We tried abbreviations, acronyms, txtspk, but they made us blue, reminded us of the things we used to say, and, not being a literary nation, we'd never quite got our heads around metaphor. We'd taken ourselves at our word, literally: so that, in everyday speech the supermarket became 'that big shiny thing where you buy other things', your house, 'the building one block from the corner, count two along'. A little later this morphed into 'that place a little way from where you go round, then a bit further on'. We began to revel in indirectness. Hunters of urban cool would show off, limiting themselves to, 'that over there,' and finally would do no more than grunt and jerk a thumb. They looked like they had something better to do than engage in casual conversation. We provincials were dumb-struck.

Grammar went second. I'm not inferring we were disinter-ested. If I was to speculate – between you and I – those most effected were people that thought too much of who they had words with. As for myself, I'd refute that our famous last words could of lingered. Irregardless of other uses, we couldn't eat them. Crumbling by the day, months went by, 'til we found our frequent grammatical errors just one thing less to lose. In other words, we began to said, 'kinda' a lot, and 'sort of' but, y'know . . . We lost heart and failed to end sentences.

We have no sayings, now, only doings, though never a 'doing word'. Actions speak louder than words (a wise saw: if only I'd looked before I ever listened to you), especially as we can't remember very far back. We have erased all tenses except the present, though for a while we hung on to the imperfect, which suggested that things were going on as they always had done, and would continue thus.

At least schooling is easier now there are only numbers and images – and shapes, their dimensions, their colours. We don't have to name them: we feel their forms and put them into our hearts, our minds, or whatever that space is, abandoned by language. We trace the shapes of the countries on school globes with our fingertips. And they all feel like tin.

Being ostensibly silent, for a while social media was still a valid form of communication, though touch-keyboards began to be preferred to those with keys. On websites people posted photos of silent activities, as well as those involving white noise – drilling, vacuuming, using the washing machine – during which communication could patently not take place.

Some questioned, in the comments boxes below, whether these photos might be staged, but doubts were put to rest when the majority began to frown even on the use of writing. Some of us wondered whether Internet forums could themselves have been the final straw: the way we'd wanted what we said to be noticed and, at the same time, to remain anon: the way we'd let our words float free, detach from our speech-acts, become at once our avatars and our armour.

Trad media was something else. The first to go 'non-talk' were high-end cultural programmes, those 'discussing' art and books. Popular shows featuring, say, cooking, gardening, home improvement, and talent contests, relied on sign language and were frowned upon by purists. On the highbrow broadcasts, critics' reactions were inferred from their facial expressions by a silent studio audience. Viewers smiled, or frowned in response, but their demeanours remained subtle, convoluted, suited to the subjects' complexities. Fashions in presenters changed. Smooth-faced women were sacked in favour of craggy hags whose visual emotional range was more elastic. As all news is bad news, jowly, dewlapped broadcasters with doleful eyebags drew the highest pay-packets. This was considered important even on the radio.

There were no more letters to the editors of newspapers. There was no Op to the Ed, then no Ed, but newspapers continued to exist. Their pages looked at first as they had under censorship when, instead of the offending article, there appeared a photograph of a donkey. But, after a period of glorious photography, images also departed, and the papers reverted to virgin. Oddly, perhaps, the number and page extent of sections remained the same. People still bought their dailies at the kiosk: men still slept under them in parks. Traditions were preserved without the clamour of print. It was so much nicer that way.

Not everyone agreed. There were protests, often by unemployed journalists and photographers, but these were mostly silent: we had internalised the impoliteness of noise and were no longer willing to howl slogans. The personal being the political, this extended to domestic life. Fewer violent quarrels were reported. With no way to take things forward, relationships tended to the one-note. Couples who got on badly glared in mutual balefulness; the feelings of those who loved were reflected in one another's eyes.

If, at an international level, there was no news, at a local level there was no gossip, so most of us felt better. We ceased to judge people, having no common standards. The first wordless president fought her (his? its? − as we could no longer give it a name, gender scarcely mattered any more) campaign on a quiet platform, gaze fixed on the distant horizon. He (she? it?) knew how to play the new silence. The opposition, opting to fill the gap left by speech with random actions, was nowhere. A more liberal, thoughtful community emerged. Or so some of us believed. How could we tell?

There were conspiracy theories: a cold war of words conducted by the international literati; uncertain terms between the word banks. Granted, old folks have always complained that a man's word isn't worth as much as it used to be, that promises nowadays are ten-a-penny, but radical economists did chart a steep devaluation. Once, they remembered, you could have had a conversation word for word, though a picture had always been worth a thousand words. That was the system: we knew where we stood, and it was by our words; but the currency went into free-fall: a picture to five thousand, ten thousand words, a million! Despite new coinages, soon it was impossible to exchange a word with anyone, unless you traded in the black market of filthy language, and, if you did, there was always the danger you'd be caught on corners, unable to pay your respects. The government reacted: 'please' and 'thank you' replaced milk at school break-time and, in order to prevent civil discontent, grown-ups received ration books of good terms. For every provision, of course, a restriction. New laws were parsed: if you didn't keep to the letter of the law, you could be had up in court for uncivil wrongs.

Some clung to individual words to fill the gaps as language crumbled, but, without sentence structure, they presented as insane, like a homeless man who once lived on the corner of my block and carried round a piece of pipe saying, 'Where's this fit? Where's this fit?' to everyone he met. Except that the word-offerers didn't form phrases, they just held out each single syllable aggressively, aggrievedly, or hopefully.

As for the rest of us, words still visited sometimes: spork, ostrich, windjammer . . . We wondered where they had come from, what to do with them. Were they a curse or a blessing? We'd pick them up where they dropped like ravens' bread on soggy ground.

Of course the big brands panicked, employed marketeers to look into whether we'd ever had the right words in the first place. Naturally, we were unable to read the results of their research. The government launched a scheme (no need for secrecy as there are no rumours): bespoke words were designed along lines dictated by various linguistic systems, and tested. As someone who, until recently, had lived by her words (if there are words to live by: as you know, I actually live by the church), I was involved or, perhaps, committed. Under scientific conditions, we exchanged conversations involving satch, ileflower, liisdoktora, always asking each other if this could be the magic word. We cooed over the new words, nested them, hoping meaning would come and take roost, but meaning never did.

A scattering of the more successful experiments was put into circulation and, for a while, we tried to spread the words at every opportunity. Despite sponsored 'word placement' in the movies (which were no longer talkies), the new words slipped off the screen: our eyes glazed over. The problem, as it always had been in our country, was one of individualism. By this stage no one expected words to facilitate communication. The experiment resulted not in a common language, but in pockets of parallel neologisms. Being able to name our own things to ourselves gave us comfort. I suspect some people still silently practise this, though, of course, I cannot tell. I have a feeling their numbers are declining. Even I have stopped. It proved too difficult to keep a bag of words in my head for personal use and to have to reach down into its corners for terms that didn't come out very often. They grew musty. Frankly it was unhygienic.

It was sad to see the last of the signs coming down, but it was also liberating. In the shop that was no longer called COFFEE, you couldn't ask for a coffee any more, but that was OK. You could point, and the coffee tasted better, being only 'that' and not the same thing as everyone else had. It was never the same as the guy behind you's coffee, or the coffee belonging to the person in front. No one had a better cup than you, or a worse. For the first time, whatever it was was your particular experience and yours alone. The removal of publicly visible words accelerated. Shop windows were smashed, libraries were burned. We may have got carried away. As the number of billboards and street signs dwindled, we realised we had been reading way too much into everything. What did we do with the space in our minds that had constantly processed what we read? Well . . . I guess we processed other things, but what they were, we could no longer say.

Some of us suspected that new things had begun to arrive, things there had never been names for. They caused irritation, as a new word does to an old person, but because there was nothing to call these new things, there was no way to point them out or even to say that they hadn't been there before. People either accommodated them or didn't. We're still not sure whether these things continue to live with us, or if we imagined them all along.

Those people who prefer the new silence are frightened that one day the word will turn. It's a feeling I share, if warily. Words, we had thought, were the opposite of actions, but, delving deeper, we found they were also opposed to themselves. Whatever we said, we knew contained the seed of its opposite. 'It's fine today,' 'I respect you,' 'Will you take out the trash?' suggested the possibility of bad weather, cruelty, and refusal. It had become so difficult to say anything. Our awkwardness got to us. In the republic of words, 'I love you,' induced anxiety. 'How was your day?' would elicit merely a sigh. I think people just got tired, tired of explaining things they'd already said to one another, exhausted by the process of excavating words with words. We were oversensitive perhaps. Do you think we have dumbed ourselves down?

The last time I saw you we spent days walking around my city. The only voices we heard were foreign: tourists or immigrant workers. You spoke their language but only I could understand the silent natives.

We walked the streets in no direction, following no signs. 'What's that billboard for?' you asked, pointing to the wordless yellow one that was all over town. I told you, 'That's an advert for the billboard company.' You were – temporarily – lost for words. We took photos of the sky disturbed by silent exhalations from the city's rigid gills – air vents linked to aircon, to the underground system – but they were all lungs and no voicebox. They couldn't breathe a word. It was cold, so cold I could see my breath next to yours, solid in the frozen air, mingling with the steam of restaurant dinners, of laundries, with warm gusts of metro dust.

The night you left, we went to a shabby bar by the station, where we drank bad wine. You talked with the people who worked there: an underclass still allowed to speak because they spoke a different language. They could effect the business we despised, butter us with the courtesies we could no longer practise. Their jobs involved asking for our orders (we would point to the desired item on the illustrated menu), telephoning abroad for crates of imported beer and vodka, telling us to have a nice day. Inside, the bar was red as a liver. We worked a little on ours. As we parted we held each other for a little too long and only almost failed to air kiss.

I am interested in failure, as are we all here, because I think it's where we're at. Words failed us a while ago. What will fail us next?

You like women who are quiet? In the end it was not so difficult to let you go; you were only interested in the sound of your own voice. Pretty soon we had nothing left to say to one another. I listened; you looped the same old tape. I tried things that were wordless; I took your hand and pressed it, but feelings meant nothing to you. We were always words apart.

Don't tell me I'm being unreasonable.

Don't talk to me about your girlfriends in the speaking world. Don't repeat the sweet nothings you whisper to them. Don't tell me about the ones you have yet to meet, who are no doubt wishing aloud for some such coincidence. Don't write back. It is no good calling me; I won't pick up. It's no good texting me, or sending me emails. There's no need to tell me anything. I know it all already. And nothing you could say to me would help.

We're in different places. I'm dead to the word, and you don't have a care in it. You're on top of it; it weighs heavy on my shoulders. So I won't go on. I love you and I'm not aloud, won't allow myself to say it any more. There's no future in it. You wouldn't want a wife who didn't understand you, whose eventual resort could only be dumb insolence – just saying. Love's a word that makes the world go round right enough. It wheels and spins like a coin unsure where to land: heads or tails. Wherever it fell, I would have gone right on to that word's end, for want of a better word, and, like other temporary Miss Words, I do most sincerely want a better word, but I can't say I've ever heard of one.

When I see they're still using words in your country I feel only half-envious, a quarter . . . I also feel a strong swinge (is that even a word?) of embarrassment and pity. Don't be offended; I'm trying to tell it like it is.

You probably think we've all gone quiet over here, that you'll never hear from us again. Yes, it is quiet, but we are still thinking. In ways you can no longer describe.

CONTRIBUTORS'
BIOGRAPHIES

JENN ASHWORTH was born in 1982 in Preston, Lancashire. She is the author of three novels – *A Kind of Intimacy*, *Cold Light* and *The Friday Gospels*. Her short stories have appeared in *MIR 9*, *The Manchester Review*, *Dogmatika*, *Beat the Dust*, *Jawbreakers* and *Bugged*, among other places. She reviews fiction for the *Guardian* and lectures in creative writing at Lancaster University.

NEIL CAMPBELL is from Manchester. He has two collections of short stories, *Broken Doll* and *Pictures From Hopper*, published by Salt, and two poetry collections, *Birds* and *Bugsworth Diary*, published by Knives Forks and Spoons, who have also published his short fiction chapbook, *Ekphrasis*. Recent stories have appeared in *Unthology 6* and the *Stockholm Review*. His first novel is due for publication by Salt in 2016.

EMMA CLEARY is from Liverpool and taught English and Creative Writing at Staffordshire University. In her critical work, she writes about maps, jazz, and the city in diasporic literature. She lives in Vancouver, BC, where she is working on her first novel.

USCHI GATWARD was born in east London and lives there now. Her stories have appeared in the *Bristol Short Story Prize*

Anthology Volume Six, Brittle Star, Southword and *Structo*, and have been performed by Liars' League in London and New York, and at the Wilderness Festival in Oxfordshire.

JONATHAN GIBBS was born in 1972 and lives in London. His debut novel, *Randall*, is published by Galley Beggar Press, and was longlisted for the Desmond Elliott Prize 2015. His short fiction has appeared in *Lighthouse, The South Circular, All-nighter* (Pulp Faction), *Gorse* and *The Best British Short Stories 2014*, and has been shortlisted for the White Review Short Story Prize. He blogs at tinycamels.wordpress.com.

JIM HINKS is an editor at Comma Press, an independent publisher specialising in short fiction. He is currently reading for a PhD in narrative structure in the short story at Edge Hill University, and writes his own stories in the name of prac-tice-as-research. He is the inventor of MacGuffin, an online jukebox for short stories and poetry in text and audio form.

TAMAR HODES was born in Israel in 1961 and has lived in the UK since she was five. For the past thirty years, she has combined teaching English and creative writing in schools, universities and prisons with her own writing. Her novel, *Raffy's Shapes*, was published by Accent Press in 2006 and she has had many stories on Radio 4 as well as in anthologies and magazines. In January 2015, she was a finalist in *Elle*'s writing competition. She is married with two grown-up children.

BEE LEWIS was born into a large, Irish family of story-tellers. She grew up in Liverpool and now lives on the south coast, in East Sussex, with her partner and their Irish Setter. She is reading for an MA in Creative Writing and is working on her first novel. She is also working on a short story collection inspired by modern sculpture.

ALAN MCCORMICK is Writer in Residence at Kingston University's Writing School. His story collection, *Dogsbodies and Scumsters*, was longlisted for the Edge Hill Prize in 2012. He also writes flash shorts in response to Jonny Voss's pictures. They work together as Scumsters, have been published regularly at *3:AM* and keep a blog at www.scumsters.blogspot. co.uk.

HILARY MANTEL is the author of numerous novels, a memoir and two short story collections. Born in Glossop, Derbyshire, she has won many awards for her work, including the Man Booker Prize twice, for *Wolf Hall* and *Bring Up the Bodies*.

HELEN MARSHALL is an author, editor, and doctor of medieval studies. Her debut collection, *Hair Side, Flesh Side* (ChiZine Publications, 2012), won the 2013 British Fantasy Award for Best Newcomer. Her second collection, *Gifts for the One Who Comes After*, was released in September 2014. Born and raised in Canada, she lives in Oxford and holds joint Canadian/UK citizenship.

ALISON MOORE was born in Manchester in 1971. She is the author of two novels – *The Lighthouse* (2012), which was shortlisted for the Man Booker Prize 2012 and won the McKitterick Prize 2013, and *He Wants* (2014) – and a short story collection, *The Pre-War House & Other Stories* (2013). She lives near Nottingham with her husband Dan and son Arthur.

K J ORR was born in London. Her short fiction has been broadcast on Radio 4 and published by the *Sunday Times*, *Dublin Review*, *White Review*, *Lighthouse* and Comma Press, among others. She is Pushcart nominated, and has been shortlisted for awards including the BBC National Short Story Award, the Bridport Prize and the KWS Hilary Mantel International Short

Story Prize. Her debut collection, *Light Box*, will be published in 2016 by Daunt Books.

JULIANNE PACHICO was born in Cambridge, grew up in Colombia and now lives in Norwich. Her stories have been published by *Lighthouse*, *NewWriting.net* and Daunt Books. She is currently completing a linked collection.

TRACEY S ROSENBERG is a novelist and poet living in Edinburgh. She has a PhD in Victorian literature from the University of Edinburgh and has published a historical novel, *The Girl in the Bunker* (Cargo Publishing, 2011), set during the final days of the Second World War. Her second poetry collection, *The Naming of Cancer*, came out in 2014 from Neon Books.

Helen Simpson is the author of *Four Bare Legs in a Bed* (1990), *Dear George* (1995) and *Hey Yeah Right Get a Life* (2000). In 1991 she was chosen as the *Sunday Times* Young Writer of the Year and won the Somerset Maugham Award. In 1993 she was chosen as one of *Granta*'s twenty Best of Young British Novelists. Her most recent collection, *Bunch of Fives*, was published in 2012. She lives in London.

MATTHEW SPERLING has had stories published in *3:AM*, *The Junket*, *The Literateur* and *The Short Anthology*. He also writes poetry and criticism; his scholarly book, *Visionary Philology*, appeared from Oxford University Press in 2014, and he regularly writes about art for *Apollo* magazine. He was born in Kent in 1982, lives in north London and is a Leverhulme Trust Early Career Fellow at the University of Reading.

REBECCA SWIRSKY has published stories in *Matter*, *Ambit*, *Litro* and the Bridport Prize anthology, and placed in competitions including the Fish, Bath, Bristol, Manchester, Sean

O'Faolain and Bridport prizes. She was awarded a bursary from the Literary Consultancy and has been mentored by Stella Duffy through a Word Factory apprenticeship. She was awarded the AM Heath Prize for her MA in Writing from Sheffield Hallam University. She contributes art criticism and book reviews to publications including the *Observer*, *Economist* and *Financial Times*.

JOANNA WALSH has had work published by *Granta*, Dalkey, Salt, Gorse and others. Her collection, *Fractals*, was published by 3:AM Press in 2013. *Hotel* is forthcoming from Bloomsbury, and *Vertigo* (selected stories) from the Dorothy Project. She reviews books for a number of publications including the *Guardian*, *New Statesman* and *The Nation*. She is fiction editor at *3:AM Magazine*, and runs @read_women. She is a member of the London Institute of Pataphysics, and also works as an illustrator.

CHARLES WILKINSON is the author of *The Pain Tree and Other Stories* (London Magazine Editions) and *Ag & Au* (Flarestack Poets). His stories have appeared in *Best Short Stories 1990*, *Best English Short Stories 2*, *Unthology*, *Supernatural Tales*, *Phantom Drift*, *Shadows & Tall Trees* and elsewhere. He is a member of the Tindal Street Fiction Group.

ACKNOWLEDGEMENTS

The editor wishes to thank Sarah Fermi of the Brontë Society, Cathy Galvin of Word Factory and Gemma Hemming of Maney Publishing.

'Five Thousand Lads a Year', copyright © Jenn Ashworth 2014, was first broadcast on BBC Radio 4 and is printed here by permission of the author.

'LS Lowry/Man Lying on a Wall', copyright © Neil Campbell 2014, was first published in *Ekphrasis* (The Knives Forks and Spoons Press) and is reprinted by permission of the author.

'Lightbox', copyright © Emma Cleary 2014, was first published in *Lighthouse* 5 and is reprinted by permission of the author.

'The Clinic', copyright © Uschi Gatward 2014, was first published in *Structo* 12 and is reprinted by permission of the author.

'Festschrift', copyright © Jonathan Gibbs 2014, was first published in *Gorse* 2 and is reprinted by permission of the author.

'Green Boots' Cave' copyright © Jim Hinks 2014, was first published in *Short Fiction in Theory and Practice* Volume 4 Issue 1 and is reprinted by permission of the author.

'The First Day', copyright © Tamar Hodes 2014, was first published in *Wiltshire View* (September 2014) and is reprinted by permission of the author.

'The Iron Men', copyright © Bee Lewis 2014, was first published in *Anglo Files* 174 and is reprinted by permission of the author.

'Go Wild in the Country', copyright © Alan McCormick 2014, was first published online in *3:AM Magazine* and is reprinted by permission of the author.

'The Assassination of Margaret Thatcher 6th August 1983', copyright © Hilary Mantel 2014, was first published in the *Guardian* and is reprinted by permission of the author.

'Secondhand Magic', copyright © Helen Marshall 2014, was first published in *Gifts For the One Who Comes After* (ChiZine Publications) and is reprinted by permission of the author.

'Eastmouth', copyright © Alison Moore 2014, was first published in *The Spectral Book of Horror Stories* (Spectral Press) edited by Mark Morris and is reprinted by permission of the author.

'The Lake Shore Limited', copyright © K J Orr 2014, was first published in the *Dublin Review* 56 and is reprinted by permission of the author.

'Lucky', copyright © Julianne Pachico 2014, was first published in *Lighthouse* 5 and is reprinted by permission of the author.

'The Tourists', copyright © Julianne Pachico 2014, was first published by Daunt Books and is reprinted by permission of the author.

'May the Bell Be Rung For Harriet', copyright © Tracey S Rosenberg 2014, was first published online on the Brontë Society website and reprinted in *Brontë Studies* Volume 40, Issue 1, and is reprinted by permission of the author.

'Strong Man', copyright © Helen Simpson 2014, was first published in the *New Statesman* and is reprinted by permission of the author.

'Voice Over', copyright © Matthew Sperling 2014, was first published online in *The Literateur* and is reprinted by permission of the author.

'The Common People', copyright © Rebecca Swirsky 2014, was first published online in Litro and is reprinted by permission of the author.

'Worlds from the Word's End', copyright © Joanna Walsh 2014, was first published in *Best European Fiction 2015* (Dalkey Archive Press) edited by West Camel and is reprinted by permission of the author.

'Fresh Water', copyright © Charles Wilkinson 2014, was first published in *Unthology 5* (Unthank Books) edited by Ashley Stokes and Robin Jones and is reprinted by permission of the author.

NEW FICTION FROM SALT

RON BUTLIN
Ghost Moon (978-1-907773-77-8)

KERRY HADLEY-PRYCE
The Black Country (978-1-78463-034-8)

IAN PARKINSON
The Beginning of the End (978-1-78463-026-3)

CHRISTOPHER PRENDERGAST
Septembers (978-1-907773-78-5)

JONATHAN TAYLOR
Melissa (978-1-78463-035-5)

GUY WARE
The Fat of Fed Beasts (978-1-78463-024-9)

MEIKE ZIERVOGEL
Kauther (978-1-78463-029-4)

ALSO AVAILABLE FROM SALT

ELIZABETH BAINES
Too Many Magpies (978-1-84471-721-7)
The Birth Machine (978-1-907773-02-0)

LESLEY GLAISTER
Little Egypt (978-1-907773-72-3)

ALISON MOORE
The Lighthouse (978-1-907773-17-4)
The Pre-War House and Other Stories (978-1-907773-50-1)
He Wants (978-1-907773-81-5)

ALICE THOMPSON
Justine (978-1-78463-031-7)
The Falconer (978-1-78463-009-6)
The Existential Detective (978-1-78463-011-9)
Burnt Island (978-1-907773-48-8)

MEIKE ZIERVOGEL
Magda (978-1-907773-40-2)
Clara's Daughter (978-1-907773-79-2)

NEW SHORT STORIES FROM SALT

CARYS DAVIES
The Redemption of Galen Pike (978-1907773-71-6)

STELLA DUFFY
Everything is Moving, Everything is Joined: The Selected Stories of Stella Duffy (978-1907773-05-1)

CATHERINE EISNER
A Bad Case and Other Adventures of Disturbed Minds (978-184471-962-4)

MATTHEW LICHT
Justine, Joe and the Zen Garbageman (978-184471-829-0)

KIRSTY LOGAN
The Rental Heart and Other Fairytales (978-1907773-75-4)

PADRIKA TARRANT
Fates of the Animals (978-1907773-58-7)